AICKMAN

TALES OF A
NORMAL CHILDHOOD

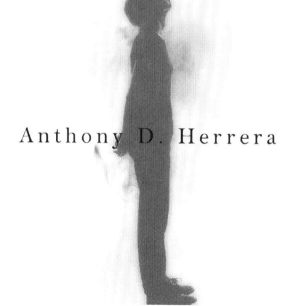

Anthony D. Herrera

Aickman: Tales of a Normal Childhood

Published by: Cloaked Press, LLC
PO Box 341
Suring, WI 54174
Cloakedpress.com

Cover Design by:
Carmilla M. Ravensworth
carmillacreates.carrd.co

ISBN: 978-1-952796-44-9

For Mom and Dad

In the summer of 1993, I became a God to vermin.

In the town of Aickman, the grass hungered for my flesh.

At the swap-meet, souls were for sale and down by the creek the severed toes floated on by.

These are the stories of the town where all my nightmares came true.

These are the stories of the worst summer of my life.

These are the stories of my best friends:

Darby

Jason Human

Eddie Gone

The Anointed One

These are the stories of a ten-year-old boy and his average American childhood.

Welcome to Aickman.

You should never have come.

INTRODUCTIONS

SEPTEMBER 1991:

HOW DARBY AND I BECAME FRIENDS

Darby scared the hell out of me.

She was two years older and a full foot taller than everybody else in our third-grade class. She'd been held back twice but that had nothing to do with her intelligence and everything to do with spite. She wore torn jeans, oversized flannels, and t-shirts of bands who were either un-American, satanic, or both. The antagonism of her wardrobe was complimented by numerous skull rings, wild hair, and refusal to go anywhere without her skateboard which sat on her lap during class like a chihuahua.

She had no friends, and the details of her life were a mystery that fueled both budding gossip mongers and conspiracy theorists. It was widely believed that she sacrificed cats at midnight deep within the Screaming Forest and had a tattoo on her back that proclaimed in blood-red lettering "I LOVE THE DEVIL." It was also assumed that she was the mastermind behind the curious incident of Mr. Durham and the exploding toilet. There was no evidence linking her with the incendiary lavatory that put the teacher who always referred to her as "my little delinquent" in the hospital, but that didn't stop the rest of the faculty from giving her a wide berth from then on.

Once the teachers stopped trying to break her, she was pretty much left to her own devices and was free to not stand for the Pledge of Allegiance or take part in the Oath of Loyalty to our mayor who, unlike most mayors I would later learn, had the head of a deer and the body of a deer. As for his mind…well, that was also very much that of a deer. Our town had made a mistake some years prior, but everyone was too embarrassed to admit it and by '91, Mayor Deer had us all in the grip of his iron hoof.

I sat next to Darby in the back because Mrs. Sherman didn't like my chubby face or tendency to cry for no reason. I was terrified for most of that September because I was certain that if I did or said the wrong thing, Darby would call on Satan to explode me like an elementary school toilet. That this avatar of terror would one day become one of my closest friends was a miracle facilitated in part by a piece of human scum known as Griffin Collins.

My fear of Darby was based on mystery, but my fear of Collins was based on misery. He was a mutant pit-bull of a little boy who was quarantined from the rest of the students except during lunch and recess. His mullet was greasy, his breath was rancid, and his laughter was always accompanied by screams.

Though the school year had barely started, Collins had already gifted me with several rabbit punches to the kidney, multiple twists of both nipples, and even managed to hawk a loogie in my mouth while I was yawning at the lunch table, a feat which was met with wild applause.

On the day that Darby first spoke to me, I showed up to school in a red and white horizontal striped shirt that was two sizes too small. It was the only clean shirt I had due to my father having neglected to do laundry for the past month. As I walked into the playground that morning looking down at my exposed pot belly and long-sleeves which barely went past my elbows, I already had tears in my eyes. I barely had time to absorb the sting of a few stray giggles when a familiar raspy voice with a sing-song southern twang cut through the muggy morning air.

"Look what Piggy's wearing, y'all!"

I didn't attempt to run as Collins and his pack of apprentice psychos rushed me because I knew there was no point. I had already factored in the oncoming humiliation before getting to school and as they grabbed me and started bongo slapping my belly and calling me blubber butt, I just took it in my stride. But I wasn't prepared for what Collins whispered to the goons after the euphoria of the initial cruelty wore off.

"Hey, I bet the goodtime gals would love to see this mess."

Goodtime Gals was the slang term for the species of ant that, as far as I know, was only endemic to the small town of Aickman. They were the size of dimes, and their exoskeletons were a brilliant emerald green that sparkled in the sun. The term "goodtime gals" was a reference to the girlish "TEE-HEE" giggle noises that the ants made as they went about their business.

Whenever Collins talked about someone meeting the goodtime gals, this meant you were about to have your face rubbed into one of the many ant hills which dotted the pathetic excuse of an athletic track behind the school. The resulting bites were twice as painful as those of a fire ant and made all the worse as the giggles of the goodtime gals always grew louder in proportion to the pain they were inflicting.

I looked to the other children for help as the goons dragged me towards the portable classrooms and the ant hills of the athletic field beyond. Every single one of them turned their back on me, which I couldn't blame them for. I had done the same thing numerous times in the past.

I foolishly held out hope that the teacher on duty would step in, but all my pleading eyes got in return was a half-smile and a hint of jealousy that they couldn't take part in that morning's schoolyard psychopathy.

"Can you hear them giggling, piggy? They know they're gonna be chawing on some lard real quick now!" Collins laughed as the goons drug me past the line of portable classrooms that marked the border of No Man's Land where students were strictly forbidden to go past before school or during recess.

Darby had, naturally, made No Man's Land her home. She was sitting against one of the portables, earphones on and reading a comic book. She wouldn't have looked up if Collins hadn't been making such a racket about how the queen ant was going crawl up my nose and lay a gaggle of gigglers inside my piggy brain. Our eyes met and though it amounted to begging at the foot of Lucifer, I mouthed the word "Help." My plea was met with a stone-faced stare.

Within seconds, Collins had me on all fours with his hand on the back of my head hovering above a large anthill. The tee-hees of the little green demons that scurried over the dirt were growing louder and louder and when a single tear fell from my cheek onto the hill, the giggles turned to squeals.

Collins mimicked the squeals as he began to force my head down. I pushed back as hard as I could, but Collins dug his long, filthy fingernails into the back of my neck and leaned in. As my face was inches from the dirt mound, I could see the goodtime gals standing on their back legs, mandibles aching to rip into my flesh. All I could do was hope that it wouldn't hurt as much after the first hundred bites.

Suddenly, the pressure disappeared from the back of my skull, and I heard a scream. I turned around to see Darby lifting Collins above her like a professional wrestler. The goons, much like myself, were speechless.

"Move," Darby said, looking down at me. I quickly rolled out of the way as she body slammed Collins directly onto the ant hill. The squeals reached an ear-piercing high as Collins screamed and flailed, shooting ants and dirt in every direction. He rolled off the hill and began running towards the school, cussing out Darby while ripping off his t-shirt and swatting at the dozens of goodtime gals that had managed to cling on. The goons remained dumbfounded and only joined their leader once Darby had taken a single, forceful step towards them.

Having never witnessed evil being defeated outside of Saturday morning cartoons, I didn't know how to react. I just lay on the ground looking up at my savior. Darby, uncomfortable with the awe in my eyes, looked away and simply mumbled, "Cool shirt," before turning around and heading back to her spot against the portable.

I laid there in a daze for another minute before the sound of approaching giggles broke me out of the spell. I got up just as a wave of gals was about to reach my left hand and I started back towards the playground. As I reached the edge of No Man's Land, I considered the world beyond: A world of rabbit punches, loogie swilling, frightened children, and teachers who enjoyed the show. I turned around and surveyed No Man's Land: No bullies, no teachers, and the only frightened child was me.

The choice was simple, really.

I walked to where Darby was sitting and chose a spot about four feet from her. We sat in silence for a few minutes very much like we did during class, when suddenly I heard her say, "Here, check this out." She was holding a comic book towards me, and I grabbed it without speaking. The book was called Sandman and had strange artwork on the cover that frightened and excited me. The bell rang and she got up and headed to class.

The next morning, Collins was out sick from gal bites, and I found myself again in No Man's Land. I sat next to Darby and handed back the comic I had read but barely comprehended the previous night. She then silently placed an issue of a comic book called Hellblazer into my hands. Because it was something I had never experienced before, it took a few weeks of us repeating this little ritual every morning before I realized that I had finally made a friend.

APRIL 1992:

HOW JASON HUMAN THRUST HIMSELF INTO OUR LIVES

All the other kids made fun of Jason Human because of his grey skin, black eyes, bulbous head, and hidden agenda, but he will always be my friend.

He transferred into our class towards the end of the year. When Mrs. Sherman made him introduce himself in front of everyone, he made a big deal about being from Ohio. He claimed that as a resident of Ohio, his speech and mannerisms would be vastly different from ours and that Ohio intellects were so far beyond the rest of America that it was almost laughable to consider him and us the same species.

"But rest assured, I am human. A real human boy. Snips and snails and puppy dog tails, that's what I like to eat. Yum Yum. Oh look, candy," Jason said as he picked up a piece of pink chalk from the chalkboard and swallowed it in one gulp.

Mrs. Sherman hated Jason immediately and sat him at the back with me and Darby. Before I could say a word of welcome, he took out a metal instrument from one of the many pockets in his shorts and waved it at me. He then looked at the bright display on the instrument's handle. "Fleshy. Small. Weak. Yes, you will be an excellent source of protein for the stronger ones when the end comes," Jason said, before turning the instrument towards Darby who simply smacked it out of his hand.

Jason spent the remainder of that year getting on Mrs. Sherman's nerves. During science lessons, Jason would invariably scream, "ARE YOU THE MISTRESS OF LIES?! WHO IS RUNNING THIS IGNORANCE FACTORY!?" and during history lessons would usually say something along the lines of, "Mrs. Sherman, none of you have a future so the past can't possibly matter."

Then there was the day he realized that Charlotte's Web, the book we had been reading in class, was a work of fiction and none of it had happened. "Wilbur...not real? IMPOSSIBLE! I love him! How can you love that which does not exist? Charlotte was more worthy of life than any of you and you tell me she never took one breath of your disgusting air?! I wept for her! My tears burn! ARE YOU TRYING TO DESTROY ME?!"

The class had found these outbursts funny at first, but when they realized that he was just genuinely odd rather than sarcastic, they soon grew tired of him. Jason did his best to ingratiate himself with the other students, but his conversation was invariably either insulting, frightening, or just plain baffling. I once heard him manage to fit all three into a few sentences when trying to strike up a conversation with a kid named Josh Gonzalez: "Ah, another beautiful day here on Earth, eh Josh? Too bad it will all end soon. And so violently! I must say, I admire the way you continue to play kickball despite the deep shame you inflict on those you love. You suck yet persist. Good for you. Hey, what's the deal with red blood? Who thought that was a good idea?"

He had quickly become the most unpopular kid in our class. One day, after the final bell had rung, me and Darby were walking out of the school when we saw Jason's legs flailing from out of a trash can. None of the students or teachers were helping, so Darby got hold of one of his flopping limbs and wrenched him out with one hand.

"Whoa, dude, you weigh like nothing," Darby said.

"I'm a vegetarian. Please put me down."

Darby gently lowered him to the ground. He scrambled to his feet, brushing off candy wrappers that had stuck to his clothes.

"Did Griffin Collins do this to you?" I asked.

"No. It was Mrs. Sherman. I was once again trying to explain to her the false premises upon which the multiplication tables are based when she let out a primitive howl and stuffed me into the rotting food house."

"Trash can?"

"I thought your name was Darby?" Jason said, confused.

"You should stop telling Mrs. Sherman she's wrong all the time," I said. "Grownups really hate that."

"As a teacher, she should be hungry for the knowledge I possess," Jason spat.

"That may be how it works in Ohio, but in Aickman, nobody likes to learn anything," I explained.

"This is, without a doubt, the longest conversation I have had since arriving here. I have observed you two. You are hated just as I am hated. I propose that we join forces so that we can better protect ourselves from the children and adults who wish to destroy us. What I lack in strength I make up for with an intellect that you can't possibly fathom and a purpose whose true goals would frighten you to even consider. The various pockets on my wonderful boy shorts are filled with tools, tools for measurement and analysis. They will help me understand this world and I will pass on this understanding to you. All I ask in return for this knowledge is your companionship, protection and, occasionally, hair, blood, and skin samples. What do you say, fellow humans, have we reached an understanding?"

As soon as I was able to close my mouth, I slowly turned from Jason to Darby.

"Yeah, you can hang out with us, I guess," she said, shrugging her shoulders.

And that is how the second friend I ever had forced himself on me.

June 1992:

How Eddie Gone Introduced Himself and The Skeleton We Destroyed Soon After

Eddie Gone didn't go to our school. Eddie didn't go to any school. He didn't have to. The Screaming Forest taught him everything he needed to know.

The Screaming Forest was what we called the woodlands on the edge of town. They were so named because of a series of caves that would ring out with what sounded like human voices begging for help. These screams, we were constantly assured, were nothing more than the wind playing off the cave system's peculiar acoustics. Sometimes, though, the screams could be heard when no wind was blowing, but nobody liked to think about those times.

It was the summer after 3rd grade and Jason Human was out collecting samples. He had invited Darby and I along for protection because we had recently told him about the legend of

15

The Spronky Man. The Spronky Man was a local mythical beast who witnesses described as bigfoot-like except shorter, with far less hair, and normal sized feet. In all honesty, he just sounded like a naked man wandering the forest which was far scarier than any missing link could ever be. If we were to run into Spronky, it was Darby's job to deal with him.

"That naked creep gets anywhere near us, I'll bash his face in with my skateboard," Darby had reassured Jason.

We had been out in the forest for about an hour. Jason was busy taking samples of flowers, rocks, and animal droppings which he stuffed into his various pockets. I'd felt uneasy ever since we'd crossed Turner's Bridge, which marked the border between the safe and well-maintained *forest* that families liked to picnic in, to the wild and dangerous FOREST where many people had disappeared over the years. Darby confirmed my dread when she leaned over and whispered, "Someone's watching us."

"Do you think it's The Spronky Man?" I asked.

Darby tightened her grip on her skateboard. "Jason, I think we should start heading back."

But Jason wasn't listening. His attention had been captured by the strangest flower any of us had ever seen. It was blood red and had fat petals that were layered like an onion. The petals appeared to be pulsing, almost writhing, and were covered in a pinkish fluid that dripped from the flower in thick strings which pooled on the forest floor in a steaming puddle. It made me sick to look at. Jason was entranced.

"A singular specimen. Hypnotic anomaly. This place, this Aickman, like nowhere else in the universe," Jason whispered as he lowered his hand to add the flower to his collection.

"STOP!" a voice rang out. Suddenly, a boy with a crew cut, black eye, and three scars across his left cheek appeared from nowhere. In a flash, he had his hand around the flower's stem, yanking it out of the ground. "What are you, crazy? Decided to give death a try? Boy, you got a big head but no brains!" the boy said to Jason.

"I don't know who you are but put my sample down this instant! I must catalogue that flower! For reasons!"

"This ain't no flower, friend. Look." As we watched, the writhing flower in the boy's hand began to swallow itself until the slimy petals disappeared into what had become a slithery and hissing stem. Jason hadn't found a blossom; he'd found a snake.

"This here's a petal snipe," the boy explained, waving the creature around in a nonchalant manner despite his own warnings. "See, the snake splits its head open and pukes up its guts in the shape of a flower to attract people and when you go to touch it, SNAP! The head closes and fills you with poison. Kills you dead. He'd be feasting on your eyeballs right now if I hadn't stopped you. My old man told me they started showing up after that chemical spill. That's the chemical spill in '28 not the one in '49. That one gave us the slugs with fingers. Anyway, get outta here, snake!" and with that, the boy lassoed the snake over his head and launched it deeper into the forest. He turned back to us, a huge grin on his face. "I'm Eddie, Eddie Gone, pleased to meet ya!" He held out his hand for Jason to shake.

"My brittle skeletal structure cannot handle the rigors of such pleasantries," Jason said, backing away.

"Huh? Was that Shakespeare? You a college boy or something?"

"He's Jason," Darby said. "I'm Darby and this is-"

"Whoah! Is that a skateboard? I've always wanted to try one. My mom would never let me on account of Jimmy, the goof next door, got a skateboard for Christmas and split his head open in the driveway. Blood was everywhere. Coolest thing I ever saw. After Jimmy got out of the hospital, he was able to play the piano even though he never had a lesson in his life. Started eating bugs too. Gotta take the good with the bad, I guess." He paused as if to ponder the truth of his statement and finally noticed our blank expressions. "I was watching you guys for a while, trying to figure out if you were worth knowing or not."

"We know," I said. "We could feel you watching. I thought you might be The Spronky Man."

"The Spronky Man? Seriously?" Eddie asked.

I blushed. "I know he's just a legend but-"

"Oh, he's no legend, he's absolutely real. I was just surprised you would think I was him because he's dead."

Darby and I looked at each other. "What do you mean he's dead?" Darby asked.

"I mean God called him up to that choir of naked creeps in the sky. Actually, he probably went the other way. I mean, I hope that's where the naked creeps go. Can you imagine a Heaven filled with naked creeps? Boy, dying sure is scary." Again, another pause, as if his brain had just processed what his mouth had been saying. He quickly shook his head to break himself of that train of thought. "Hey, do you guys want to see The Spronky Man's bones?"

As we followed the strange child we just met deeper into the dark and forbidding woods, where many people have been lost and never found, so that we may see the Earthly remains of a legendary local monster, we did not once stop to question the wisdom of our actions. On the way, Eddie regaled us with stories of his exploits in the forest. He considered the woods his second home and claimed he could draw a map of the entire Screaming Forest from memory. He said he once heard a cave whisper the Emancipation Proclamation and swore that he saw a flying saucer crash somewhere in the deep woods. Jason was quick to point out how ridiculous that story was.

I asked him about the scars on his face and his black eye which never healed during the entirety of our friendship.

"Oh this?" he said. "This was a…a bear. Yeah, a bear."

"I thought there weren't any bears around because the caves were too loud," Darby said.

"Koala bear," Eddie said. "Escaped from the zoo in Ellingville. I was the one that caught it. Mean mother. Wasn't in the papers cuz the bigwigs hushed it up." Before any of us could question his story, Eddie shouted, "HERE IT IS!" and ran towards a clearing which was inside a perfect circle of trees where a ring of dazzling light shone down on a thick field of bright green grass. In the center, sunlight sparkling off the ivory white bones, lay a skeleton. We approached it slowly. "Lady and gentlemen, I give you The Spronky Man," Eddie proclaimed grandly.

As I stared down at the bones, I realized that this was the first time I had ever seen a dead body. Before the enormity of the moment could hit, however, a voice inside my head pointed out that it wasn't a dead body, it was a skeleton. Another voice chimed in to say that a skeleton WAS a dead body. The first voice violently disagreed. The argument continued in my head for a bit with the pro-dead body voice insisting that a skeleton is the remains of a human being, so it was, by definition, a dead body. The pro-skeleton voice countered by saying that for it to be a body, there had to be meat on the bones and further argued that a zombie and a skeleton were two different kinds of monsters based entirely on meat quotient thus proving their point. The argument would have gone further if not for a third voice, my own speaking voice, interrupting them.

"Wait, how do you know that this is The Spronky Man?" I asked Eddie.

"He ain't got no clothes. Who else could he be?" Eddie shrugged.

"Good enough for me," Darby said as she lifted her skateboard into the air and smashed it down into the skeleton's face.

"WHOA! What did you do that for?" I asked, shocked.

"Naked creeps get their faces smashed. Those are the rules," Darby said, wiping bone powder off the edge of her board.

Jason then reached down and ripped the middle finger off Spronky's left hand and put it in one of his pockets.

"Why!?" I shouted in disbelief.

"Research," Jason stated flatly.

"Oh man, if you guys ain't the biggest bunch of weirdos I ever met," Eddie said. "You mind if I pal around with you?"

For the rest of the summer and every day after school, we would meet Eddie at the edge of the forest where he would introduce us to the terrible wonders of a cursed woodland that lay on the edge of an equally cursed town.

SEPTEMBER 1992:

THE ANOINTED ONE MOVES IN NEXT DOOR

I had never had a vision until The Anointed One bit me with their snake hand.

There were three moving trucks. The first two had been opened immediately. The third sat idle and the moving men didn't want to get anywhere near it.

I watched all of this from my porch. I had lied to my dad that morning about being sick and stayed home because I didn't feel like going to school. You were allowed a certain number of sick days per semester, and I always made sure to take advantage of all of them. I was using my precious free time to catch up on weekday television and the consumption of pizza rolls when I heard the trucks pull up. I spent the next couple of hours watching the movers unload the first two trucks and made guesses about our new neighbors based on their blandly tasteful furniture. I worked out that they were a family with at least one child though none of them seemed to be present.

Once the first two trucks were empty, the men gathered in the street and gave skittish glances towards the third. Nobody seemed to want to make a move until the tallest mover took charge.

"Ok, fellas," he said, "We got to do this now. I don't want to be messing with whatever the hell that thing is after sunset. Let's get it in the house and get out of here."

What emerged from the last truck was a gigantic, shiny black altar that measured over seven feet long and six feet high. It was one solid piece of stone that had been carved in such a way to make it appear as though a giant snake had wrapped itself around the immense structure. The eyes of the serpent were made from sparkling rubies and its mouth was sprung open in a silent scream revealing rows of razor-sharp teeth. The combination of hideousness and beauty compelled me to leave the safety of the porch to get a closer look. As I reached the edge of the yard, I could make out several strange symbols chaotically scrawled across the stone surface as well as many tiny humanoid figures dancing along the body of the colossal snake. I was so lost in the detail of the monstrosity that I was not prepared for the voice which spoke so close to me.

"Beautiful, isn't it?" came the soft whisper.

I jumped about a foot into the air and let out a yelp as I landed. I looked around to see where the voice had come from but saw nothing.

"Cast your eyes down, pilgrim," the whisper said.

I was hesitant to follow the whisper's advice. The sight of the leviathan crushing the stone altar and the soft hiss of the whisper had convinced my mind that when I looked down, I would find that slithering horror made flesh ready to rip out my throat with its jagged teeth.

"Be calm. You will not be harmed. By me at least. I cannot make the same promise for the chaos of the universe."

Reluctantly, I let my eyes roll down. Standing next to me, barely as tall as my belly, was a tiny figure dressed in robes of the deepest crimson. The fabric spread out from the figure in a circle like a pool of blood. Miniscule hands peaked out of the cavernous sleeves of the robes, and I could see a drawing, possibly a tattoo, of a snake wrapped around the left one. The figures' face was hidden by a mask that blended seamlessly with the robe. There was a strip of either plastic or glass running through the middle of the mask that allowed the wearer to see, though I could not make out the eyes staring up at me.

"Uh…hi," I finally blurted out.

The figure tilted its head to the left and right as if it was studying me. It then lifted the hand with the snake tattoo and whispered into the palm. Suddenly, the hand struck out like a snapping viper and wrapped around my wrist. I flinched but was soon overcome with a wave of drowsiness as if the tattoo had emptied a wonderful poison into my veins.

"I have dreamt of you," the being whispered.

"Oh?"

"Many times."

"That's cool."

"Not of your physical reality, but of your soul. Do you understand?"

"Yep," I lied.

"Fate has ordained that we should meet. Through you I will meet the others: A stoic warrior, an idiot from another place, a lost boy, and you, who sees and remembers."

"See…what do I see?"

"You see me here and now. But you are also watching from a great distance. As I speak, you are in the future, writing these words as I am saying them. This moment of time has long passed, and the two of us as we are now have ceased to exist. But through your simple act of remembrance and retelling, we live forever. For that I thank you and also thank the you that is yet to be." The figure then released its grip, raised its arms to the sky, and chanted incomprehensible words that made my head spin. The incantation seemed to drain the venom from my system, and I soon came back to my senses. The figure lowered its arms and looked me right in the eyes.

"Do you have any candy?" it asked.

"What?" I answered, confused.

"Snickers or peanut M&Ms? My parents won't let me have any because they say it makes me too hyper."

That's when it finally hit me that I was talking to a child. A child that seemingly had the ability to paralyze with the touch of their hand and see into the future, but still a child.

"Sorry, I don't have any right now."

"But you will have some at a future date?" they asked, a note of hope breaking through their dark whisper.

"Probably."

"This is wondrous news."

The child then began to smack their lips to an uncomfortable degree, so I asked them a question to get them to stop. "So, your family's moving in next door?"

"For a time, yes."

"Where'd you move from?"

"Parts unknown."

"Like Wyoming?"

"No. Further away. Beyond the veil."

"What's your name?"

"My true name is far too powerful to speak. You may refer to me as The Anointed One."

"The Anointed One? What does that mean?"

"It is the title bestowed upon me by the followers of The Book of The Never."

"Book of the what?"

"Words are useless. I will show you."

For the second time within a matter of minutes, the tattooed hand shot out, but instead of my wrist, it covered my heart. There was a flash of light, a scream, and the smell of copper.

And I Saw…

I saw our universe nestled inside the mind of a great serpent as nothing more than a lie the beast was dreaming up. I saw The Serpent, fangs overflowing with poison and eyes like fire, gorging itself on oceans and oceans of blood. I saw the oceans pour from the cup of a king who was made of infinite eyes and everlasting light and had been driven mad by the prison of eternity. I saw the wastelands of Antarctica and multitudes of robed pilgrims braving the desolation. I saw The Dagger, a mile-high black obelisk that erupted from the wastes. I saw the pilgrims gather and praise The Serpent at the foot of The Dagger. I saw an infant, tiny and sick, brought before The Dagger and the infant placed its frail hand on The Dagger and the stone did writhe and scream and from it erupted black blood which bathed the infant but touched nothing else. I saw the infant raised up and I saw the pilgrims kneel and I saw the black blood disappear and I saw on that frail hand there was the mark of The Serpent and the pilgrims rejoiced and exalted, "THE ANOINTED ONE!"

And I no longer saw.

"Now do you understand?" The Anointed One whispered as I came back to reality.

"Um…" I was blinking rapidly, trying to get my bearings. "Well, no, not at all. Not in any way, but…hey, can I ask you a favor?"

"Certainly."

"Can you please stop touching me with your snake hand and making me see visions?"

"Oh, did you not enjoy it?"

"It was…fine, but you should really ask first before you touch someone or mess with their mind."

"Thank you for making me aware of the customs of your people. You have much to teach me."

After some more painful awkwardness I learned that The Anointed One was not only going to be attending Aickman elementary, but they were also going to be in Mrs. Hackett's 4th grade class along with me, Jason, and Darby. On their first day, Mrs. Hackett had them introduce themselves in front of everyone. "Like everything else, this will end in tears. Now, I must go meet my new friends as The Serpent has ordained," was all they said before they marched to the back of the classroom to join the three of us, which suited Mrs. Hackett just fine. After school, we took them to meet Eddie out by the forest and there was an immediate feeling of completion, as if we were five fingers on a hand now wrapped in a soft, warm glove that protected us from the icy winds of Aickman township. It is no exaggeration to say that the school year that followed was one of the happiest times of my life.

But that is not what we're here for. We're here for the summer that came after.

SUMMER 1993

TOES

I was ten years old the first time I saw a severed human toe. I was also ten years old the second time I saw a severed human toe. And the third. Same for the fourth. As for the fifth severed toe, well, I was still ten years old. It was quite a day.

Summer break had begun and me and my friends sought the shelter offered by a particular stretch of God Help Us, They're Killing Us Creek. The name of the creek predates the town of Aickman itself and is associated with the first settlement of the area, the name of which has been lost to history. When the Aickman town founders arrived, the only trace of the first settlement left was a wooden marker on the banks of the creek with the words "God Help Us, They're Killing Us" written in blood. The name just sort of stuck.

We hung out under a tall willow tree. Years ago, young lovers had carved a giant heart into the tree with "Dennis + Kathy" written inside. Sometime after that, one of the lovers, or possibly a third party, put a giant X through the heart and carved the word LIES twenty times all around it. The sad, drooping branches and turbulent history tattooed into the bark led me to trust the tree and feel at home in its shade.

That morning, Jason Human and The Anointed One were having an argument. This was not unusual. Though we were all friends, we rarely seemed to agree on anything. Just the week before, me and Eddie had gotten into a screaming match over what would be worse: Eating puke or eating snot. I had strong feelings on the matter and the crux of my argument was that puke had once been food. Eddie's counterargument was that boogers were delicious. It ended in a stalemate.

Jason and the Anointed One's argument was about a similarly important issue: The very nature of reality. Jason contended that the universe was made of matter and could be understood through observation and experimentation. The Anointed One was of the view that the universe and everything in it was a lie told by the pet serpent of a god-king to trick the god-king into feeding The Serpent more blood. They both made valid points.

"I am not a lie!" declared Jason Human. "My smooth, grey skin and juicy knowledge brain are a fact!"

"You are a beggar," The Anointed One intoned. "A beggar who dances a fool's dance for his Lord Science as The Serpent starves. If it doesn't get the creamy blood which it desires, it will tell a new lie and that will be our final doom. So says The Book of The Never."

"That book again!" Jason said, flailing his arms. "Why do you never provide me a copy of this book so I may study it and prove you wrong about everything you hold sacred?"

"I cannot," The Anointed One said.

"Why? Is it forbidden to give the book to outsiders? How convenient."

"No, it is not forbidden. I cannot give you the book because there is no book."

"Wha…" Jason's bulbous head was pulsing now. "You mean to say that the book you constantly reference doesn't exist?"

"The Book exists. It's just not a book."

"How is a book not a book?"

"Hmmm, I've never heard this riddle before." The Anointed One stroked the chin of their mask. "I give up. How is a book not a book?"

"How should I know?"

"That's a terrible riddle."

"GAH!"

"You following this?" I asked Eddie. We were both lying on the bank of the creek, Eddie with a fishing line tied to his toe.

"Yeah," said Eddie. "It's hard to know who to believe. On the one hand, Jason has a very stupid head. On the other hand, The Annoying One is very short. Frankly, I don't trust either of them."

"What do you think the Universe is about?" I asked.

"It's big. I'm little. Who cares?" Eddie yawned.

I looked up the willow tree to the branch that Darby was laying on. I was going to ask her what she thought of all this, but she had her headphones in and was reading a comic book, once again proving herself to be the most sensible out of all of us. I closed my eyes hoping to nap through the rest of their argument when Eddie shouted.

"Hey! I got a bite!"

I sat up. Jason and The Anointed One stopped their bickering. Darby took off her headphones and jumped down from the tree. We gathered around Eddie in a state of shock. We had been telling him for the past year that he would never catch anything. How could he? For one thing, he never used any bait because he had a deep sympathy for worms, even going so far as to claim that they're the animal he feels closest to. For another thing, there were no fish in the creek. The textile mill had dumped mysterious barrels into God Help Us about ten years ago which meant that the water was delicious and made your skin tingle, but it also exterminated all life in the creek from that point on. None of these facts, however, had deterred him in his quest and now we could all see the dark shape bobbing up and down on the end of his line.

"And you bozos said I'd never get a bite!" Eddie trumpeted, reeling it in. "Nobody ever believes in ol' Eddie Gone. But look at your faces now. Well, you ain't getting a taste of this fish. It's gotta be a twelve-pound bass at least, and all for me! Butter grilled, pan fried, I can't wait to get my mouth arou…"

It took a lot to make Eddie shut up once he got going, and a big, fat severed toe impaled on the end of a fishhook was certainly a lot. He stood there, mouth agape, so still that it seemed like he was posing for a picture with his record-breaking catch. The toe swung like a pendulum on the end of the line. Our eyes followed it as though we were part of the world's sickest hypnotist act.

It was a big toe off the right foot of a large adult. It was swollen to the point of bursting and the flesh had turned purple. The toenail was long, thick, and yellow. There was no blood but the chunks of meat and bone poking out from the severed end made me simultaneously nauseous and, worryingly, a little bit hungry. What the heck were we supposed to do about this?

Jason was the first to act. He grabbed the toe from Eddie and inspected it with a magnifying glass. He made a series of "Hmmm…" and "Ahhhh…" noises as we watched. If anybody could figure out what was going on, it was Jason.

"I have a theory, but I need to test it," Jason said. "I need complete silence."

We held our breath.

Jason rolled the toe between his thumb and forefinger and brought the severed appendage closer to his large black eye. He then lowered the toe to his thin slit of a mouth and licked it with his blue tongue.

"Just as I thought," Jason announced. "Toes taste bad."

Eddie snatched the toe away from Jason. "Of course it tastes bad! It's a rotten toe!" Eddie railed. "What the heck is a toe doing in the creek?"

"It is a gift, Eddie," The Anointed One explained. "A reward for your patience and determination from the power that controls this creek."

"I WANTED A FISH!" Eddie screamed at the creek.

"You have to be realistic, Eddie," Darby said. "There aren't any fish in this creek."

Eddie examined the toe in his hand thoughtfully. "You really think it's a gift?"

"NO!" Jason shouted. "Don't listen to this tiny fool! That toe is not a reward. It is simply proof that one of our fellow humans has become acquainted with a water-based calamity and is minus one salty toe."

"Are you claiming that Eddie hasn't worked hard for this toe?" The Anointed One accused.

"Yeah, you saying I ain't earned this toe?" Eddie asked, wagging the toe at Jason.

"Toes are not earned! Water based deities do not exist and even if they did, they would have no dominion over toes!" Jason loudly reasoned.

"The Book of The Never states quite clearly th-"

"We need to call the cops," I said, snapping out of my toe induced daze.

"No cops!" Darby barked. "We take this to the cops and they're going to arrest us for grand theft toe or some other made-up crap. They'll send us away til' we're 21."

"Yeah, and I'll never see my toe again. No cops," Eddie said flatly.

"Then what are we supposed to do?" I whined. "We can't just ke-"

"HEY, THERE'S ANOTHER ONE!" Eddie shouted as he ran into the middle of the creek and picked up a second big toe out of the water. He held them both in the air, one in each hand. "A matching set! Must be from the other foot. Wait! No. Would ya look at that? It's another right toe! Two right toes…that's got to be good luck, right?"

"Eddie, stop touching the toes!" I pleaded.

"Why? It's like the Annoying One said, this is my reward. These toes are in recognition of all the time and effort I have put into this creek."

"They are human toes! They should be on human feet!" I reasoned.

"These toes belong to me now. I'll give them a good home and I will never lose them like their irresponsible owners. Now find me a bucket or someth- HOLY COW!" Eddie exclaimed, looking upstream.

It was like salmon battling against the current, endless pink flesh flopping over each other, to return to their ancestral mating grounds. But instead of fish, it was toes. A swarm of water toes coming straight for us.

"The creek must really like me!" Eddie said. "You guys need to get in here and help me catch them!"

"We shouldn't be touching rotten toes," I said.

"C'mon, I can't catch em' all on my own," Eddie pleaded.

The Anointed One waded into the ankle-deep water.

"What are you doing?" I asked.

"Sharing in the bounty of my friends' reward," The Anointed One said, moving to stand by Eddie.

Jason went in next.

"Guys, they are rotting human toes!" I screamed, trying to make them understand.

"I don't believe there is an intelligence behind this scenario, but Eddie asked for our help and toes are just flesh and bone. Human niblets. Fingers of the feet. Why, we homo sapiens touch fingers all the time, right?"

"When they're attached to a hand!" Again, my logic was faultless.

Darby joined the rest.

"Why are you helping them?"

"Because it's rad, Weirdo. Now get your butt in here and help," Darby commanded.

I felt her eyes burning through me, accusing me of being a bad friend. It was peer pressure plain and simple. You should never do something you don't want to just because your friends are doing it, but aside from being gross, was there really any harm in touching the toes?

Yes, yes there was. Decomposing human flesh is host to all kinds of bacteria and if any of them got into my system I could get sick and die. What they were doing was incredibly dangerous, I knew this for a fact. But I got into the water anyway. What was I supposed to do? They were my friends. I stood next to Darby and the five of us lined up reached both banks. Eddie hunkered down and we all joined him, waiting for the oncoming school of toes.

Water toe catching is very much like an Easter egg hunt. Granted, it's an Easter egg hunt taking place in a creek, which is unusual, certainly. Also, instead of searching for the eggs, the eggs are coming right at you and the eggs are toes and there are absolutely no bunnies involved. But aside from all those points, it's very much like an Easter egg hunt.

When the wall of toes hit us, we adopted various methods of capture. Eddie scooped as many as he could into his hands and threw them onto shore once he ran out of room. Jason Human moved at lightning speed, stuffing each one into his many pockets. The Anointed One lowered the sleeves of their robes into the water and caught the toes in them like a net. Darby was able to hold on to her toes in her huge hands without dropping any. I snapped the toes up with my index finger and thumb, dropping them in a little pouch that I made by lifting the bottom of my t-shirt up with my free hand. The onslaught of toes lasted about a minute. Once every toe was collected and counted the total came out to sixty. Sixty big toes off sixty right feet. They sat in a pile near the willow tree.

"Sixty. Man. I wonder where the creek got all these toes," Eddie pondered.

"The Book of The Never speaks of a great eye whose tears are the toes of traitors. The power of the creek must be in league with the eye. Or they at least know the same people," The Anointed One said.

"Schplerbang!" Jason exclaimed.

"Schplerbang?" Darby repeated.

"Yes, it is a common word where I come from."

"Ohio?" I asked.

"Yes…Ohio. Obviously. We from Ohio use this word whenever we are in the presence of nonsense like The Anointed One keeps spouting. This creek has no intelligence, eyes don't weep toes, and our universe is not a serpent's lie!"

"We fear what we don't understand," The Anointed One said.

"Then you must live in a constant state of fear because you don't seem to understand anything. Schplerbang! Schplerbang!"

"The Book of The Never states-"

"That not-book and everything you believe are the biggest pieces of Schplerbang in this or any other solar system and you are the tiny messiah of nothing save for mountains and mountains of the most fetid Schplerbang imaginable!"

Jason fixed The Anointed One with a vicious stare. The Anointed One stared back but said nothing. Darby, Eddie, and I were held prisoner by the tension. After a few seconds of the stare down, The Anointed One turned, picked up a toe from the pile, and threw it at Jason Human's head. The toe bounced off his skull, which jiggled from the impact, and landed at his feet. Jason, face twitching, never broke eye contact with The Anointed One as he reached down, picked up the toe, and hurled it at their mask, leaving a toe print on the eye port.

Everything was still. We could all sense that the future of our friendships depended on the next few seconds. Luckily, one of us had a plan.

"TOE FIGHT!" Eddie screamed as he scooped up handfuls of toes and began lobbing them at everybody.

Two or three bounced off my head before I got over my reluctance to touch the dead flesh again and began hurling toes back at Eddie. Darby grabbed a handful and scrambled up the tree, raining toes from above. Soon we were all running and screaming and throwing toes at each other.

"Yes! Hijinks! Child Time! This is what it means to be young!" I heard Jason say at one point.

"We live in a beautiful nightmare," The Anointed One said right before nailing me between the eyes with the bone end of a toe.

As we ran out of breath and the toe fight ended, I could sense that the anger that Jason and The Anointed One felt towards each other had been eaten up by the exhilaration of lobbing body parts at good friends. Darby then forced Jason to apologize, which he did and added that while the beliefs of primitive cultures are ridiculous, they should be tolerated even by the far more advanced people of Ohio. The Anointed One also apologized and admitted that Jason's master, science, had to be admired for all the cruelty and suffering that it had helped unleash on the world. They shook hands to their new understanding.

Eddie was so moved by this display that he decided to throw the toes back into the creek. "These toes aren't a gift for me," Eddie explained. "They obviously travel the waterways of America helping people overcome their differences and bring communities together. Keeping them would just be greedy, and if there's one thing Eddie Gone ain't, it's greedy." As Eddie placed the last toe into the water, he gave them a salute. "God Speed," he whispered.

A few days later Jason would reveal to us that he hung on to four of the big toes and ran some tests. According to his findings, all the toes were genetically identical which meant there were either sixty identical people all missing a toe or one person that was missing sixty toes. Either way, I had nightmares about it.

IT:

THE DISEASE THAT THINKS IT'S A GAME

To this day, medical science still has no explanation for the mystery of It. We know that It will spontaneously appear in certain populations, mainly children, and that the infection can be passed on by a two-part process:

1: The current host of It makes physical contact, usually using the hand, with a non-infected party.

2. The host shouts "Tag! You're It!" at which point the infection leaves their body and moves into the new host.

There seems to be no immunity. If you've been It before, you're just as likely to be It again as anyone else. In fact, there are only three known ways for children to avoid the infection:

1. Run Fast
2. Hide Well
3. Never go outside

One of the biggest obstacles to further research into this phenomenon is the fact that most, if not all, scientists do not consider It to be a disease. The doctors I have spoken to on the subject wave me off with explanations like "It's only a game," or "It's just a bit of fun," or "Leave me alone." But if they had seen what I saw on that Sunday in June over 30 years ago, they would know that It is real and will destroy your life.

My friends and I wouldn't have been involved in these events at all if my house hadn't become our unofficial meeting spot. We'd been hanging out on the porch for about an hour trying to decide what to do with the day. Darby mentioned that she had spotted an abandoned toilet on the side of the road and Eddie thought it would be the perfect thing to throw off a bridge.

"We'll never get this chance again," said Eddie. "You ever seen a crapper fly? Me neither. You ever see a crapper explode? I have. At my aunt's house. It was disgusting, but worth it."

"I'm in, but I get to chuck it," Darby said.

"DEAL!"

Jason suggested that we let him take samples of our blood. "You know. For fun. Blood fun. That's a phrase. Right? Let's have blood fun?" he explained.

The Anointed One spoke of a dream they'd had about a door in a cave and the darkness beyond it. They wanted us to find the cave and harness the darkness for our own ends. "Beyond the door, beyond the light, lies the key to eternal night," they intoned, possibly as an enticement.

I suggested that we watch videos in my basement and eat pizza rolls.

The sky was overcast, and the weatherman had predicted rain. We were debating the relative dryness of each suggested endeavor when Chad Pennington approached us. This was surprising because Chad was one of the most popular kids at our school. He had, at the age of ten, mastered the art of perfect hair and possessed the confounding ability to smile at all times. He was tall but not freakishly so, athletic though he never seemed to sweat. His shirt and shorts were wrinkle free and his sneakers were a brilliant white. He was the kind of kid who was going to grow up to be either a salesman, politician, or some other kind of menace. We lived on the same street, so we had to wait for the school bus together in the morning. He wasn't mean or anything, but he had a habit of talking at you and never to you.

"Hey man, did you see the thing on TV last night? Crazy, right? It's like, what the heck was that? Hey, I heard you like to write. That's cool. I was thinking about getting into it. Maybe we could hang out sometime and write a story. I have this idea about a kid who finds a knife that makes him really good at soccer. You play soccer? I bet you'd be fantastic at it. I'm not just saying that. Oh, here comes the bus, you sit at the back, right? Ok man, I'll see you at school," is an example of the one-sided conversations we would often have.

"Oh wow, the gang's all here! All right, very cool," Chad said, flipping his perfect hair out of his left eye. "Listen, we're about to get a monster game of tag going. It's going to be epic. For sure. And I was talking to everybody, and they all really want you guys to play. So many kids actually said that to me, no joke. There's already a bunch of us down on Grapevine, we'd really love it if you came," he lied to us.

His lying wasn't based in cruelty. We all knew the other kids didn't like us and, at their most charitable, did not care if we played or not. Chad was saying this because he wanted the game to be as huge as possible. He took pride in organizing massive see-saw wars and one of his famous water balloon fights had caused $20,000 worth of property damage. He had a gift for convincing others into joining his massive affairs and the more you said no, the more he enjoyed getting you to say yes. And he was good, very good. So good, in fact, that I cannot remember the series of further lies, flatteries, and hair flips he pulled out to get five of the most unpopular kids in town to take part in a group activity. All I know is that one moment I was on my porch and the next I was in the middle of the biggest game of tag in the history of Aickman.

I'm not sure exactly how many kids took part. The closest estimate I have is between 30 and 917. It was a mixture of 2nd through 5th graders. An army of kids who would usually have nothing to do with each other coming together in the name of It. Of course, this was all down to Chad. He had run the same sales pitch to everyone. The sheer size of the game was a testament to his powers. If he wanted, he could have talked that mob into overthrowing the town and proclaiming him king and I would have gone along with it even though I didn't like the guy.

Chad got two of the taller 5th graders to let him sit on their shoulders as he announced the rules to the mass of children he had gathered. Over this, I could hear the shutting of windows and the turning of locks all up and down Grapevine Street. The adults had seen the sea of children and knew there was nothing to be done. A storm was about to be unleashed and all that they could do was pray that their homes would survive it.

With his pronouncements finished, Chad was lowered back to the ground. He began his inspection of the crowd. The task of choosing the first carrier of It was his and he took it seriously. Some kids shied away from his gaze, others stood their ground and met it. I was hiding behind Darby and Jason. After a few minutes, he settled on Daryl Holtz, a freckle afflicted 3rd grader who was one of the fastest kids at school. It was a good choice. A slow kid would have killed the momentum of the game right out of the gate. He wanted this event to be legendary and he was making all the right moves.

Having thus been infected, Daryl closed his eyes and counted the customary 100 seconds, which is the time it takes for It to mature in the original host's body. While Daryl stood in the middle of Grapevine Street allowing a strange concept to grow within him, the rest of the mob scattered in search of hiding places. Some hid behind porches. Others clambered under cars. I saw Eddie climb into a trash can, an innovation that failed to catch on with anyone else. Then there were those, like Darby, that didn't even try to hide and would face Daryl, or anyone else, head on. As for me, I waited till no one was looking and climbed up a tree.

It is here that I must make a confession: I am a bad person. I'm sorry I didn't tell you earlier, but I didn't want to scare you off. I try to be good. I try to follow the rules. But that day I didn't. Y'see, one of the biggest rules was DO NOT CLIMB TREES. This rule was put into place because not everybody could climb trees so it would give certain people an advantage. I didn't break this rule because I was a rebel, or I thought I was better than everyone else; It was simple self-preservation. I was the slowest kid at school. If I had gotten tagged, which I assuredly would have, I wouldn't be able to catch anyone. This would have meant that for the game to continue, someone would have had to take pity on me and let me tag them. This had happened too many times in my young life, and I wasn't going to live through that embarrassment again. So, I chose the more dignified route: Illegally hiding in a tree and hoping no one would notice.

From that vantage point, I had a perfect view of the game. Daryl had finished his count and with the ritual intoning of "READY OR NOT, HERE I COME!" was soon on the hunt. The people who stayed in the open scattered and the hiders hunkered. The first person that Daryl found was a 4th grader named Rebecca Hall who was hiding behind a bush. She had been so wound up in anticipation that when Daryl tagged her, she let out an ear-piercing scream that made everyone jump and abandon their hiding places. The mob was on the move. It was complete chaos.

Kids were running right through hedges. A couple knocked over the garbage can Eddie was hiding in and he spilled out like a stray cat. One kid crashed into a mailbox ripping the post right out of the yard. I heard glass shatter. There was smoke coming from somewhere. Did I hear a donkey or was the donkey only in my mind? A shirtless kid had grabbed an American flag off someone's porch and was now waving it proudly over his head. A little girl was kneeling in the middle of the street praying to whoever would listen.

There were so many kids that It was passing from person to person at an incredible rate. A whole group of boys collapsed in a yard and were frantically passing It from one member of the pile to another. Back and forth. Each one of them had to have been It at least 10 times before It escaped that huddle. What kind of effect was all this rapid transmission having on It?

I kept an eye out for my friends to make sure they were doing okay. Nobody seemed to be interested in tagging Eddie even though he was right in the middle of the action. I think this was because he didn't go to our school so most of the kids didn't know him. Also, he was probably covered in garbage juice and smelled horrible.

Jason Human was the only other person who ran as slow as I did. This was entirely down to his technique which was to lean back at a 45-degree angle with his arms flailing out behind him while emitting a scream that was a combination of a cat yelp and a turkey gobble. At one point he almost got tagged but, in the panic of his pursuit, Jason ran face first into a metal garage door leaving a perfect imprint of his huge head. He fell back unconscious to the driveway and his pursuer, not certain of the ethics and legality of tagging a comatose individual, moved on to another target. I almost climbed down to see if he was ok, but as soon as no one was around, Jason's eyes popped open and he began to wiggle down the driveway, onto the street, and eventually squeezed into a storm drain to ride out the rest of the game.

Darby got tagged once. But only once. A kid named Danny Royce slapped her way harder than necessary on the right arm and even from a distance I could see her eyes fill with rage. She wanted to get Danny back immediately, but there were no touchbacks, that is the tagging of the person who just tagged you, allowed. So, Darby grabbed a third grader and tagged him, then with her other hand, grabbed another third grader and forced the first third grader to tag the new one. Having no use for the first third grader, she let him go and made the remaining one tag her. Now, with the ammunition she needed, Darby mounted her skateboard and gave chase to Danny.

When he saw her coming, he let out a curse and ran for his life. He tried jumping over fences, knocking trash cans in her path, but Darby swerved or jumped over everything. All the kids had come out to watch the spectacle. I could see Chad clearly happy with his decision to rope the weird kids into the game. People were going to be talking about this for a long time.

Danny was screaming at this point and running out of steam. He made one last attempt at escape by sliding over the hood of a car, but Darby just sped up and launched herself over the automobile. The mob let out a collective gasp as Darby came down and slapped Danny hard across the back, sending him flying out of the street and into a yard. Darby gave the peace sign and rolled away. There were cheers.

I didn't see anything of The Anointed One until the end. The game had reached an ebb. Everyone was tired but didn't want to stop. They had all posted up in new hiding places and there was some confusion as to who was currently It. In the driveway across from my tree, I could see Chad hiding behind a car. Even after all that had happened, he wasn't sweating, and his clothes had the same crispness as earlier in the day. Everything had become still.

The clouds were ready to burst. The rain would be the end of the game.

"Who's It?" a voice shouted.

"The kid in the robes!" came another shout.

The Anointed One. Everybody peeked their heads up trying to catch sight of them. I moved myself as quietly as possible around the tree trying to get a bead. I couldn't find them. I could sense a nervousness growing in the mob.

"The freak probably went home!" somebody offered.

"No, look, over there!" came another voice, but it was a false alarm.

This shouting went back and forth. A sighting here. A theory there. Some were proposing that they designate someone else as It. Another contingent said to stop and go home before the rain came. Chad announced that everyone needed to stay put. He said The Anointed One was somewhere nearby. He could feel it.

He was right.

As soon as he made that declaration, I spotted them. They were right behind Chad. They lifted their left hand, the one with the snake tattoo, from under the robe and slithered it silently through the air. The snake hand got closer and closer until The Anointed One spread their fingers as if the hand were a mouth and ever so gently nipped at Chad's right arm. He must have jumped at least 5 feet. I couldn't hear what The Anointed One was saying, but my guess was something along the lines of, "Tag. You're it. May the Leviathan's Eye remain blind to your presence in the next life," as they slowly glided away.

The sight of a frightened Chad would have been enough to make me laugh and give my location away but unfortunately it was given away by the sudden breaking of the branch I had been standing on. I tumbled down the tree and was only saved from crashing into the ground by my pants which were caught on one of the lower branches. I hung uselessly, unable to free myself, like a chubby piñata.

Chad had been in a state of shock. He had so far avoided being tagged and it was obvious that he had not been expecting the indignity. He turned his head. I could see his eyes. He was mad. Madder than Darby had been.

"Cheating, bro? Not cool, my man," he said as he started running straight for me to relieve himself of his failure. I began to shake and shimmy to get off the tree. Finally, there was a rip and I fell to the ground. I didn't have time to register the pain. I just got up and started running. I don't know why I bothered. The impact had already knocked out my breath and I didn't get more than 10 feet before I felt him slap his hand across my back and announce, "TAG! YOU'RE IT!"

No amount of explanation can make sense of what happened next. It was nothing you could see with your eyes. It was all instinctual, interpreted through sensory organs that science is not prepared to admit exist. Right after being declared It, I stopped in my tracks, confused. Chad had made it a few steps past me before he stopped as well. He turned. We were looking at each other. Something was off. Neither of us felt right but we couldn't quite explain why. Then Chad looked down at the hand he tagged me with, and realization hit us both at the same time.

I wasn't It; Chad was. It was still in Chad.

He walked back to me. I was so dumbfounded that I didn't move. He slapped me on the arm. "Tag. You're It." I wasn't. He slapped my arm harder. "TAG! YOU'RE IT!"

"Okay, yeah, I'm It, I'm It," I said, breaking out of my daze, trying to calm him down. But it didn't work. We both knew the truth. He grabbed me by the collar of my shirt with his left hand and raised his fist, ready to punch. I braced myself.

"TAG! YOU-" but before he could strike, Darby grabbed his arm and pushed him off me. He stumbled back. Darby was about to get in his face, then stopped. She took a step back and looked down at me.

"What…what's wrong with him?" she asked.

"He's…It," I answered.

Slowly, all the other children began to emerge from their hiding places and gather around. Some of them tried to approach Chad to see what was wrong, but they all stopped. They could sense it. He was sweating now and there was no smile on his face. His clothes now seemed ragged and torn, stains appeared out of nowhere. His hair wasn't perfect. It looked the same but only in the way that a stuffed bobcat looks like a living one.

He lunged at the group and began tagging. He tore through them in a panic, both hands slapping wildly at any living thing, hoping that It would leave him. But it did no good. It was apparent that whatever It was, It had chosen Chad.

The rain started to fall. The kids began heading home. Chad was still trying to tag them, but they ran to avoid his unclean touch. As he was about to tag a 5th grader, the kid pushed him to the ground. Chad just stayed there. Darby and I stayed with him as everyone else left. After the three of us had gotten thoroughly soaked, I reached my hand out to touch his shoulder.

"DON'T TOUCH ME!" he screamed. "It was you! You and your friends did this to me! This is why everybody hates you!" and with that, he got up and ran away.

Nobody saw Chad after that. In the days that followed, several strange noises could be heard coming from his house. Black handprints suddenly appeared on the windows of his bedroom and a bolt of red lightning struck the roof one night. I would occasionally see his parents out on their porch. Their eyes were sunken and blood shot, like they hadn't been sleeping. They installed several padlocks on their doors and had apparently stopped going to work. I heard from another kid on my street that they saw Father Agostino go in one night and then come running out a minute later, praying all the way back to his church.

Eventually, a For Sale sign appeared in the front yard and Chad and his family were gone.

ALONE PART 1:

THE TALL GRASS BEYOND THE CAR WASH

B ehind the car wash there lived a killer and it was beautiful. Cleanliness was never a priority for either me or my father, but on that Sunday morning in June the filthiness of our car could no longer be ignored once we read the message that someone traced into the dirt on the back window: "WASH ME! My name is Dan and I live at 27 Apple Valley Rd and I would like you to come to my house and bathe me. Food and drinks included. Guests Welcome. It will be fun!"

This troubling invitation had finally convinced my dad to do something about the state of the car and to forbid me from ever walking down Apple Valley Rd again.

The car wash sat on a concrete lot on the outskirts of town near The Broken Monument. The monument had been a brass statue of some kind, but an obscure calamity had destroyed it so that all that remained were the feet of a human, four legs of a pig, and the large claws of an unidentified creature. There was a plaque at the base of the ruined statue that simply read, "We must never forget" and indeed every 3rd Monday of March there was a town

51

wide holiday so that we could remember those that might have once existed and may or may not have done something worth remembering on the day it could quite possibly have happened.

Being summer, dad wanted to get to the car wash early to avoid the heat. All of dad's planning was about avoiding things like the heat, traffic, conversations, people, and reality in general. I went along because I had never been to the car wash before and I also wanted to get away from the newest stench in the house which neither of us could determine the origin of nor were particularly interested in dealing with.

The car wash consisted of six concrete bays with a faded orange roof. The asphalt lot was already shooting up heat haze from the morning sun when we pulled in to the third bay. When I got out of the car, I immediately froze as I saw that beyond the car wash, past the coin-operated vacuums, was a giant wall of immense grass. Each blade was at least seven feet tall and incredibly thick but undulated and swayed like spider silk. The blades were a candy green and danced with a delicate grace that was completely alien to the sweaty, hunch-shouldered world of Aickman. It was so beautiful that it felt like I was standing on the border between my ugly little life and a realm of emerald wildfire that would burn the stink of Aickman from me forever. I summed up these new and inexplicable feelings that were so suddenly unleashed within me by whispering "Cool" to no one in particular.

It was dad's command of "Go Play" that broke me from my trance. I immediately set out towards the grass, not just because I felt a need to be closer to its loveliness, but because I knew dad was about to freak out. He wasn't good at things like washing cars, mowing lawns, cooking food, keeping jobs, or really any verb and noun combination you can think of. Halfway across the lot I turned around to let him know where I was going. He didn't hear because he was screaming and punching the machine that activated the sprayer.

As I got closer, the details of the grass became clearer. The blades shimmered in the sunlight and their sheer size was incredible. I had already planned to snap one in half to make a rad sword, but what was really drawing me was a conviction from seemingly nowhere that I needed to explore the hidden worlds within that grass. Something inside me was certain that past those towering blades were sights and sounds beyond my imagining: strange creatures that put the mutants in The Screaming Forest to shame (yes) riches to fund endless weekends of video rentals and pizza rolls (yes) undiscovered countries from whose bourn no traveler returns (YES)

(All those things and more)

My mind was suddenly so filled with possibilities that I didn't even notice that the blades were beckoning like fingers-

(come on...)

-or that I had started swaying back and forth with the motion of the grass.

(come in...)

I felt weightless, floating. Getting closer and closer-

(Come see...)

-swaying...dancing... the rustle of the grass in the wind like sweet music.

(Come be...)

I was almost there...

(...with ME!)

I stopped a few yards from the beckoning blades. Was somebody saying something?

(No...it was probably just your imagination.)

I figured that it was probably just my imagination, but I didn't feel right. My head was aching as though something enormous had squeezed itself into my brain which wasn't even large enough to grasp the concept of fractions or how to divide them. Suddenly, my dad, the car wash, and the entire world seemed miles away. I felt very alone.

(I'm here.)

I hated that feeling. I wanted my dad. I wanted my friends. I wanted to be near people.

(But why? Don't you remember?)

As I turned to head back, the image of Mrs. Levinson, my second-grade teacher, popped into my head. She would make me stand in front of the class while holding up my homework so everyone could see how bad my handwriting was and laugh. Then suddenly I could hear the wheeze of coach Tumor who smoked cigarettes while teaching P.E. and loved to throw kickballs at my head to get me to run faster, jump higher, or simply to amuse himself.

(It's different in here.)

The ache in my head had spread to the rest of my body which began to shake. The memories of my classmate's laughter and kickballs bouncing off the bridge of my nose so the smell of rubber stuck with me all day were so crystal clear that I felt like crying. I was about to call out to my dad-

(Go Play.)

-but what good would that do? He would just tell me to Go Play. He was always telling me to Go Play. Go Play just meant LEAVE ME ALONE because that's all he ever wanted, to be left alone.

(Does He Even Love You?)

The immense thing in my brain grew bigger and bigger, my skull on the verge of exploding. I couldn't move. I couldn't scream. My body was clenched as though I were about to vomit up all my organs. In the small part of my mind that had yet to be enveloped by the invading immensity, I called out to my friends-

(Selfish. Dumb. Dangerous.)

-so I could tell them how selfish, dumb, and dangerous they were. They never listen to me. They always make me do what they want to. We could have caught a disease off those toes. We could have died!

(A Parade of Horrors...)

As the immensity continued to eat away at everything inside me, all the worst things I could possibly imagine slithered their way into my mind: Mrs. Levinson, Coach Tumor, Griffin Collins. The world was an endless parade of horrors. Mayor Deer, Broken Promises, Diarrhea...why do these things exist?!

(They don't exist in here. In here, you'll find no more of that. No more sickness! No more forgotten birthdays! No more sitting front row at your grandfather's funeral!)

No more wet beds! No more sucking at everything! No more fat fat flesh!

(No more nightmares! No more fear! No More pain!)

No more crying! No more sadness! NO MORE!

(No more father! No more friends! NO MORE!)

NO MORE!

(NO MORE!)

(NO MORE!) NO MORE!

NO MORE! (NO MORE!)

NO (NO MORE!) MORE!

(All the NO MORE you could ever want!)

All I could ever want…

Suddenly, the pain in my head stopped, replaced by cool, calm certainty. Slowly, I turned away from the world and its nightmares to face The Tall Grass Beyond the Car Wash. Several blades were reaching out, welcoming me. I lifted my hands as I got closer to my deliverance.

(yes… YES!)

Just as my fingers were about to caress the nearest blade which would gift me with an infinity of no more, a boot smashed into the back of my head.

(NO!)

"HEY KID! GET AWAY FROM THAT GRASS!" came a voice like a dump truck. The impact of the boot instantly knocked the enormity from my skull. I saw that my hand was inches away from a bowing blade and, realizing what it wanted to give me, I pulled back. Suddenly, there was a low growl and the blade reared up like a snake. Before it could whip out and grab me, I felt several small objects whizz past my head, and the face of the thick blade exploded with several large gashes. I could see brown coins sticking out of the middle of the fresh wounds which oozed with a viscous green fluid. The candy color of the blade began to sicken and pale before turning a desiccated brown. The other blades recoiled and shrank away from me as the wounded blade crumbled into a powder, the deadly coins dropping to the asphalt. So much had happened in so little time that I didn't know quite what to do.

That's when the second boot hit me in the back of the head.

"What is wrong with you?! Get away from that grass and bring me my boots!" came the dump truck voice again. I turned around to see a large, bootless man in an orange baseball cap who resembled a pile of garbage wearing ill-fitting clothes. His legs and feet seemed too small to support his immense frame and his eyes were hidden by a shock of white hair that exploded in all directions from under the cap. He was as ugly as the grass was beautiful.

"Listen, kid, there's glass everywhere because punks have been smashing bottles and I haven't been able to sweep it up cuz I broke my only broom on the heads of the bottle smashing punks. It's a real vicious circle. The point is, I don't want to cut my feet open and get one of these new diseases going around SO BRING ME MY BOOTS!"

I reached down and picked up the tiny boots from either side of me and walked slowly towards the man. He snatched the boots from me and gingerly, with a surprising nimbleness, slipped them on.

"You here with someone?" he asked.

"My dad," I replied.

"Where's your dad?"

I looked over to the third bay where my father was inside our car, crying. "He's in our car. Crying," I said.

"Why's he crying?"

"Probably couldn't make the hose work."

"Course he couldn't. You need to buy tokens from me first. There's a sign out front that says See Garvey Towne For Tokens.

That's me. I'm Garvey Towne," he said, patting the two huge coin bags that lay either side of his gut.

"There wasn't a sign out front when we drove up."

"There wasn't?"

"No."

"You sure?"

"Yes."

"Lousy punks," he fumed.

A dizzy spell came over me and I rubbed at the sore spots on the back of my head. "Why did you throw boots at my skull?"

"To get your attention, of course."

"Why didn't you just yell at me?" I asked, fingers tracing the lumps sprouting on my head.

"You wouldn't have heard."

"Why wouldn't I have heard?"

"Because of that grass," he said, looking at the dancing field of green. As he stared, the muscles of his jaw slackened, and his breathing got heavier as he added in a whisper, "That grass…it waves against the wind."

"What?" I asked, perplexed.

Garvey Towne stared at the field for a few more seconds, then shook his head violently. "I mean, I threw boots at your head because that grass ain't our property and you don't belong there. Don't go near it. Stick by your dad, wash your car, and leave. Those are the unwritten rules of the car wash."

"Why don't you write the rules down?" I asked.

"What for? All our signs just get stolen, apparently. You need to stop and think before you ask dumb questions."

I took his advice and thought for a few seconds. "Mr. Towne, did you just save my life?"

Garvey Towne looked startled. "Course not. My job is to get people tokens, carry the key to the bathroom that no one can use, and smash the punks. I don't save lives."

"Well...thank you, Mr. Towne."

He shuffled uncomfortably. "You're a weirdo, you know that? Look, I'll get your dad the tokens he needs but you got to calm him down first. I don't like emotional people. The car wash is no place for emotions. Save that for the movies or a gazebo. And don't go saying anything crazy like I saved your life. It's weirdo crap and it's bad for business." He looked towards the grass. "There's nothing weird going on here." He looked down at me. "Got it?"

I nodded, more confused than ever when just at that moment, there came a rustling from the grass. We both turned to see a tall man in an expensive suit emerge. He was carrying a briefcase and had an impossibly large smile with more teeth than could reasonably fit in a human head. Even more striking than the ocean of pearly whites were his dead eyes. They were beyond hollow and worse than empty. They were nothing less than windows into the beating heart of nothingness.

"Hi there!" the thing shouted. "I'm a businessman and I come from a wonderful place. Perhaps you've heard of it, or seen it in a dream? Regardless, I have been sent by head office to offer that young man right there a wonderful business opportunity," it said, pointing directly at me.

"OH NO YOU DON'T!" Garvey Towne screamed as he shot both fists into the coin bags on his gut and pulled out handfuls of brown tokens. "You get back in there, businessman! You go back where you belong! We don't need your kind out here!"

The businessman held up the briefcase to shield itself from the storm of tokens. It hissed as the tokens cut into the exposed flesh of its hands. Thick green ooze leaked from the gashes, the same as I had seen dribbling from the grass.

"I can see this is a bad time," the businessman chirped. "We'll call again when circumstances are more amenable." The businessman then lowered the briefcase to look me right in the eyes with its empty stare. "We are so looking forward to working with you." Its impossible smile seemed to grow even wider as the creature's eyes exploded into green puddles when a fresh barrage of tokens tore through its face. It then turned and ran back into the grass. Garvey Towne looked down at me. He was out of breath.

"Remember…nothing…weird…happened…here…today," he puffed.

PIÑATAS OF BLOOD

The doorbell rang and I knew immediately that it was The Anointed One. Where anyone else who pushed the doorbell would send a pleasant, high-pitched DING-DONG floating through our house, The Anointed One's touch unleashed a noise that was akin to the low growl of a dying behemoth whispering the words DOOM NOW.

I ran downstairs as soon as the behemoth spoke and opened the door. The Anointed One was standing there in flowing blue robes with four black envelopes in their tiny, snake-covered hand.

"Greetings my neighbor, my friend, my soldier," they whispered.

"Soldier? What are you talking about?" I asked.

"I have a mission for you," they said, handing me the black envelopes which had a name scrawled across each in dull white chalk: Darby, Eddie, Jason, and my own.

"What are these?" I asked.

"Invitations."

"To what?"

"My birthday party."

"It's your birthday?!"

"Tomorrow. I need you to deliver them."

"Why didn't you just mail them?"

"Because I have no idea where any of our friends live."

"Neither do I."

"Then you must go forth and find them. I would go, but there is much to prepare. If on the course of your quest you should perish, a piece of birthday cake shall be provided to your father as payment for your bravery."

Now, you may think that in a town as small as Aickman it would be downright strange to have no idea where three of your best friends live and, on this point, I can only agree. But as a kid I just never thought about it. They didn't bring it up, I never asked, and we just got on with our lives.

I headed straight for the willow tree. That was the place where I was certain to run into at least one of our compatriots. The general rule with our circle was that the more of us gathered in one place, the stronger the magnetic pull on the absent ones to join. All friend groups have their own algebra, and each member takes their turn being A or B or whatever else the equation demands. As variables go, Eddie was always the most unpredictable, but you could always count on him to show up at the willow tree. Always. Without fail. He would never be there first, and you would never hear him creeping up, yet within seconds of your arrival he would just appear.

"What's the story, morning glory? Wanna go spit in cups and see whose is thickest?" was Eddie's opening gambit that day. I handed him his envelope which he opened quickly to find the bright crimson card that I had already seen inside mine. Written on it was the following:

WHO: The Anointed One
WHAT: Birthday Party
WHERE: My House
WHEN: Tomorrow at 8:00 PM
WHY: Difficult to say. Was my coming foretold or am I merely a result of the chaotic circumstances that brought my parents together resulting in my random and ultimately pointless existence? A birthday party invitation is not the place to contemplate this. Of all questions, WHY is the most terrifying. I wish I had not included it.

P.S. We require no presents except your presence

"So, it's the Annoying One's birthday, huh?" said Eddie. "I'll tell you this much for free, I ain't drinking no blood. Nuh-uh. No sir. Eddie Gone does not drink blood. Never has, never will."

"They're not going to make us drink blood," I said, disgusted at the thought.

"And don't be saying I'm a blood bigot."

"Blood bigot?"

"I'm as open minded as the next fella."

"There's nothing to be open minded about."

"I mean, what's the big deal, really?"

"There's no deal."

"It's just blood. It's natural. Probably better for you than soda and all that junk, right?"

"No."

"Yeah…yeah, I'm probably gonna drink some of that blood."

"There won't be blood."

Eddie gave me a look like I was the biggest dope on Earth and before I could offer a rebuttal, Jason Human approached. He had a porcupine on a leash which was a new development.

"Greetings my 17th and 43rd favorite persons I've ever met. You seem much the same as always. Inertia looks good on some.

I, however, am always looking towards the future. Notice anything new?"

"Cool porcupine," I said.

"What?" Jason asked.

"The spike hog, bubble brain. Your new thing," Eddie said, pointing at the porcupine.

"This?" Jason said, indicating the indifferent animal lying placidly on the ground. "No, this is experiment 2787. He's not my new thing. Ignore him."

"What are you talking about, stretch?" Eddie said. "He's new and he's a thing and how the heck are we supposed to ignore a little prickly cutie pie on a leash?"

2787 let out a tiny yawn. Eddie and I swooned.

"I knew this would happen!" Jason declared. "This little diva has been upstaging me all day! Nobody has even noticed my new thing!"

"Ok, Jason, what's your new thing?" I asked.

"MY BASEBALL CAP IS BACKWARDS! I AM VERY COOL NOW!" Jason shouted.

After Eddie and I calmed Jason down and assured him that he was very cool, I handed him his envelope which he read and contemplated for a second.

"Hmmmm. I will of course drink the blood, but do you think they'll let me take some home?" Jason asked.

"It doesn't say anything about blood on the invitation. Both of you are just jumping to conclusions," I whined.

Jason and Eddie gave each other a look like I was the biggest dope on Earth.

"Look, The Anointed One and their beliefs might be a little strange but they're not going to make us drink blood." I was getting very annoyed at all the blood talk.

"Okay, pal. No blood. Sure," Eddie said sarcastically. "Just to be safe though, I'm going to grab a bib cuz all's I got are white t-shirts."

"For the sake of our continued friendship, I will indulge you in your bizarre fantasy where you will not be drinking blood tomorrow you fragile, deluded, unattractive fool," Jason added.

We waited around to see if Darby would show but she never did, so we decided to head into town. We found her walking down Poplar Street. She was hugging her skateboard to her chest and had a smile on her face which gave the three of us pause because the whole scene was very un-Darby. She considered life in Aickman to be a waking nightmare and always carried herself with a mean look and tense shoulders to let the nightmare know that she was ready to fight back. But for those few seconds on Poplar Street, it seemed as though she'd forgotten all about the nightmare and was instead walking in a dream. As soon as she spotted us, though, the dream bubble burst and the smile instantly disappeared.

"Rad porcupine," she said, waving at 2787, who ignored her.

Jason began making a grumbling sound, so I intervened. "And hat," I said, pointing at Jason's head.

"Oh yeah, cool style Jason."

"Thank you, Darby. I knew you, out of everyone, could appreciate what I was going for."

I handed Darby her envelope. "Do you think they're going to make us drink human blood or animal blood?" she asked after reading the invitation.

"What's the difference? Humans ARE animals. Filthy animals," Jason said.

"Gotta be human or else what kind of lame-o religion we talking about here?" Eddie said.

"Or they could just have cake and ice cream," I blurted rather sharply. "Why do you assume that just because it's The Anointed One that it's going to be gross?"

All three of them, and I swear even 2787, gave each other that look that was really starting to bug me.

"Whatever," I said, walking away. "Just be there tomorrow at eight." I'd had enough of the insinuations. My friend was not going to make me drink blood. The party was going to be fine. I had nothing to worry about. I kept saying this over and over to myself for the rest of the day until I drifted off to sleep.

I, of course, had nightmares.

I dreamt that we walked into The Anointed One's house, which none of us had ever been inside of, and suddenly we were in the middle of a vast black stone castle. The Anointed One's parents, whom we had never met, were over seven feet tall and adorned in leather robes covered with spikes. They had sharp claws and jagged teeth and as soon as we were inside, giant snakes wrapped around our bodies, squeezing us so tight that our mouths were forced open. The Anointed One's parents then brought over goblets overflowing with blood and poured them down our throats. The parents laughed as we guzzled and choked on the thick, coppery liquid. We became so engorged with the blood that our bodies bloated out like balloons and soon we were lifted into the air with ropes. That's when The Anointed One appeared with a long stick in their hands.

"It's just not a birthday party without piñatas," The Anointed One whispered. Their monstrous parents began singing the birthday song as one by one The Anointed One batted at Darby, Eddie and Jason until they popped like ticks sending waves of blood and candy crashing to the ground. I wiggled and squished around in my rope like a manic waterbed, but I could not get free. The Anointed One approached, lifting the stick.

"Please!" I screamed.

"It's my party and you'll die if I want you to!" The Anointed One bellowed, bringing the stick down against my swollen side and just as I was about to burst open, I woke up screaming. I could taste blood.

Evening came and there was fear in my heart.

We met up on my porch, as was our custom, before heading over to The Anointed One's. I was visibly sweating, partly due to the heat, but mostly because I had not been able to get my imagination in check. I'd slowly been able to cast away thoughts of being transformed into a macabre party game, yet I couldn't completely shake the idea of being forced to swallow blood at some point that night.

The mini-panic attack I was having went unnoticed by the others who were all rather gussied up for the event. Darby had drawn an Egyptian pattern around her eyes, tied her hair back in black ribbon and was wearing a men's dress shirt and pants. Eddie was wearing his usual garb, but his skin was fresher and pinker, like he'd actually bathed. In addition to that, his ever-present black eye had taken on a luminous, almost pastel-like quality and the scars seemed to shimmer. Jason's huge head had a similar shine to it, as if it had been buffed, and he was wearing an ill-fitting tuxedo that only went out to the elbows and knees. He had brought along 2787 who was wearing a pink bow on their collar. I also noticed that his baseball cap was turned towards the front again.

"Why did you abandon the style, Jason?" Darby asked.

"I haven't. I have turned the hat a whole 360 degrees. I am on a level you cannot imagine," Jason declared.

Despite the fear gnawing at me, I couldn't help but bring something up, "Why are you guys so dressed up? You didn't get this dressed up for my birthday party."

"Did you see the invites?" Eddie asked.

"Yeah," I replied.

"Yeah, well, they put the fancy in schmancy and I ain't gonna look like no bum for this soiree."

"It's The Anointed One's turf. Elegance is expected," Darby added.

"What do you mean?" I asked. "You guys spent all yesterday talking about how they were going to make us drink blood!"

"Exactly," Eddie said. "And you know who else drinks blood? Dracula. That's who."

"Dracula is a monster," I said.

"Yeah, but he's classy," Eddie retorted.

"Dracula's got a dress code for sure," Darby nodded.

"So, you're saying me and my dad aren't classy?" I huffed.

"Not Dracula classy," said Eddie. "You and your dad are more like a couple of…uh…blobs."

"Blobs!" I snapped.

"Not blobs," Darby said. "More like…Creatures From the Black Lagoon."

"That makes more sense," Eddie agreed. "You guys live in a black lagoon. No shirt, no shoes, no problem. A real Bless This Mess situation. As close to nature as you can get in a house."

"Leave him alone!" Jason screeched. I was shocked but moved by the completely unprecedented display of compassion from him.

"Thank you for defending me, Jason." I said, putting my hand on his arm.

"I wasn't. You and your father live in filth. There's just no more time to continue accurately describing your home situation through monster metaphors. It's 8:00 PM. The party has started," Jason announced.

The Anointed One's house was much the same as any other on our block. Two-story with a wraparound porch. White paint with red trim. Neatly manicured lawn. All in all, it was a lot nicer than my house, with our peeling paint job, untamed grass, and duct tape over the cracked windows. If you were to ask somebody which house on our block was home to the adherents of a chaos snake cult, they were more likely to pick mine than the genuine article.

We stood at their door unsure what to do. Like I said, none of us had ever been inside before. Nobody seemed to have the courage to knock.

"What do you think their parents are like?" I asked nervously.

"Dead. That's why we've never met them," Darby said.

"We've never met your parents," I reminded her.

"Wishful thinking, then," Darby said.

"Prolly got big heads," said Eddie.

"What, like Jason?" I asked.

"No, I mean they're probably full of themselves. If I'd given birth to the savior, I'd sure as heck be a real snob about it."

"I imagine they are covered in ritual scars," said Jason. "That's why our tiny friend is always robed and masked. Sacred mutilations all over their bodies. Teeth filed to points. There will be whips, of course. Always whips. Scrawlings on the walls in one of your ancient dead languages. The smell will be horrendous. The homes of believers are all the same."

Jason's description, though ludicrous, got my heart racing a bit more and the fact that still no one had bothered to knock assured me that they were all feeling the same fear I was. We would have probably stayed on the porch looking at the door all night if the handle hadn't suddenly turned and the door swung slowly open into complete darkness. We stared into the lightless house unsure what to do. The only one of us who had any sort of plan was 2787 who immediately marched through the doorway dragging Jason with him. Jason let out a little cry as he grabbed at Eddie's t-shirt dragging him who then grabbed at my hair pulling me and I instinctively reached for Darby's hand and once we were all inside, the door swung shut.

Darkness surrounded us. There was the sound of drums. They were beating a primal rhythm. It grew louder and louder and I could feel Darby squeezing my hand as hard as I was squeezing hers. Suddenly, a light flashed from above. It was a brilliant crimson that illuminated two figures standing 10 feet in front of us. Their robes were exactly as I dreamt. Black leather. Spiked. The taller figure raised its hands to reveal massive metal claws. It pointed right at us.

"TINY FOOLS!" it said in a booming voice.

"WHAT HORRIBLE TURN OF FATE HAS GUIDED YOU HERE ON THIS MOST SACRED OF NIGHTS?" blasted the smaller figure. They paused as if truly expecting us to respond. None of us made a sound. Instead, we began to bunch up closer and closer as if trying to merge into one giant creature that might stand a chance against the two nightmares before us.

"YOU ARE TRESPASSERS!" the tall one screamed.

"DON'T YOU KNOW THIS MEANS YOUR DOOM?!" the small one wailed, bunching its metal claws into fists.

The tall one glided towards us. "PREPARE YOUR SOULS FOR OBLIVION!" it bellowed as it lifted its claws high in the air, ready to shred our flesh.

We screamed and screamed and screamed.

At the very height of our terror, the red light disappeared and was replaced by the soft glow of standard indoor lighting. We were standing in a simple yet tastefully appointed living room. The two figures were laughing. We stopped screaming but were frozen to the spot in a mixture of fear and bafflement.

"Sorry about that," said the taller figure in a much softer manner, stifling a giggle.

"It was The Anointed One's idea," the shorter one intoned in a lilting voice.

"We certainly didn't mean to give you kids the willies," the taller one said while removing their hood to reveal a bald, smiling middle-aged man. The shorter figure removed their hood to reveal a slightly younger woman with cascading raven black hair.

"Welcome to my party," came the whisper from behind that sent us all jumping two feet in the air. We turned to see The Anointed One in swirling, multi-colored robes with a party hat atop their mask. Though most of us were still too stunned to speak, Eddie managed to capture our mood perfectly.

"HOLY MOLY WHAT THE CRAP WERE YOU THINKING?!" Eddie shouted. "You trying to give a ten-year-old a heart attack?! Are we playing send my friends to the hospital!? Gonna pin a donkey tail in my eyeball next?! JEEZ LOUISE!"

"You must be Eddie," the tall one said, holding his huge metal claws out to shake hands. "Oh, sorry about that." He removed the gloves that the claws were attached to and held his hand out again. "I'm Eric, The Anointed One's father."

Eddie reluctantly held out his hand and they shared a manly shake. "Eddie. Eddie Gone. Not sure but I might be standing in a pee puddle. I won't be cleaning it."

"No puddle. No problem," Eric laughed.

"I'm Alora, The Anointed One's mother," said the woman as she approached to shake Eddie's hand. "They're always saying so many nice things about you."

"Really?" Eddie said, shocked.

"Mother, please." The Anointed One had sidled next to Alora, hugging her hip, careful to avoid the spikes on her robes.

"Calls you the jungle boy. Says you were raised by wolves," Alora continued. "You hold the spirit of the forest within you. Says you can hawk a loogie over 20 feet."

"Welp, can't argue with any of that," Eddie concluded.

"From everything The Anointed One has told us, the incredibly stylish young woman with the rad eye makeup has to be Darby," Eric said.

"I guess," Darby said, letting a half-smile cross her face as she shook Eric's hand.

"Guess, nothing," Alora said. "You look absolutely amazing. You're the first person The Anointed One has ever met that has made them reconsider wearing the sacred robes. All we hear about sometimes is how Darby wore this or Darby wore that. You're a fashion icon in this house."

The Anointed One was doing an uncomfortable wiggle and making a low moan out of embarrassment. We all enjoyed that very much.

"I mean, I'm like whatever, but nothing compared to what you guys are rocking," Darby said, referencing their spiked robes, desperately trying to get the attention off herself.

"Oh, these?" Alora said. "These are just our ceremonial robes. Only supposed to be used for our most sacred of rituals. Technically, outsiders are never supposed to see them but when The Anointed One told us about their little plan, we just thought, what the heck!"

"Speaking of spikes," Eric said. "I see from the fact that you brought a porcupine into our house that you must be Jason. We've heard...about you." Eric extended his hand to Jason which Jason grabbed and brought up to his non-existent lips to kiss.

"The porcupine is part of an experiment that is beyond even my understanding. It is called 2787. Ignore it."

"Yes, we'll ignore the porcupine on a leash that you brought into our house. Of course," Alora said.

Eric looked at me. His smile grew wider. "This man needs no introduction." His grip on my hand was soft and warm. It felt like a hug.

"It is so good to finally meet you," Alora said in a soft whisper, leaning over and taking my hand in hers. "Y'know, The Anointed One is always saying-"

"Enough of these pleasantries!" The Anointed One declared, throwing their hands in the air. "It is time for CAKE."

What followed did not involve blood, torture, or death in any way. It was just a typical birthday party. We ate a cake that was shaped like a giant serpent biting the throat of a humanoid figure that represented "Time" and then played a game similar to Pin The Tail On The Donkey called Stab The Frog In The Face. After that, Eric and Alora took us down to the basement to show off the black stone altar I had seen when they first moved in. Jason was very curious to learn how they managed to get such an immense object into their house let alone down to the basement. Eric and Alora just laughed and told him it was their little secret. Things got a little ugly when Jason demanded to know these secrets.

"ALL OF THEM! RIGHT THIS SECOND!" he screamed. None of us were surprised that it was Jason who would ruin the party, but what was surprising was how easily Eric dealt with him.

"Nice hat," Eric said.

"What?" Jason asked, lowering 2787 who he'd been brandishing as a weapon.

"Your hat. It's super cool. I meant to mention it earlier, but I was just intimidated, y'know."

"I do know," Jason said. "It gives off power. Do you know why?"

"Boy, I sure don't."

Jason leaned towards Eric and whispered, "I've turned it 360 degrees. It has never been done before."

"Well, I'll be darned."

"Would you like to know more facts about my hat?"

"I can't think of a better way to spend my night," Eric said, giving a little hand signal to Alora who ushered the rest of us out of the basement.

Once upstairs, The Anointed One opened their single present which was a life-sized doll of themselves with unsettlingly realistic hands.

"Technically, as the leader of our sect, The Anointed One is not allowed gifts of any kind," Alora explained. "That's why we didn't ask you to bring any. But we had a scholar friend of ours look through the sacred texts for a loophole and using some rather loose interpretations of certain passages we discovered that they are allowed to receive effigies of themself. We have them made special from Belarus. Gets one for every birthday. Keeps them in their room."

"Can we see them?" Darby asked The Anointed One.

"You are not ready to meet the Army of Me," they responded.

By the time Eric, Jason, and 2787 had come up from the basement, Alora had tried to get a dance party going but it turned awkward very quickly. Darby spent the whole time commenting on the radness of their record collection and The Anointed One would only slow dance with their doll. Alora tried to get me and Eddie to join in, but we were boys, and everyone knows that boys don't dance. Jason took this opportunity to teach 2787 about a new fad called moshing and ended up with 5 spines in his abdomen which he removed with no fuss despite Alora and Eric's alarm.

"We can call you an ambulance, Jason," Eric told him.

"Your science cannot possibly fix what is wrong with me," Jason assured him.

Besides that, nothing worrying occurred for the rest of the night...until the end. And it was partly my fault.

I couldn't stop thinking about the red light that shown on Eric and Alora when they were pretending to be monsters. I saw no lamp or projector that could seemingly have made that happen, so I finally asked them where the light had come from.

"The Ruby," Alora said.

Eric gave her a look.

"Don't you dare," Alora said. "It was your idea to use it. You broke the rules first."

"What's the ruby?" I asked.

"Well, it's a sacred relic put in our charge," Eric explained. "It exists in both this and another realm. It has strange, mystical properties that no one quite understands. Alora and I have the power to make it appear with our minds which we're never supposed to do. But I knew it would add the perfect effect to The Anointed One's practical joke."

"He has a flair for the dramatic," said Alora, rolling her eyes.

"Don't tell anyone, okay?" Eric said, winking at me.

The completely baffled look on my face in light of this revelation seemed to jumpstart Eric's "flair for the dramatic" and as soon as Alora walked away to deal with the 2-litre of soda that Jason had just spilled on the floor, he leaned closer to me and asked, "Do you wanna see it?"

I absolutely did not, but before I could say so, Eric's eyes rolled back white and suddenly a giant red ruby appeared floating just beneath the ceiling. It was shining down a beam of hazy crimson light.

"ERIC!" Alora shouted.

"What?" Eric shrugged. "He forced me!" he lied, giving me a little nudge on the shoulder.

We all stared at the beauty of the ruby as it spun in the air. Sparks of energy leapt from it, and I could hear the drums again, but the beat was less savage and more like a heart. It was such a distracting sight that no one noticed that Jason had let go of 2787's leash and the porcupine headed straight for the beam of light. Eric had time to let out an "OH NO!" before 2787 was engulfed in the ruby's beam. Almost immediately, the porcupine stood on his hind legs and spread his front paws out to his side. The eyes of the once placid porcupine became filled with the energy of the ruby and sparks were now jumping off its body. He began to levitate up to the ruby and as soon as his paws touched it, the ruby seemed to melt and be absorbed by 2787's body. The ruby was gone. All that remained was 2787 who still floated and emitted a red glow.

"2787, you get down here right now!" Jason demanded.

"Silence, skinny fool!" 2787 announced with the same booming voice that had come out of Eric earlier. "My name is not 2787! It is Dumpling O'Whiskerson! Of the clan Stab Back! Of the family Knife Rat! I am no longer your test subject. I have been infused with the power of the Ruby of Sarnoth. With this power I will return to my people and rally all the animals of the forest to overthrow humankind who destroy our living world daily. Quake with terror you fools for the age of man is at an end!" and with that, Dumpling O'Whiskerson launched himself through the ceiling leaving the most adorable porcupine shaped hole behind.

"That's…worrying." Eric said, then turned to Jason. "Well, Jason, I hope at the very least this taught you why you should not bring porcupines into people's homes."

"Don't listen to him," The Anointed One said. "That was the coolest thing I have ever seen. You have made this the greatest birthday party of my life."

"Yes, I am a very good friend," Jason agreed.

The ascension of the porcupine marked the end of the party. I was the last one out. As I was walking down the steps of the porch, I heard a "psst." I turned around to see Eric and Alora standing in the doorway.

"Is something wrong?" I asked.

"No, nothing's wrong," Alora said. "Except of course for the porcupine with untold power out to destroy humanity." She was giving Eric the stink eye.

"We shouldn't blow that out of proportion," Eric said.

"Sure," Alora scowled.

"No, we just wanted to thank you," Eric said.

"Thank me?"

"For being so nice to The Anointed One. For becoming their friend," Alora said.

"Also, for introducing them to the others," Eric added. "We move around a lot. They've...never really fit in anywhere."

"Honestly, they don't fit in here," Alora said sadly.

"We had high hopes for this town," Eric said. "The stories and reports we got about...phenomena."

"It seemed like we would fit right in, but..." Alora didn't finish the thought.

"Anyway," Eric continued. "You were the first kid their age to meet them and not run screaming. I know our ways are different and The Anointed One is certainly different."

"It's not their fault," Alora corrected Eric. "They didn't choose to be chosen."

"I know that I'm just say-"

"Well, you don't need to say anything."

"Can we not do this in front-"

I could see that this was going to turn into a real grown-up type situation, so I just interrupted them. "HEY!" They both stopped. "You don't have to thank me or anything. The Anointed One is cool. I like them. I'm glad you guys moved in next door."

"So are we," Alora said, smiling.

"Don't be such a stranger," Eric said.

I walked back to my house. I was surprised to see The Anointed One waiting on my porch.

"How did you get here?" I asked.

"I saw your dream," they whispered.

"What?"

"Last night. The blood piñatas."

"How do you know about that?"

"You dream very loud."

I didn't know how to react to this. I just stood there, silent.

"I don't want to kill you. I don't want to make you drink blood," they said.

"I know. It was just a dream. I couldn't control it."

"It hurt." They turned away from me.

I wanted to argue that maybe they should stay out of my dreams then, but that would have just made things worse. So, I said the only thing worth saying at moments like that: "I'm sorry."

They turned back to look at me. "It's ok. I had my revenge," they giggled.

Realization dawned on me. "That's why you had your parents do that to us?!"

"It was very funny."

Before I could refute this blatantly false statement, there was a loud boom above. I ran off the porch to see what it was. High up in the clouds I could see a red streak barreling through the night sky. I couldn't see him clearly, but I knew that it had to Dumpling O'Whiskerson trying out his new powers. In the past, momentous occasions were always marked by eclipses or other such celestial phenomena. It was fitting that The Anointed One's birthday would be capped off by the appearance of an angry porcupine tearing up the stratosphere.

"Happy birthday," I called back but was answered with a thud. I turned to see The Anointed One lying on the porch. I ran back up and tried shaking them. As soon as my hand touched their shoulder, I realized that it wasn't them but their life-sized doll. I looked up just in time to see The Anointed One waving at me from their bedroom window as the lights in their room went out.

I left the doll on the porch, went to bed, and tried not to dream so loud.

For more information about Dumpling O'Whiskerson, go to Wikipedia and look up The Great North American Forest Rebellion of 1997.

ALONE PART 2:

THE GARBAGE MAN

The story of Mr. Garcia and the garbage cans ended that summer, but, as far as I'm aware, it started the previous September.

That first night began with a nightmare. I dreamt that a worm in a top hat was following me around town. He was well-spoken and used his dexterous vocabulary to loudly proclaim the many ways in which I would make a fine meal after I died. He rhapsodized about the fruit soft flesh falling from my bones and marinating in my natural juices to make a graveyard stew that would put all the chefs of France to shame. His talk of me as a rotting delicacy was turning the heads of everyone in town, and they were starting to look at me with hunger in their eyes. I could see my first-grade teacher licking her lips and behind her a mailman was salivating so much that his uniform was sopping wet. The worm had whipped everyone up into such a frenzy that they started chasing me down the street ready to rip me to pieces. Just as the hungry mass of Aickman was about to make me their dinner, I was woken by the sound of metal scraping concrete.

My pajamas were soaked with sweat from both the nightmare and the hot weather which September had promised to end, but, as usual, failed to deliver. It was midnight and my window was open in the vein hope of catching a breeze that didn't exist. The racket that had woken me up was coming from outside, so I went to the window to investigate. That's when I saw Mr. Garcia.

Mr. Garcia lived across the street. He was an older man who kept to himself. Occasionally you would see him out in his customary brown slacks and white undershirt mowing the lawn or trimming the hedges. He wasn't fastidious about yard maintenance, and I got the sense that he only did it so that no neighbors would bug him about it. If you waived at him, he would pretend not to see. If you said hello, his ears would no longer work. He couldn't be called a cranky old man because cranky old men love to yell at children and complain to anyone that'll listen. Nor could he be called a lonely old man because loneliness is an affliction, and he didn't seem to be suffering at all. He simply preferred solitude and every decision he made was based around the principle of avoiding contact with other human beings.

The year before, my school had run a candy sale. I was, of course, a terrible salesman. I was so lacking in the instincts which make a successful salesman that the very first door I knocked on was Mr. Garcia's.

"Yes," Mr. Garcia had said.

"Um, yeah hello, um, Mr. Garcia. Um, my school is having um, eh, my school is-"

"Are you trying to sell something?" Mr. Garcia asked.

"Um, y-yes."

"You're not very good at it."

"Oh, ummmm…."

"What are you selling?"

"Uh, chocolate bars."

"You shouldn't sell candy to old people. It could kill us," he said, and then he closed the door on my face. It was the only time we had ever spoken.

From my window on that hot September night, I watched Mr. Garcia drag a huge silver garbage can down his driveway and couldn't help but take note of four things:

1. It was extremely late to be taking the garbage out.
2. That silver garbage can was not his normal garbage can.
3. It was Thursday and garbage day was on Monday.
4. The garbage can was wrapped up in heavy chains with a giant padlock securing them on top of the lid.

I found the whole scene incredibly unsettling. The night was so still, and the sound was so loud, but I seemed to be the only one it had woken up. Mr. Garcia was struggling to pull the can; his labored breathing was almost as loud as the grinding metal on the driveway. The chains, which looped underneath the can, seemed to snag and send the can twirling off in unpredictable directions. When he finally reached the curb, he collapsed in a heap on the street. It took him a while to catch his breath and when he finally sat up, he leaned back on the trash can for support. His white undershirt was almost transparent with sweat and there was a rip up the left leg of his trousers. He must not have realized that he was using the can to rest on because when he opened his eyes and saw that he was leaning on it, he quickly scuttled back in fright. He lifted himself onto the curb and sat there just breathing, sweat falling from his forehead.

He sat there for two hours. I know because I watched him the whole time. I couldn't look away. What was in the trash can? A dead body? Then why bring it to the curb? Also, if it was a dead body, why was it chained like it's keeping something from getting out? Or was it stopping something from getting in?

It was about 2:00 AM when the truck pulled up. The markings on it designated it as an official vehicle of Aickman township waste management. Two men in dark overalls got out. The taller of the two approached Mr. Garcia who finally stood up. They spoke for a few seconds and then the tall man handed Mr. Garcia an envelope and then extended his hand to shake, but Mr. Garcia declined. The two men struggled to lift the can and placed it in the bed of the truck. Mr. Garcia stood in the street and watched the truck drive away. Once it was out of sight, he turned and looked directly at me.

"Go to bed," he said.

I jumped straight from the window to my bed and screwed my eyes closed tight.

I didn't tell my friends. Or my father. In fact, this is the first time I have ever told anyone about Mr. Garcia. I don't like to inflict my troubles on others and, knowing my friends, I was sure they would want to get involved. But what I witnessed that night seemed somehow so wrong that to breathe a word to anyone else risked them becoming stained by those cursed and baffling events. I decided that the best course of action was the standard procedure for dealing with anything in Aickman: push it to the back of my mind and hopefully forget about it within two weeks. As usual, the plan worked. For a while at least.

Then, around Halloween, I dreamt about the worm again.

This time I was at a doctor's appointment and the worm was telling Dr. Evans that my bones were too shiny. The worm was worried that when I die and all my flesh fell off, the light from my bones would be a navigational hazard to passing airplanes. Dr. Evans had many questions, but the worm assured him that he had spoken to several experts who were certain that I would die out in the open and in such a manner that my corpse would be irretrievable for several generations. Both Dr. Evans and the worm concluded that the best course of action was to remove my skin and dull my shiny bones. Before Dr. Evans could skin me with his scalpel, I woke up and, remembering the events that followed the worm's last visitation, headed for the window.

The air was crisp, and fall had well and truly banished summer, but there was that same stillness, like time suspended. The Jack O'Lanterns on the Smith's porch were lit but the candles didn't seem to flicker as if the flames were frozen in place. There was no racket this time because Mr. Garcia was now using a dolly to move the chained can. It looked like the first garbage can but had none of the dents and dings suffered the previous month and now had the number 2 sloppily spray painted across the front. Mr. Garcia had aged dramatically. His formerly salt and pepper hair was now completely white and there were dozens of liver spots that had sprouted across his face and chest. He set up a folding chair by the curb and placed the can down next to it. He collapsed into the chair and for the next hour we both waited. Eventually, the same men in the same truck appeared, relieved Mr. Garcia of the can, and drove away.

"Go to bed," Mr. Garcia said, and I did.

This pattern would repeat over the course of the school year. Once every month, I would have a dream about the worm who would convince people to harm me based on some property of my decaying corpse and I would wake up before they could kill me. I would then go to the window and watch Mr. Garcia tow a chained garbage can with ever increasing numbers spray painted across it to the curb and then the men from waste management would take it away. He would then tell me to go to bed and I would do just that.

This ritual was monthly but had no set date or span between pick-ups. For instance, the pick-up for February, can #6, was on the 28th and the pick-up for March, can #7, was on the 1st. Weather also seemed to have no effect on when he had a new can to dispose of. I remember that night in January, can #5, was the coldest in a decade and Mr. Garcia sat shivering and miserable under piles of coats and blankets for over four hours. I wanted to go over and offer him some more blankets, but a combination of fear and respect for this little tradition we'd built stopped me.

That was nothing compared to April, can #8, though. That night, the worm had barely been able to explain to the President of the United States how my spinal fluid could cure stupidity forever, when a peel of thunder woke me up. A violent storm had moved in, and each thunder strike shook the house. The electricity in the neighborhood had gone out. The only illumination was the constant lightning that showed me not much of anything because the wind and rain had created a blurry wall through which I could perceive that the tree in the front yard was bowing over, ready to snap. I thought there was no way that Mr. Garcia could be out in that chaos.

But he was.

Through lightning strobes, I could just make him out. He was wearing a yellow slicker and using his arms to protect his face from the lashing rain. He could barely stand from the onslaught of the wind and looked like a sailor in the middle of a hurricane.

Eventually the wind blew so hard, and the street flooded so much that Mr. Garcia climbed on top of the trash can to anchor both himself and it. He started pounding the can with his fist and, without even thinking, I began punching the wall in the dark, matching every one of his blows. When the punching became too painful for both him and me, he stopped and began screaming at the sky above. It seemed to me that he was demanding something, most likely answers. The only reply he got was stinging rain and vicious, howling wind. Being no match for the storm, Mr. Garcia curled into a ball to wait it out.

The men from the city arrived shortly after the storm passed. They helped Mr. Garcia down from the can and escorted him to his front door. Before he went in, he turned to look at me. He was so drained from the night that he could not muster the energy to vocalize his command. I dutifully went to bed anyway.

May's pick-up went without incident, but I could see that this terrible responsibility was exacting its toll. Mr. Garcia's skin was stretched tight over his bones and all his teeth had long since fallen out. His hair consisted of a few greasy clumps that sprang wildly from his skull. He no longer sat his monthly vigil in silence, instead he had begun conversing with the can. His moods swung wildly from boisterously laughing and slapping the can on the back one minute, to openly weeping and hugging the can the next. He even pointed at me several times and seemed to whisper conspiratorially into the can's nonexistent ear.

I was the only person, besides the two men from waste management, who saw him those last few months. He never went outside at all anymore except to move and guard the cans. His yard had become wildly overgrown, and he didn't even bother to bring in the pile of newspapers that collected and rotted on his front porch. Several people in the neighborhood had said they'd contacted the authorities to complain and had been assured that someone would investigate. No one ever did.

That last night in June, the worm spoke directly to me. This time he came to my bedroom while I was wide awake. I felt him inch his way across my pillow and nuzzle up to my left ear.

"It's time to talk to Mr. Garcia," the worm whispered.

I sat up and went to the window. Mr. Garcia was in his fold out chair next to the can. He had his head in his hands and was either crying or laughing; possibly both. I put on my shoes and headed downstairs, stopping at the kitchen to grab a knife to put in my pocket. I walked out the front door and slowly approached Mr. Garcia.

He lifted his head from his hands and gave me a toothless smile. "This is new," he said.

"Mr. Garcia, what is going on?" I asked with a slight tremble in my voice.

"You should know. You've been watching for months. Keeping me company. Sharing my burden. I think you just might be my best friend." A thin stream of saliva fell from his lips. "What's your name by the way?"

I was shaking. Tears had begun to well up in my eyes.

"What? What do you want me to say?" He rose up from his chair. "Do you want me to make sense of this?" He took a step towards me. "How can I make a child understand when I don't?" He let out a high-pitched laugh. "Did you know the town has a protocol for this? Do you know what a protocol is?"

I shook my head. He took another step towards me. My hand tensed around the handle of the knife in my pocket.

"It means official procedure. This whole situation," he swept his right hand around to indicate himself, me, and the can. "This has happened enough times that they've got it figured out. I called 911 and they transferred me to a special line and next thing I know there are people coming to my house with their chains and cans and pamphlets. PAMPHLETS!"

I flinched.

"They have pamphlets with a smiling woman on the front. The pamphlet's got no whys, but it has plenty of whats, wheres, and whos. You're one of the whos, did you know that?" he giggled.

A tear escaped and rolled down my cheek. He didn't notice.

"Not you specifically. People like you. Built different. On a different frequency. That's why you see when no one else does. You're a freak...a freak...just like me." He seemed to become lightheaded and stumbled back before quickly snapping to attention. "All these pamphlets, they tell you disposal procedures and ways to cope but they have no idea how to stop it. Their only advice is to just get used to it." He was getting closer. "How the hell am I supposed to do that?" He put his hands on my shoulders.

"You tell me." He leaned down and pulled me closer so that we were face to face. "How am I supposed to live with this!?"

I pulled the knife from my pocket and waved it in front of his face. He let go of my shoulders and took two steps back.

"Maybe…maybe that'll work. At the very least I'll have to go to the hospital. Might get an infection. Might have to be in there a few months. A break at least. A vacation…I'm so tired." He closed his eyes, rubbed his head, and then let out a bark of laughter which made me flinch and drop the knife. He picked it up. I was too scared to move. "Hell, I'll just show you," he said then turned the knife handle towards me. "You might need this." I took it with my shaking hand.

Mr. Garcia walked over to the trash can and took a key from his pocket. He unlocked the padlock and the chains fell away. He grabbed the handle of the lid, pulled it off, and dropped the lid to the street. "Get up," he said to the contents of the trash can.

A pair of hands reached up and clasped the rim of the can. Slowly, with an odd grace, a second Mr. Garcia raised himself up.

The Mr. Garcia in the can looked more like Mr. Garcia than the man who was guarding it, like the Mr. Garcia from before. Head full of hair, mouth full of teeth. His white undershirt and brown slacks were perfectly laundered and crisp as opposed to the ratty and torn rags worn by the other.

"Hi, I'm George Garcia, retired homeowner, pleased to meet you," the man in the can said to Mr. Garcia, right hand extended.

"It's your lucky day, Mr. Garcia," Mr. Garcia said to himself, ignoring the offered hand. "Get out of the can."

The clean Garcia stepped out with one fluid motion and stood next to the decrepit Garcia.

"Help me," the decrepit Garcia said to his double. The clean Garcia held out a steadying arm so that the real Garcia could climb into the trash can. Once inside, the decrepit Garcia turned to look at me.

"Hey…whatever your name is, have you been dreaming about a worm?"

I just stood there silently.

"He's in the pamphlets too. But this isn't," he said as he handed the padlock key to the clean Garcia and lowered himself into the can. The clean Garcia wasted no time and quickly got the lid on and the chains secure. He then swallowed the key and let out a yip like a coyote. He began looking all around as if everything were new. He sniffed at the air and began sucking on his fingers. He looked down at the street and lowered himself to his knees, resting his left cheek on the asphalt before turning his head and licking the black road. Another yip escaped his lips as he jumped back to his feet and looked at me.

That's when I realized that I had met the creature in front of me before, or some aspect of it at least. The body was different, but I recognized that impossibly large smile which wasn't quite as empty as the nothingness in its eyes.

"The Tall Grass," I whispered to myself.

The empty thing turned to me. "Hi, I'm George Garcia, retired homeowner, nice to meet you!" It extended its hand in greeting. Instinctively, I swiped at it with the knife. Two of its fingers fell to the ground despite the weakness of my slash. His smile grew wider as thick green fluid poured from the wounds.

I turned and ran back inside my house. When I got to my bedroom, I looked out the window to see if it had followed me. It was still standing where I left it. It was waving at me with its wounded hand, the green liquid spraying everywhere. I felt the worm nuzzle up to my left ear.

"It came for him, not you…this time. Now, wake up."

I opened my eyes, and the sun was shining. I went to the window. The pile of newspapers on Mr. Garcia's porch was gone. In the middle of the freshly mowed lawn stood the second For

Sale sign that had gone up on our street in as many weeks. I never saw Mr. Garcia or Mr. Garcia again.

THE AICKMAN COUNTY SWAP MEET

There were many signs dotted along the dirt path that led up to the Aickman County Swap Meet:

FRESH BABOON MILK!

Ghost Blood, No Questions

Father Belial's $50 Weddings/Exorcisms

Designer Nightmares For Personal & Private Use

Bucket O' Guns! Guns By the Bucket!

But I think the sign that most accurately summed up the experience of visiting The Meet was written on a modest tombstone that sat nestled against the entrance:

RIP
SANITY

The Meet was located about 15 miles north of Aickman and occurred on the last weekend of every month. When people from outside the area stopped to ask directions, we locals would instruct them to go north on Addison which would soon become Farm Road 1168. Keep north on FM 1168 for about five to ten minutes until you see an old homestead. At this point, locals had two options: Either instruct the stranger to take a right just past the Old McKinley Place or give the exact same command, but in lieu of saying "...the Old McKinley Place" you say "...where the murders happened." If you have chosen the second option, you would then wait for the stranger to ask, "What murders?" which gave you carte blanche to relate the horrible saga of the McKinley Machete Massacre. Though I am of a somewhat morbid bent, I will refrain from recounting the horrible events of that hot August night in 1956 when a perfect storm of misunderstandings, jealousy, and a song about the many uses of peanut butter drove a man to commit the unthinkable. There are countless volumes already dedicated to that particular tragedy and I only bring it up as an example of the type of story that the people of Aickman loved to tell.

It's a tale they had a lot of practice telling, particularly to outsiders who were drawn to the area by the whispers and rumors about The Meet. These whispers and rumors were all the advertising available because officially The Meet didn't exist. I don't mean to say that it was a fantasy or a shared delusion, but the 3 square mile field where The Meet was located lay outside of all local, state, federal, and world jurisdictions. No entity on Earth wanted to lay claim to the land. It appears on no maps, save for one made by early German settlers that simply marks the field in a black circle with the word NEIN written over it. With no authority willing to claim the land, it had achieved a state of non-existence and as such it was bound by no laws. Anything could be bought or sold there. There were no restrictions. The lure of such freedom is irresistible to any real American and our town would see adventurers from all corners of the country come on down to check out if the rumors were true. They came cocky and curious. They left shaken and shattered.

I remember one day giving directions to a portly gentleman in aviator sunglasses and a camo hunter cap. He jumped the curb right in front of me in his blue pick-up.

"Hey ugly, where this Meet y'all sposed t'have at?" he shouted out of the passenger window. When I gave him the instructions, he let out a "YEE-HAW!" and peeled off, sending bits of gravel into my face. The next day, I saw the same man wandering the streets, bloodied, and wearing only boxer shorts. He kept repeating the same phrase: "The dang ol' Mist…"

This was a reference to the thick blanket of haze that covered the entirety of The Meet. The haze always stayed perfectly within the geographical boundaries of the field. Some claimed that it was smoke from an underground fire that would continue to burn for centuries. Others were certain that it was composed of the decaying particles of all the souls that had been destroyed there. I always tended to believe the latter explanation because of something my grandfather once told me at a Dairy Queen: "A dead soul will burn the eyes and sting the skin. It'll choke you but never kill you. Hell, my soul died 30 years ago and I'm still alive."

I had grown up with stories about The Meet my whole life but had never been until that summer. My father disliked commerce and wasn't a huge fan of freedom so there had been no reason for us to visit. He had been in one of his moods since our trip to the car wash. He'd go days without speaking and hardly left his room, which confirmed for me that he no longer had a job. I had learned from experience that these moods were always punctuated by a sudden manic insight. Sure enough, one Saturday he stormed into my room declaring his intentions to finally see The Meet for himself. He'd become convinced that the answers to all our problems could be found there.

"If we just buy the right thing, we'll be happy. I know we will," he said with that smile that always let me know that doom was just around the corner.

On the drive up, he decided to relate to me the full story of the McKinley Machete Massacre. He included several details that I had never heard because most people leave them out. Murder stories in polite society are supposed to be gruesome but never graphic. My father did not believe in polite society. When he finished, I made him pull the car over so I could puke. He was a very good storyteller.

The Meet had no parking lot, so you had to find a spot somewhere along the dirt path that led up to the entrance. This was the first time I had seen the signs that I mentioned earlier. I was particularly taken with one that read:

MONKEY RACES! HOT DAMN! LOOK AT THOSE
PRIMATES GO! EVOLUTION SUCKS!

That sign helped to alleviate a great deal of dread that had been building in my chest. To my young mind there was something reassuring about the prospect of monkeys in little shorts competing for what had to be a whole hell of a lot of bananas. It wasn't until later in life that I would learn that when man pits monkey against monkey, everyone loses.

The entrance was a tall, rusted archway with equally rusted iron letters nailed to it that read:

A KM N
OUN Y
SW P
ME

There was no ticket booth or fee to enter. There was only the arch, the tombstone that rested against it, and the impenetrable wall of mist that lay beyond. My father looked down at me. I looked up at him. We both took a deep breath and entered.

We weren't there long.

From what I was able to piece together on the car ride back, my father had managed to enrage a collection of large men. This is something he did quite often. His ability to anger and annoy had led to the end of certain long-running feuds in town by bringing people together in their mutual hatred of him. On that day, in circumstances he was never clear about, he managed to unite several large men in the shared goal of skinning him alive. Luckily, he was faster than them. It couldn't have taken more than five minutes between entering The Meet and my father dragging me out pursued by strangers who wanted to kill him. But in those five minutes I saw something that changed everything.

I saw Mr. Sandwiches.

Mr. Sandwiches was a teddy bear. Mr. Sandwiches was my teddy bear. From the time I was born to the age of 6, that raggedy brown bear with the green marble eyes and missing left ear went with me everywhere. He witnessed my first steps. He heard my first words. He had been my confidant, co-conspirator, and protector in the dead of night. That bear was the only friend I had in my whole life until I met Darby and the others. When he disappeared shortly before my seventh birthday, I was devastated. When my dad tried to replace him with a blue elephant named Jocko, I bit Jocko's trunk off. Mr. Sandwiches had been my entire world and was my first lesson that not even the world lasts forever.

In the years since, I'd completely forgotten about him. I've never understood the mechanism of the mind that made such things possible. There are people who say that without the ability to forget, the pain of loss wo

uld shatter us and leave us unable to survive. I've always felt that the ability to lose the most important parts of yourself makes survival a pretty bum prospect. But I'm not in charge of the universe so I guess we're stuck with the way things are.

As soon as we entered, the mist stabbed my eyes and clawed at my throat. I let go of my dad's hand to cover my face to try and block the assault. My dad, of course, hadn't noticed and wandered off. I stumbled around trying to find the exit but there was no point of reference to get my bearings. There was only the mist and the voices within it. I could hear vendors calling out things like "TIGER FOR SALE!" and "FIGHT ME FOR CASH PRIZES! The shadows of figures loomed in the acrid fog but never burst through, always just staying beyond my field of vision. I tried calling out to my father. Only wet coughs would come. I was at that moment convinced that I was about to choke to death on the air of the freest place on Earth.

That's when the suffocating haze parted. A bubble of fresh air seemed to bloom right in front of me, pushing the smoke or the souls or whatever I had been drowning in away. The epicenter of this bubble was a ramshackle booth. It was made of rotting, waterlogged wood, and tilted lazily to the right on the verge of collapse. A sign, written on dirty butcher paper and nailed across the front, read "Rennie's Lost & Found: I Have What You Want." Sitting behind the booth was a man with a sallow face and one completely black eyeball. He wore a leather cap that clung to his bald skull. He smiled at me. Half the teeth on both the upper and lower gums were missing in exactly the opposite proportion so that the top teeth could touch the lower gums and vice versa. He lifted a wiry hand, and I could hear the bones creak and snap as he beckoned to me.

"Wanna see something, kid?" the old man croaked. I was too frightened to respond. "S'matter? Somebody steal your tongue? Young tongue like yours would fetch quite a nice price here at The Meet. Much more than mine." He then stuck out a bulbous, black mass of flesh from between his rotting gums that had more in common with a tumor than a human sensory organ. I gagged. He pulled the tumor back into his face, giggling. "Isn't that wild?" he leered, not expecting an answer. "But enough fun. Let's get down to business. There's somebody that wants to say hello." He lifted his other hand and sitting on the palm was a mangy, pudding-stained stuffed bear that my mother had named Mr. Sandwiches.

A neutron bomb detonated in my heart.

The shockwaves broke a seal in my brain.

A tsunami of memories swallowed me whole.

I remembered the feel of his rough, sticky fur on my face.

"He's different, daddy! He doesn't want to be soft!"

His sickly aroma like a mildewy garbage can invaded my nostrils.

"He eats bad seaweed for breakfast and kisses skunks because they're lonely!"

In a flash I recalled the story of how he lost that ear.

"The Ear Fairy got him, daddy. SHE MUST BE STOPPED!"

Memories of the countless times I would cry at night, burying my face into his chest, his fur absorbing the tears.

"….bath time, Mr. Sandwiches…."

All of it came back. All at once. Fresh tears were falling down my cheeks, yet my brain didn't even realize I was crying. I was focused on my long-lost bear to the exclusion of all else. A switch had flipped inside me. Nothing mattered but him. The old man let out another giggle. "That's right. Was lost, now found. Let's make a deal," he hissed.

My brain had become completely rewired. I no longer found that disgusting man frightening. In fact, I would have done anything he asked. No price was too high. I would have gladly pushed a button to blow up the entire world to get my bear back. But just then, my dad came crashing through trying to escape the men he had angered. He picked me up in his arms and bolted to the car.

As we peeled out, I had already made up my mind to return as soon as I could. By the time we got home, I had devised a completely fool-proof plan:

1. Somehow get back to The Meet
2. Somehow find Rennie's Emporium
3. Somehow get Mr. Sandwiches
4. Somehow get back home

It was perfect.

The only one of my friends I related any of this to later that day was Darby. This was a practical consideration. She was the only one that I could count on to get me back to The Meet. My father was too frightened to go back and none of the others had the experience this mission required. I was more than willing to try to walk back alone, but I viewed myself as a liability in my own quest. My incompetence would probably get me killed before I got there. My mania was such that I didn't care if I lived or died but dying before getting Mr. Sandwiches back was not an option. Darby was the only person who could keep me alive long enough to achieve my goal. Also, I was certain she was the only one who wouldn't laugh at me about all this. On that count, I was wrong.

"Mr. Sandwiches?" she said, stifling a giggle while leaning on the railing of my porch.

"My mom named him."

"Does he, like, eat sandwiches all the time?"

"No. He eats seaweed. Rotten seaweed," I huffed.

"What?"

"It's why he stinks."

"So, you want me to help you rescue a stinky teddy bear from some sort of witch-man with a tumor tongue?" she giggled.

"He's my friend. He needs my help."

Darby gave me a puzzled look. "It's not actually him, y'know? There's no way it can be."

"I would recognize a piece of my soul anywhere."

"Whoa. Ok, Weirdo, you're getting a little TOO weird right now," she said, standing up straighter as if on her guard.

"Loyalty isn't weird," I said, my face getting redder by the moment.

"Dude, I don't know why you're getting so upset but…"

"BECAUSE YOU'RE NOT LISTENING TO ME!" I screamed. "You're laughing like everyone else in this town laughs."

"I am not like everyone else in this town," she spat.

"You are. You don't care. What if it was Jason or Eddie out there?"

"It's not, though! It's just a stupid teddy bear!"

"Is your stupid skateboard just a skateboard?" I spat back.

Darby stopped. She looked down at her board which she had instinctively been hugging to her chest once the screaming began.

"How would you feel if some creep was holding that hostage?" I sneered.

Darby slowly lowered the board to the ground. She put her right foot on top of it and tentatively rolled it back and forth. She seemed to be considering my point. When she finally came to a decision, she flipped the board back up to her hands and looked at me.

"How much money you got?" she asked.

"None."

"How are you going to pay for him?"

"I don't think he wants money."

"What does he want?"

"Nothing good."

"Then why are you going back?"

"Because Mr. Sandwiches needs me."

She didn't try to talk me out of it. She just told me to meet her at the stop sign at Addison and Mayflower the next morning. If we didn't get there on Sunday, we would have to wait a month for another chance.

"Are you sure you don't want to bring the others?" she asked as she was leaving.

"This is too important. I can't count on them."

She gave me a look but said nothing.

I barely slept that night. Every time I would drift off, I would see Rennie and his hellish tongue licking Mr. Sandwiches and I would snap awake.

We met at the stop sign at 8:00 like we agreed.

"Dude, you look terrible," Darby said as a greeting.

"Couldn't sleep. Tongue dreams," was the only explanation my rattled mind could give. "How are we getting to The Meet?"

"Hitch-hike," she said.

"Have you ever hitch-hiked before?"

"All the time. How do you think I get to the city to get my music? You think I can find Suicidal Tendencies tapes in Aickman?"

The caravan of out-of-towners to The Meet was already well underway. We stuck our thumbs out and it didn't take long for a beat-up old Cadillac to pull over. The driver was an older, chubby man with a bouncy pompadour wearing a pink tuxedo.

"You going to The Meet?" Darby asked.

"Absolutely am," the man said. "Got urgent business, in fact. You kids shouldn't be hitchhiking, though. All sorts of weirdos heading out that way."

"You a weirdo?" Darby asked.

"Hell yeah," the man laughed. "But I'm probably the safest weirdo you'll find all day. If you kids insist on going out there, better me than someone else. Hop in."

I sat in the back while Darby sat in the passenger seat. The man said his name was Martin Candy and that it was a very special occasion.

"Getting hitched. Tying the knot. Nice Day for a White Wedding and what have you."

"You're getting married at The Meet?" Darby asked.

"Got too. Reverend Belial is the only man within 500 miles who has no qualms about my blessed union."

"Why, what's the problem with your…" just then Darby was cut off by a banging coming from the trunk. We looked at each other in horror. Martin Candy let out a laugh.

"Ha Ha! Don't worry, I don't got no person tied up in my trunk."

Darby gripped her skateboard ready to swing it at Candy's face. "What do you got in the trunk, then?"

"Well," Candy said. "It's kind of hard to explain. See…" and before Candy could finish, a huge tentacle covered in red suckers tore out of the back seat and started wiggling around wildly. I was frozen in place. Darby stood up in her seat, board raised ready to swat at the slimy protuberance. Candy stopped her.

"WHOAH! WHOAH! WHOAH!" Candy shouted. "She don't mean no harm. She's just hungry."

"She?" Darby asked, perplexed.

"My bride to be." Candy lovingly sighed. He then reached over and pulled a corndog out of the glove compartment. He waved it in front of the tentacle. "Right here, darlin', lunch time." The tentacle wrapped around the fairground food and then immediately shot back into the trunk of the car. The chewing noises sounded like slugs in a meat grinder.

"My baby loves corn dogs," Candy smiled.

When we finally arrived at The Meet, it was already so busy that Candy had to park close to the farm road. We jumped out immediately.

"Good luck with…uh…everything," Darby said.

"Don't need it. I'm already the luckiest man in the world," Candy beamed.

We hurried towards the entrance. On the way, Darby pulled out a pair of red bandanas and bright blue swim goggles from her backpack. "This'll help with the mist," she said.

I tied the red and white diamond patterned bandana around my face and slipped the goggles on. They were tight, almost perfectly cupped to my eyeballs. It felt good to be prepared.

Halfway to the entrance, the path became a bottleneck caused by a grove of wild thorn bushes growing on each side. Our progress was slowed by a gigantic man waddling in front of us. He was as round as he was tall. The majority of his girth was being used as some sort of mobile armory. Every available inch of his body was covered in holsters and sheaths for handguns and blades of all shapes and sizes. What couldn't be sheathed hung loosely from fishing wire all around his enormous belt so that he resembled a walking Jupiter orbited by moons of antique pistols, flare guns, and sawed-off shotguns. In each hand he had an AK-47. His stubby legs seemed barely able to hold the weight and he moved about as fast as a tortoise that was also covered in guns. There was no way around him until we reached the clearing ahead. The whole time we could hear him muttering to himself.

"You will respect me. You will respect my rights. I am a big boy, mommy. A big boy. I get McDonald's when I want. Not when you say so."

It was hard to tell through the goggles, but I estimate that Darby rolled her eyes about 231 times for the five minutes we were stuck behind him. As soon as the path widened, we took off running to get away from Mr. Guns & Ammo. We reached the entrance a minute or two later.

"You said he's somewhere near the front, right?" Darby asked.

"He was yesterday. He might not be now. Rules don't matter in there," I reminded her.

We each took a deep breath and walked into the haze. The goggles and bandanas worked. I could see far more clearly than last time. I led Darby in the general direction of where I thought Rennie's Lost and Found had been. We walked for ten minutes, only managing to find booths that sold things like flamethrower fuel, pungent crab meat, and loose asbestos.

"It had to have been right around here," I said. "He must have set up somewhere else."

"He might not even be here today." Darby had to yell this over the sound of the vendor at the clown horn booth honking off his merchandise to the delight of a shirtless man.

"He's here. He's waiting for me." I was certain of this, which was saying something because certainty never came naturally to me. This search-and-rescue mission I was on had given me a lot of clarity and I was enjoying the feeling of purpose. This feeling, however, was getting me no closer to Mr. Sandwiches.

"I don't know how we're going to find him in all of this," Darby said, scanning as much of the horizon as she could. "It looks like it goes on forever."

"We'll have to split up," I said.

"I don't think the two of us could cover all of this in one day." She swept her hand across the void. "We should have brought the others."

"Jason would have got killed quicker than my dad and The Anointed One…well who knows what kind of effect this place would have had on them," I reasoned. "Eddie might have been useful though."

"For sure," Darby agreed. "I really wish that Eddie was here."

Just then, a gust of wind blew through the haze, sending it billowing in all directions before it collapsed back on us.

"I don't know what genie you've been talking to," came a voice from behind. "But here I am."

We turned to find Eddie standing with his fists on his hips in that Peter Pan pose he was so fond of. He wasn't wearing any eye or mouth protection, yet the haze didn't seem to bother him at all.

"What's with the disguises? You guys rob an underwater bank or something? Don't you know fish money is useless on land," he said, pulling my goggles and letting them slap back to my face.

"Ow!" I exclaimed. "What the heck are you doing here?"

Eddie didn't answer immediately. He looked all around as if for the first time registering his surroundings. "Oh, this place?" he said, waving his hands around. "Yeah, I'm always here. Always here at the good ol'….uh…."

"Swap meet?" Darby finished for him.

"Yeah! That's it. The good ol' swap meet. You know me, I always beat my feet to The Meet. Been here since before dawn. Can't pass up the opportunity to buy…" He looked at the closest booth visible through the haze. "Dioramas…of dead squirrels…in scenes of winter's wonder? Yeah, can't get enough of that stuff." He got a troubled look on his face as if realizing something, but then he shook his head, as he often did, and looked back at us. "Anyway, I should be the one asking what the heck you two are doing here."

Darby gave me a look asking for my permission to tell Eddie about Mr. Sandwiches. I gave her a nod. We then took turns relating different parts of the story. I fully expected Eddie to laugh and make fun of me, but he just listened in rapt attention. When it was over, he stroked his chin.

"You were right not to involve Jason and The Annoying One. They would have been liabilities." He then stuck a finger in my face. "But it hurts that you didn't trust me enough to tell me about this."

"I thought you would just laugh," I said.

"And I probably would have if it wasn't for Bill Myerson."

"Who's Bill Myerson?" Darby asked.

"He was a little yellow donkey," Eddie said, wistfully. "The best stuffed animal I ever had. I named him Bill Myerson as a tribute to the man who killed my grandpa. We were inseparable. Did everything together." Eddie's eyes began to tear up. "Then one day my aunt Delia drowned Bill Myerson in the toilet. I tried to save him, but it was too late. We buried him in the backyard. My sisters Penelope and Irma helped. Then, in the middle of the funeral, my Aunt Delia told us that he wasn't actually dead, and me and my sisters tried to dig him up before he suffocated. We dug as fast as we could, but it was too late. So, we had to bury him again." Eddie let out a sigh. "The point is, I got to say goodbye to Bill, but you never got that chance with Sandwiches. I'm gonna help you find him. The only problem is, what happens if me or Darby find this Rennie first?"

"What do you mean?" I asked.

"You're the one that has business with him," Eddie said. "How are we supposed to find you? We don't got no walkie-talkies and even if we did, how are we supposed to give directions in this soup?"

"I think I know what to do," Darby said, looking past us. Heading our way was Mr. Guns & Ammo. His mutterings had turned to screaming.

"THESE ARE MY GUNS, MOTHER! YOU CAN'T HAVE THEM!" he was bellowing.

"Stay here. If he starts shooting, hit the dirt," Darby said, heading towards the gun mountain.

"Is Darby going to fight that guy?" Eddie whispered.

"I don't know what she's thinking," I admitted.

Darby walked towards the screaming man. She was about to pass right by him when she seemed to get tripped up and fell into his side. The impact threw the man off his balance, and he screamed, "THE GOVERNMENT, MOTHER! THEY'VE COME FOR ME!" as he threw his two machine guns in the air in fright. A few rounds blasted off as the guns hit the ground, but no one seemed to get hurt. Mr. Guns & Ammo fell on his back and began to squirm. Darby tried helping him up. He swatted her away and started crying. She came walking back and pulled us away from the troubled man.

"What the heck was that about?" Eddie asked, confused.

"This." Darby produced two flare guns.

"Cripes, you stole those off that gun show?"

"Yep. I'll take one and you take the other Eddie," she said and handed him the flare gun.

"NEAT-O!" Eddie began aiming and making laser beam noises. Darby grabbed him by the arm.

"Careful, it's only got the one shot," she chided him.

"Why don't I get one?" I asked bitterly.

"He only had two," said Darby. "Besides, if you find Rennie then you can deal with him. If either Eddie or I find him, we'll fire these off, you can see it in the haze and follow the direction of the light."

"Dang Darby, that's smart thinking," Eddie said. "After this, we should actually go commit underwater crimes."

"You okay going alone?" Darby asked, putting a hand on my shoulder.

"I'm getting my bear back," I answered.

We split up and began our separate odysseys. I made my way through the dizzying chaos of booths that seemed to stretch on for an eternity. The food stalls mixed the odors of frying meat and bubbling fat with the sulfur sting of the haze. Delicacies available for consumption included penguin tartar, otter on a stick, poached condor eggs, deep-fried chimpanzee hearts, and funnel cakes. One vendor even claimed to be selling dodo jerky that was centuries old. That was the first time I ever thought about what extinct animals must have tasted like.

Weapons were a hot item. Rocket launchers, land mines, grenades, tank shells, tasers, throwing stars, harpoon guns, crossbows, bear traps, stilettos, iron maidens, nerve gas, and Molotov cocktails were all sold at one of the more modest booths I came across. Most other weapons vendors weren't quite as reasonable.

There were also the ADULT booths whose services I didn't understand at the time and, now that I do, I envy my younger self his ignorance.

Then there were the vendors that didn't fit any category. This included a booth that sold stolen mail by the pound fronted by a shifty man with a slimy mustache. "Take your chances, folks! Could be a treasure trove! Why there might be birthday money from grandma in there! Or maybe a social security card! Become a new man! Mail! I am compelled to steal it!"

There was also the woman who was selling Angel Hooves which looked like severed horse feet covered with glitter. "The angels get rid of their old hooves so that new hooves can grow in. They dump them on my lawn. I wish they would stop. But I am taking these lemons and making lemonade. Bless a friend or loved one with the gift of these hooves."

Despite how clearly unhinged most of the people at The Meet were, I approached anyone I could and asked about Rennie. The mere mention of his name seemed to fill everyone with fear. They would shoo me away or lie unconvincingly about having never heard of him. The man who sold mice guns, functional firearms for your pet mouse, became so upset that he flipped over his booth and set it on fire. The woman who ran The Ball Pit, which was a 20-foot-deep hole filled with colorful plastic balls where parents could drop off their children for the day, was so frightened by my questioning that she accidentally fell into the pit. The children were on top of her in seconds. I had to turn my face away from the violence that followed.

The only person who provided me with any useful information was a man sitting behind a simple fold out table with no signage. He was in his late fifties and wore a red cardigan that, coupled with his soft features, radiated a warm kindness. As I approached him, he was immersed in a large leather-bound book and sipping from a teacup.

"Hello," I said.

He put the book down and smiled. "New to The Meet, eh?"

His pleasant demeanor was in such a stark contrast to everyone else I had encountered that all I managed to say to this was, "Huh?"

"The mask and goggles," he said, pointing at my face. "Not used to the smog yet? Don't worry, after a few visits it coats the lungs. You'll learn to love it better than the fresh stuff."

"This is smog?"

"That's what I call it. People have all sorts of words for it. Smog, haze, mist, smoke, dragon's breath, acid damp, hell clouds, etcetera. None of them quite capture it. Need to get a poet down here to invent a new word. Possibly a new vocabulary," he said and began to stare off into the distance. "Lord knows this place deserves it." The faraway look in eyes lasted a few more seconds before he came back to reality. He let out a little laugh. "I'm sorry, young man, you have to excuse my wandering mind. As you get older it's harder and harder to focus on the here and now. How can I help you?"

I liked this man immediately, so I didn't want to spring Rennie on him. "Look, I have a question and it might just freak you out."

"Well, you certainly know how to get a fellow interested," he chuckled.

"I'm serious."

"I believe you. The goggles alone tell me what a sober individual you are."

"What I'm about to ask has upset several people at The Meet today," I warned.

"Not surprised. This is a high-strung lot." He indicated the Meet with a twirling motion of his left hand. "The folk round here don't do well with reality. That's why they come to a place like this. A hidden place, far from the eyes of the world. Doesn't take much to spook people like that."

"You're here."

"So I am." He lifted his teacup and brought it to his lips. "Please, don't leave me in suspense."

I took as deep a breath as I dared. "Do you know Rennie's Lost and Found?"

He stopped mid-sip. Slowly, he lowered the cup to the table and cleared his throat. "Yes, I am familiar with that particular booth." He didn't show any further signs of agitation, so I continued.

"Do you know where it is today?"

He swallowed. "No. I am not aware of its present location."

"Do you know who Rennie is?"

"No, but that's the wrong question," he sighed. "When it comes to Rennie, the only useful thing to ask is what he is."

A vision of that ghastly tongue flashed in my mind. "Do you know what Rennie is?"

The Kind Man sat up straight. "Rennie is the natural consequence of The Meet. A place like this, a place beyond anyone's control, could be whatever we wanted it to be. It could be a beautiful thing. We, that is human beings, do not like beauty. Oh, we like nice shiny things that are pleasing to the eye, we can't get enough of that. Pure beauty, though? Fundamental beauty that strikes at the heart of all things? We can't comprehend it. So, we make everything small. Superficial. Settle for less. That's how we end up with a place like this. A blight. An open wound. Let such a wound fester for too long and it leads to infection. Pus. Gangrene. That's what Rennie is."

"He has my teddy bear."

"I am truly sorry to hear that."

"How can I beat him?"

"By not falling for his tricks in the first place," he exhaled sadly.

"Can you help me, sir?"

"I wish I could, my young friend. I truly do." He then looked past me. "However, I got a business to run, and I see a customer coming up now."

A man in an all-white suit and sunglasses approached the table. Without saying a word, he flopped down a stack of 100-dollar bills. The Kind Man looked down at the stack and licked his lips.

"Couldn't stay away, could ya?" The Kind Man said as he reached down beside him and brought up a pair of pliers. "You need that good stuff, huh?" He reached the pliers into his own mouth and latched onto a tooth. There was a loud crunch and after a good yank, he pulled out one of his back molars. The man in white held out his hand and The Kind Man dropped the molar into his palm. The man in white closed his fist, smiled, and walked away. The Kind Man turned his head towards me and winked. "Vaya con Dios." He smiled as blood poured down his lips. I turned away in disgust just in time to see a flare explode in the sky. I ran toward the fading red glow.

I reached Rennie's booth about 2 minutes later. Both Eddie and Darby were already there. From the smoke trailing out of Eddie's gun I knew that he had found Rennie first. Darby must have just beaten me there. They were both mesmerized by Rennie's awfulness. His skin had somehow become even more jaundiced and vicious looking sores had bloomed around his nose.

"Isn't this a nice surprise?" he smacked. "I thought my day had been made when this...boy?" He was pointing at Eddie. "Close enough, I suppose. When this boy appeared. But then he fires his gun, and this enchanting young lady makes the scene." He winked his dead eye at Darby. "And now, out of nowhere this little pudgy fella comes along and I just don't know what I'm going to do with myself," he said while he clapped his hands in delight.

"Where's Mr. Sandwiches?" I demanded.

"What's that? Some kind of mascot? Like that rich peanut with the monocle? Or the leprechaun that worships that devil cereal?"

"His bear, you creep," Darby snapped.

"Young miss, I am no zookeeper. I am merely a simple businessman looking to feed himself today."

"Enough of this crap, old man," Eddie cut in. "You were flashing Mr. Sandwiches like a hotshot yesterday and now you're playing the shrinking violet? The only plant you resemble is a stinking weed. Now tell us where the bear is, or we'll teach you the meaning of sandwiches. KNUCKLE SANDWICHES!"

Rennie brought his hand down violently to the table. "Don't YOU threaten me!" His finger was an inch from Eddie's nose. "I see right through you." He cocked his head at me and Darby. "They could too if they really looked. I have nothing to fear from the likes of you." Eddie took a step back.

"How about me," Darby said, brandishing her skateboard. Rennie pointed at it.

"Now that there, that's got some power all right. Yes, you could kill this old body of mine with that no problem. But it won't get the twerp his bear." Suddenly, Mr. Sandwiches appeared on the table. Without thinking, my hand shot out to grab him, but Darby stopped me.

"Don't!" she screamed.

"Smart girl. You try to grab that before our business is done and you'll lose those plump lil' fingers of yours."

"You hurt him; you die," Darby threatened.

"If I die before granting him ownership of that bear then he can never have it. That itch I put in his brain can never be scratched. It'll spread and consume him. He will never know a moment's happiness again."

I knew he was telling the truth. I could barely stop myself from grabbing Mr. Sandwiches. All the nerves in my body were telling me that everything would be ok once I had him in my arms. "What do you want?" I asked, shaking uncontrollably.

"You know what I want," Rennie leered.

"No…I don't," I whimpered.

"Good lord, you're dumber than I thought. And weak. I never saw a fly bumble into my web quick as you did. Didn't have to say anything. One look at this," he patted Mr. Sandwiches on the head, "And you were gone. Would have had you yesterday if not for your father. If he hadn't been in such a hurry, I would have had him too. Weak men make weak sons."

"I am not weak!" I shouted. Darby and Eddie flinched. Rennie let out a phlegm filled chuckle.

"See there? That fire in your gut? You should thank me. That's my gift to you. The gift of purpose. Turned a scared piggy into a man on a mission. You'll never know courage like that again. Once I get what I want, I'll take that too. You'll go back to the way you were. Minus your SOUL, of course."

I'm certain that Rennie had expected a bigger reaction from me about this revelation. He had just confirmed that I, and presumably everyone, has an immortal soul and that in order to get Mr. Sandwiches I would have to somehow have it ripped from my body. The cosmic implications of this would be enough to drive the most hardened philosopher insane, let alone a ten-year-old boy. But without even giving it a second thought I blurted out, "Okay, fine, how do we do this?"

Everybody, including Rennie, looked shocked.

"Holy Hell, boy," Rennie said. "You have absolutely no will, do you?"

"Guess not," I blurted. "Do I sign something or what?"

"JEEZUM CROWE!" Eddie shouted. "You can't give this creep your soul!"

"Kinda takes the fun out of it," Rennie lamented.

Darby grabbed me by the collar. "I am not letting you do this!" I didn't struggle to get out of her grip, I just went rag doll and slipped out of my shirt. My bandana came off as the shirt went over my face. The haze no longer bothered me. It smelled kind of sweet, actually.

"Okay, let's hurry this up. How's it done." I knew I had to make the trade before Darby and Eddie could stop me.

"Simple." He pulled out a thin gold tube. "Just stick this in your hand, press a button, and in a few seconds, it'll suck that soul right out."

"DO IT!" I stuck my hand out. Rennie lifted the tube and brought it down. Just before it reached my palm, Eddie wrapped his arms around my waist and dragged me to the ground. I began to flail and kick. Why couldn't my friends understand how much I needed Mr. Sandwiches?

"Cripes, man!" Eddie screamed. "No bear is worth this! Do you know how rotten a soul has to be to equal a stuffed animal!?"

At that moment, Darby had an epiphany. She turned to Rennie. "Hey, creep."

"Yes, darling?"

"Gross. You know I'm not letting you have his soul," she said. "I'll kill you. That's a fact."

"I believe you. But if the twerp doesn't get his bear, it will destroy his mind," Rennie beamed.

"PLEASE DARBY! I NEED IT!" I screamed.

"You're going to get it, I promise," she said, looking pitifully at me. She swung back around to Rennie. "You're not getting HIS soul. But what if I gave you A soul?"

"Darby, No!" Eddie screamed. I'm ashamed to admit it but at that moment I really did not care if Darby gave up her soul, just as long as I got what I wanted.

"Interesting." Rennie rubbed his hands together. "You'd give your soul for the twerp?"

"I said A soul. Not my soul."

"The only soul you got to give is your own, little girl."

"Don't call me that." Darby reached into her pocket and pulled out her wallet. She peeled open the velcro and removed a piece of scrap paper which had JASON HUMAN'S SOUL written on it.

I stopped struggling. So did Eddie. "Oh wow!" we both exclaimed at the same time.

Last October, Jason and The Anointed One had got into an argument about life after death. The Anointed One believed that we would all meet up again someday in the never-ending river of blood within The Serpent's gullet. Jason firmly believed that the whole notion was nonsense and was so confident that he challenged The Anointed One to a bet.

"If it does turn out that this ridiculous river of blood is real," Jason tried to snort derisively but ended up shooting a purplish fluid from his mouth. "Then I will be your slave in this so-called afterlife. If, however, we don't go anywhere when we die, then you will not exist and that will be very satisfying to me. Do you agree to the terms of this wager?"

The Anointed One happily accepted the terms but wanted assurances that Jason would stick to it. To that end, Jason officially signed over his soul on a piece of notebook paper making The Anointed One its legal owner. This was his insurance that they could boss him around in the next life. Less than a week later though, The Anointed One traded me Jason's soul for a can of orange soda. Then that Christmas I had given it to Darby as a present because I knew she would think it was funny. I had completely forgotten all about it.

"What's this? Trash?" Rennie waved it away.

"Take a look. It's a soul. It's the only one you're getting today," Darby said.

"That's no soul, that's just..." Suddenly Rennie began to sniff the air. He tilted his head back to take in a big nose full. He snatched his hand out and grabbed the paper from Darby. He held it up to his face. "I'll be. It is a soul. Something strange about it, but it's an immortal soul. Not the one I want, but I am finding this little saga tiring. Plus, I really don't feel like getting my skull beat in today." He looked at me. "A weakling like you doesn't deserve the friends he has. Take the bear." Rennie waved his hand over Mr. Sandwiches' head, and he tumbled off the table straight into my arms. I squeezed him tight. I breathed in his rotten mildew stench and for the first time in over 24 hours I no longer felt a gnawing gap at the center of myself. I was complete.

"Isn't that sweet. Makes the job worth it. Now if you'll excuse me…" Rennie took the golden tube and looked at the paper. "Actually, I think I'll take this one straight." He put the tube down and stuck out his tumor tongue. Both Darby and Eddie gagged. Rennie placed the paper on the writhing mass and pulled it back into his head. He made a theatrical gulping noise and then patted his belly.

"Interesting flavor. With just a hint of…" Suddenly his smile disappeared. A strange noise, like wet feet stomping into a bucket of cow brains, began to emanate from within him. He stood up, clenching at his belly.

"What…what have you done to me?!" His body began to spasm, limbs jutting out in all directions. His head snapped back and forth. I could see from his one good eye that he wanted to attack, but he couldn't get his body under control. We stared in astounded horror.

"WHAT KIND OF SOUL IS THIS?!" Rennie screamed. He opened his jaws and stuck his fingers in his throat, trying to induce vomiting. Nothing would come. In a panic he reached for the golden tube and shoved that into his mouth and pressed the button. It immediately exploded. A cloud of flame and smoke started to rocket out of Rennie's mouth. The cloud gathered above him and glowed with a deep, pulsing light. Within the cloud I could see a field of stars, planets in motion, black holes swallowing galaxies, and other astronomical phenomena that scientists on our planet would not know about for hundreds of years. Suddenly, the cloud seemed to solidify into an orb of pure energy and with a flash of light and clap of thunder, it was gone.

All that was left behind was Rennie. Blackened. Charred. Darby walked up to the still figure and raised her skateboard. Before she could strike, the figure collapsed into a pile of ash.

I was so entranced by the spectacle of what just happened that it took Eddie's scream of terror to alert me to the horror in my arms. Where Mr. Sandwiches had been there was now a slick, oily and vaguely humanoid shaped….thing. Its slime was covering my arms and bare chest. I quickly pushed it away from me and got up off the ground. The thing's stomach began to grow and expand like a wad of bubblegum. The belly ripped open with a squelch and strands of thick, coarse black hair began to stream out. I was too terrified to move but without a second thought, Darby lifted the remaining flare gun she had, took aim, and fired. The thing burnt up within a minute and with it, every remnant of the spell I had been under. I remembered everything I had seen and done that day and immediately peed my pants.

"WHAT THE HECK AM I DOING HERE?!" I bellowed.

"Looks like he's back to normal," Eddie said.

I grabbed Darby by the collar and pleaded, "Don't let me die!"

"I won't." She handed me my shirt, which I quickly put on to cover my pudginess. "Can you find the exit for us?" she asked Eddie.

"Sure thing, follow me!" Eddie said.

As we made our way out, I thought of something. "Did we just kill a guy?"

"Technically, I think he killed himself," Darby said. "Either way, he sucked and there are no laws here, so I think we're good."

"It's kind of messed up that we just gave him Jason's soul," I admitted.

"Yeah, well, my plan was to jump him later and steal it back," Darby said. "I didn't think he was going to eat it."

"Why do you think it did what it did to him?" I asked.

"Jason's a science boy. He was a magic man. Science beats magic…I guess?" Darby shrugged.

"I peed my pants."

"I know," Darby said.

We told Jason about what we did the next day.

"Hmmmm," he said. "That would explain the orb of pure energy that struck me and which my body seemed to absorb. It must have been my soul. Souls must be real." He thought about this for a few seconds and then began screaming. He didn't stop for three days.

FIREWORKS AND THE FACE AT MIDNIGHT

We were running blind and scared through the dark of the Screaming Forest. Darby had her hand around mine, dragging me so that I wouldn't fall behind. She said she could still see Eddie and that if we followed him, we would be safe. I didn't know if Jason Human or The Anointed One were ahead of us, behind us, or had already been captured. All I knew was that the screams of our pursuers were getting closer by the second and if we were caught, it meant pain and possibly even death.

Happy 4th of July.

What you have just read is a storytelling technique whereby a narrator starts their tale with an exciting and, at this point, mysterious section from later in the narrative to hook you because the actual beginning of the story isn't nearly as compelling. I will eventually explain how the five of us ended up being chased in the dead of night by a mob of murderous children with baseball bats, but for any of it to make sense, this story must begin with a history lesson.

In the town of Aickman it was a crime to not pop fireworks on the 4th of July. Like most children, I never questioned this law or the reasons for its being. I just did what I was told because I didn't like getting in trouble. As an adult, I would come to find out that this law existed in no other city in America and have since spoken with my father who explained how this extraordinary piece of legislation came to be.

The true power behind Mayor Deer was a local businessman named Big Beef Burlington. Burlington was a huge man with a sweaty pink face which barely contained his bulging eyeballs that always seemed on the verge of launching out of his skull. When he spoke at Mayor Deer's biweekly rallies, he would cover everyone within a 20-foot radius with a sheet of spittle and fine spray that launched from his mouth like seawater ejected from a whale's blowhole. His tirades on these occasions were at worst nonsensical and at best made no sense.

"You don't kill a gopher with a hammer! You kill it with your hands! That's what's missing from the world today! This new generation is soft and lazy! I've worked hard every day of my life! It is why my hands are so strong! It is why I can crush a gopher's skull in seconds! The gopher hides. It hides among us. You may be working with a gopher. You may be married to a gopher. My friends, there is only one answer: Hands. Hands like steel."

Burlington was a clown that wore no makeup and brought no joy. The people of Aickman loved him.

In the midst of one of our country's many military adventures across the globe, Beef Burlington introduced a bill to make the exploding of fireworks on the anniversary of the nation's founding mandatory for every man, woman, and child of Aickman.

"Our brave soldiers are out there on the front line fighting for your freedom and yet some of you, gopherlike, hide away in your burrows while the true patriots celebrate. Why? Why do you hate America?"

Burlington had whipped Aickman up into such a patriotic frenzy that his bill soon became law and the refraining from the popping of fireworks was punishable by two days in jail and a $2000 fine. But nobody had read the fine print of the bill which required that each individual had to provide proof of purchase for said pyrotechnics.

"We cannot have our citizenry disrespecting those who have given their lives by combusting artillery that was procured by illegal means or purchased through unauthorized, possibly foreign, sources."

This meant that you had to provide a receipt for each member of your household to prove they had purchased fireworks. But you couldn't use any old receipt from any old fireworks stand. The receipt had to include an official stamp from the town that designated the fireworks as legal, and you could only get that stamp from one vendor: Big Beef Burlington.

"You know me. You can trust me. My rockets' red glare, my bombs that burst in the air, are made by hard working Americans in America and I am the only dealer in the state who can guarantee it. If any other vendor, fly by night hucksters all, can provide documentation to this effect, they will be given the stamp. Until then, Big Beef's Bang Bang Emporium is here for your needs."

Burlington made a fortune every 4th of July and had the city bring on extra men who were dubbed The Deputies of America to police the town and make sure that everyone had their correct documentation. He even created a force of children known as The Future Deputies of America who were authorized to arrest kids that did not have the proper paperwork. It was truly Government in action.

This was The Anointed One's first 4th of July in Aickman, and that afternoon we were on my porch trying to impress upon them the chaos that was to be unleashed at 10:00 PM, which is when Burlington had convinced the town that the Declaration of Independence had been signed. We each tried to capture the magnitude of a frenzied population setting off huge quantities of explosives simultaneously.

"Truly there is nothing else like it," said Jason. "Like being at the center of a supernova or a gamma burst. You should be dead...yet you live!"

"There's so many Got Dang bang-a-booms and wheeeeee-BLAMS it's like World War I, II, and III all rolled up in one!" Eddie exclaimed.

"Last year, I went blind for an hour just from looking at the sky," I added.

"It's...pretty cool," Darby reluctantly admitted.

My dad had already taken me, Eddie, Jason and Darby to Big Beef's Bang Bang Emporium to pick up our requisite firecrackers. He bought us all assorted bottle rockets, black cats and roman candles, making sure that each of us had a receipt. Dad always did well at holidays because they came with a strict set of instructions that he could easily follow. It was those other times of the year, when he had to figure out what to do himself, that he was left floundering. Burlington had been at the Emporium that day, flanked on either side by The Deputies of America who wore their official red sashes proudly. He was shaking hands and congratulating his customers on being patriotic and right-thinking Americans. He even shook my hand.

"Son, I can't tell you how proud I am to see an obvious gopher like you casting off your burrowing tendencies and taking your place in the world of light."

My hand smelled like raw pork for the rest of the day.

The Anointed One didn't seem too impressed by the pictures we were painting, so we began planning out the evening's festivities. Eddie wanted to make sure we worked in a Roman Candle fight, and I made Jason promise not to add any special ingredients to the firecrackers like he did last summer which caused the instant incineration of over 10 acres of forest.

"You don't know how fortunate you were," Jason declared. "If I wanted, I could've split this pitiful planet in two."

In the middle of all this excited talk about what we would and would not blow up that night, I noticed that The Anointed One was acting strange. Well, strange for them. They sat on the railing that surrounded my porch, turned away from us and looking towards their house. Their head was bent to the left and their shoulders slumped in a manner that was completely alien to the usually rigid and imperious stances that befitted the future leader of a serpent cult. Every now and then, I could hear them let out a sigh over Eddie and Jason's fevered descriptions of the glittering fire that was going to tear apart the night sky. Not understanding what could be getting them so down, I finally shouted over, "What kind of fireworks did your parents get you?"

Back still towards us, The Anointed One responded flatly, "I do not have any fireworks."

We were all stunned. "What do you mean you don't have any fireworks? That's…impossible," I sputtered.

The Anointed One slowly twisted around to face us. "My people do not believe in celebrating anything as trifling and insignificant as a country or its birthday. The death of a star? Yes. The birth of a goblin? A joyous occasion. The imaginary unity of a human population spread across land masses both connected and unconnected? Not a priority. Early this morning, The Deputies of America came to our home. I was in the back shed performing my morning blood rituals, and, as I came out, I saw my mother and father being loaded into the back of a van. I understand that they will be in custody for the next two days. I fully expect to be apprehended by The Future Deputies of America before nightfall."

None of us knew what to say. Nobody had been arrested for non-compliance in years. A feeling of dread was building in my chest. I didn't want my friend to go to jail, but an even more craven part of me didn't want to get in trouble by association.

"The emporium's still open," I said in a panic. "My dad can drive you over and get a receipt no problem."

"No. I will not betray my beliefs. I will serve my time. It is only two days. What is two days in the ocean of eternity?"

The dread in me kept increasing. The Anointed One was right, it was only two days, but watching someone flagrantly breaking the law right in front of me when they could easily avoid trouble made no sense. I was not raised around belief and at that moment it seemed like an incredibly inconvenient and rather stupid thing to base your life around in the face of actual consequences. I wanted to shake them and make them see sense.

Just then, Darby took her receipt out of her pocket and ripped it up.

"What are you doing?!" I screamed.

"If The Anointed One's going down, then I'm going down," Darby shrugged.

"Darby, my friend, you do not have to put your freedom in danger for the sake of my beliefs."

"I'm not," said Darby. "I'm putting my freedom in danger for the sake of my beliefs."

Darby's talent for saying the coolest things anyone has ever heard always lit a fire under Eddie. "Yeah. YEAH!" Eddie exclaimed, taking out his receipt and shredding it to confetti. "Who needs fireworks anyway? We're the fireworks! Butch and Sundance! Billy the Kid! Bona fide outlaws!"

"Outlaws..." Jason rolled the word around his tiny mouth. "Yes, the time has come." He reached into one of his pockets, pulled out his receipt, and began to strut and fret up and down the porch, waving it grandly. "I have always feared that I would one day turn to a life of crime. My vast intellect, my cunning vision, my natural leadership abilities would all make me quite unstoppable. A true kingpin. Al Capone on a galactic scale." He collapsed against the railing as if being crushed by the tremendous force of his destiny, holding the receipt aloft, like the skull of Hamlet's friend Yorick. "I do not wish to be a criminal! But...it seems inevitable." He bolted up, crushing the paper in his fist. "This, my friends, is the first step down the dark path," he declared and then swallowed the receipt.

"You didn't have to eat it," Darby said.

"Paper tastes good," Jason countered.

After these extraordinary displays of friendship, I couldn't help but notice them avoiding looking in my direction. It was no secret that I was the biggest scaredy-cat of the group. I was always filled with a sense of shame whenever I was too scared to join in with things like sticking my head in a mysterious hole or investigating the voices coming from the burnt-out ice cream truck by the river. I felt that shame now. I couldn't handle jail. The thought of people being mad at me made me sick to my stomach. I kept picturing Big Beef Burlington spitting the word "gopher" into my face over and over until I was covered in a thick mass of mouth slime. I wasn't brave enough to handle that.

The worst part was they weren't expecting me too. This wasn't like the toes; This was serious. There was no peer pressure, they were just waiting for me to make my excuses. The shame pressed so heavy on my heart that I couldn't come up with any. I was on the verge of just walking back inside my house and leaving them to it when Darby put her hand on my shoulder.

"It's ok, Weirdo," she said.

The understanding and pity in her face made me feel so small. Like a baby. All at once I got a vision of what I must look like in their eyes: Naked except for my huge diaper and lil' blue bonnet around my head. My cheeks were rosy red and my eyes watery, constantly on the verge of tears. I was sucking on a bottle, milk leaking down my chin and dripping onto my potbelly, waving my rattle around like the useless little toddler I was.

Something in me snapped. I was no baby. I WAS A BIG BOY! Sure, I wasn't strong like Darby, or smart like Jason, or wily like Eddie, or…whatever the heck The Anointed One was, but I was no baby! I reached into my pocket, took out the receipt and ripped it up. Eddie cheered. Jason congratulated me on becoming a crime boy and offered me a job as a goon in his forthcoming criminal empire. Darby gave me a half smile.

"But let's at least try not to get caught," I said, as a concession to my cowardice.

We agreed on the willow tree by God Help Us, They're Killing Us Creek as our hideout for the night. We were to bring sleeping bags because The Deputy's authority lasted until sunup the next day. Jason tried to make us take a vow that if any of us were caught on the way, we would not snitch out the others and, if we did, then we would be, "Sleeping like the fishes. In water. Which is very uncomfortable. For us humans. Because it's cold. And wet," but Darby made him cut it out.

I told my dad I was going to spend the night at Eddie's, which was a terrible lie because I had never been to Eddie's house and had no idea where it was. This turned out to not be that big of an issue because my dad asked absolutely no follow up questions. At that moment I wished I was the kind of kid that liked to go out and break the law every day because I had the perfect father for that kind of lifestyle.

I stuck to the back alleys and ditches to avoid The Future Deputies, who were out in force. Their red sashes shone brilliantly in the sun, and I noticed that one or two of them were brandishing baseball bats, which was a new development.

We had all reached the tree around sunset. Eddie didn't have a sleeping bag because he said the ground was good enough for him.

"Nice and cool and comfortable. Boy oh boy, you can't beat the ground and that's a fact," Eddie said.

Jason was now wearing an eyepatch and had drawn beard stubble on his face as well as a scar across his right cheek. He was chewing on a toothpick and attempting to flip a quarter like the gangsters did in the black and white movies that played on tv every Sunday, but he was incredibly bad at it and often sent the coin straight into his uncovered eye.

We got settled in and waited for 10:00 PM when Aickman would put on a light show like no other. It was about an hour before we realized that nobody had brought any food and our stomachs were rumbling.

"Boy, I wish we could roast some mallows or wieners. Being an outlaw sure makes you hungry," Eddie said.

"Even if we had any, we couldn't build a fire. It'd attract the deputies," said Darby.

Jason spit his toothpick out. "I say let the coppers come, see?" We could take em'. We could take em' all! I got the brains and you got the muscle. Eddie'll be the driver. WE'RE GOING TO ROB A BANK! Or take Mayor Deer hostage! Or paint the school buses red and the fire trucks yellow!"

"Jason, what's wrong with you?" I asked.

"Crime!" Jason declared.

"Calm down," Darby said, rolling her eyes. "Honestly, I couldn't think of a worse gang of criminals in the world."

"Or a better group of friends," The Anointed One whispered.

We all turned to look at them. Their head was cast toward the ground and their right index finger was tracing around the tattoo of the snake on their left hand. I don't think they meant to say that out loud and they felt embarrassed about their sudden display of emotions. Luckily for them, the moment was interrupted by what sounded like the end of everything.

10:00 PM had come.

It is impossible to convey just how monumental the Aickman 4th of July fireworks truly were. The sheer amount of sound concussing up and down the basin and the pandemonium of light dancing across the overcast night sky was such a shock to the senses that you could only lie back and take it in with slack jawed and uncomprehending awe. I was dimly aware of my hair being blown back by the shockwaves that originated over a mile away from us and I could feel tears that I'm sure tasted like fear and wonder slide down my face. Confronted with such a terrible and breathtaking spectacle, all you could think about was your own insignificance and hope that the enormity wouldn't decide to swallow you whole. It was this total absorption of our senses that allowed The Future Deputies of America to sneak up on us.

"Looks like we got ourselves some gophers over here, deputies." said their leader, Griffin Collins.

In the nearly two years since that morning with Darby and the green ants, Collins had only gotten bigger, uglier, and stupider. He had begun sprouting vicious acne across his face which he constantly picked at. He'd also cultivated a greasy rat tail that slimed down the back of his neck. He and his goons hadn't been able to touch any of us because we were under Darby's protection, but he wasn't just with his goons tonight. There were twelve deputies in all, mostly made up of kids who usually had nothing to do with Collins. They were shining their flashlights directly into our faces and each one had a shiny metal baseball bat. Collins was smiling.

"As official law enforcement representatives of the town of Aickman, I demand to see proof of your patriotism." Collins said, smacking his bat into his right hand.

Darby had gotten out in front of us, brandishing her skateboard. There were ten feet between her and Collins.

"We don't have any receipts, Grif."

"My name is Deputy Collins, you anti-American piece of trash," he said, smile growing larger.

"See here, copper!" Jason Human began shouting, marching up to Collins. "You don't know who you're dealing with, do you? We're a criminal organization more powerful than anything you can imagine in that feeble little brain of yours! I'm Mr. Big, see, and we got cops like you in our pocket. We go all the way to the top! You can't touch us so why don't you-"

With one quick swipe of his bat, Collins sent Jason flying. Darby caught him with one hand, and he scrambled on to her back, arms wrapped around her throat, shivering.

"Being outside the law is cold and lonely, I wish for the warm embrace of society once more!" he whimpered. Darby shook him off and he retreated with the rest of us.

"Why don't you try that with me, Collins?" Darby spat.

"Why do you think I came out here for? Big Beef gave us special orders. State says he can't lock up kids anymore. He told us to spread the law in any way we see fit." Collins extended his bat, pointing it at Darby's head. "I'm going to smash your face in Darby, and there's nothing you can do about it."

"The rest of you okay with that?" Darby screamed at his mob.

"The law is the law," came a voice from the crowd.

"It's your own fault," came another.

"You've left us no choice," a final one said.

From the way they were gleefully swinging their bats and giggling with each other, we knew that these kids were going to hurt us and that they knew that they would be considered heroes by the town for doing it.

So, we ran.

As fast as we could.

As far as we could.

Deep into The Screaming Forest.

The Future Deputies, knowing that their powers to do whatever they wanted to whoever they wanted were going to expire by tomorrow, gave chase.

We followed Eddie. He knew the forest better than anyone. It was too dark to see anything, so he guided us by memory. We ducked into hollow logs and hid behind immense trees. He avoided the caves for fear that we may get trapped, but every hiding spot was only a brief respite as the Future Deputies kept at us doggedly. They had walkie talkies and flashlights whose hateful beams were always catching one of us and giving away the rest.

After almost two hours of that hellish hide-and-seek, we ended up in a small dry creek bed that cut through the middle of the forest. We lay in it, shielded by the banks, trying to catch our breath.

"I…can't…keep…running," I puffed.

"You have too. If they catch us, we're dead," Darby said, fear in her voice which made me even more hopeless.

"crime doesn't pay crime doesn't pay crime doesn't pay crime doesn't" Jason had begun repeating this over and over while rocking himself gently on the creek bed.

"Jason, be quiet!" Darby hissed. "Eddie, where are we?"

"This is Bonesaw Creek which means Cavendar rock is over there, and Blood Canyon is over there." None of us could see where he was pointing, and it didn't matter anyway. None of those places could offer us the safety we needed.

"I apologize for getting you into this," The Anointed One whispered. "I shouldn't have said anything. I should have taken on this burden alone."

"Don't say that," Darby said. "Who knows what those animals would have done with you. They haven't caught us yet, and they're not goi-"

"FREEZE!" came a voice from above, flashlight shining down.

I froze, curled up in a ball, fully expecting the blows of multiple bats to come down on me. But all I heard was a scuffle, a scream, and a thud. I opened my eyes and saw that the flashlight was now lying in the creek bed. From its light I could see one of the deputies moaning on the ground about 10 feet from us. Darby was holding his baseball bat in one hand and her skateboard in the other. It had only been the one, given false courage by his shiny sash.

"HERE! THEY'RE OVER HERE!" the prone deputy screamed. All at once, several flashlight beams turned towards our direction.

"What are we going to do?" I yelped.

"Fight," Darby said, grip tightening on both bat and skateboard.

"There are too many!" I pleaded.

"That's how it goes sometimes," Darby said, eyes on the deputy lying in the creek bed. Her mind was made up on who was going to get it first. She started walking towards the red sash when Eddie grabbed her sleeve.

"Hold it, Darby! Jason, what time is it?" Jason had an infallible sense of time and was always correct to the precise second.

"crime doesn't pay crime doesn't pay crime doesn't pay cri-"

"JASON SNAP OUT OF IT!" Eddie shook Jason and his body flopped around like an out-of-control firehose. He seemed to come back to his senses.

"Please…my bones…my delicate, beautiful bones," Jason whimpered.

"What time is it, bubble brain?" Eddie said. The flashlights were getting closer.

"Eleven…fifty…two…my bones."

"I know what to do. Follow me!" Eddie declared.

And that's where you came in. We had no idea where Eddie was leading us or what we were going to do when we got there. This was going to be the end of it no matter what.

As it happened, it turned out that Eddie was leading us to a dead end. It was a sheer cliff face that was closed in on both sides by a long-ago rock fall. We were inside a horseshoe of rubble with no possible means of escape. Trapped.

"Eddie! What have you done!" I blubbered.

"Jason, what time is it?" Eddie was grabbing Jason by the collar.

"What does it matter? My brains are about to be dashed across the rocks of the 2nd worst planet in the solar system!" Jason flailed.

"THE TIME!" Eddie screamed.

"Eleven Fifty-Seven!"

"Three minutes," said Eddie.

"What happens in three minutes?" Darby demanded, but Eddie didn't get to answer.

The flashlights were on us. The Future Deputies surrounded the opening of the rubble alcove. Their faces were hidden in shadow, but I could feel their smiles through the darkness, bringing that absence of light to life so that the night itself seemed to be delighting in the horror to come. Collins approached, shining the flashlight in his face so we could see his triumph.

"It's over, freaks. You're going to come out of there one at a time and you're going to face justice. The other freaks will watch. Then we're going to march you back into town and you will apologize to Big Beef personally for what you've done. If you don't come out, we'll go in, and it will be a bloodbath. I promise."

"Two minutes," Eddie whispered.

Darby pushed us all against the rock wall and stood facing Collins, bat and board held out in front of her like twin samurai swords. "Grif, no matter what happens next, I am going to hurt you."

The briefest spasm of fear danced across Collins' eyes, but his fingers caressed the fabric of the red sash, and his bravery was restored. "Naw, I don't think so. Deputies!" Collins commanded, raising his hand, "Get ready to charge."

"One minute," Eddie whispered.

"WAIT!" The Anointed One cried out, stepping in front of Darby.

Collins lowered his hand. "You ready to come out, freak?"

"Griffin Collins, you are the most passionate servant of the god cruelty I have ever met. But you also swore allegiance to the god justice. You wear his banner. It is to this god that I appeal. My friends had the proper receipts. They chose to throw them away in a show of divine friendship. A creature like you can never comprehend the beauty of such a sacrifice." The Anointed One looked back at us. "Their bravery should not be punished." They turned back to Collins. "I am the cause of all of this. Please, I beg you, punish me. Let my friends go."

Collins began to rub his chin in a pantomime of deep thought and then raised his hand again. "Naw, this is more fun."

But before Collins could drop his hand, the Earth began to shake violently. Both groups tumbled and swayed, trying to keep their footing. Behind us, the rock face began to pulse with a brilliant shade of green and, from somewhere deep within the rock, there came a high-pitched whine that was building to a roar. I covered my ears and screamed. Just as a particularly nasty judder was about to send me into the rubble face first, Darby grabbed me and held me close and tight. I could just about hear her yell "HOLD ON, WEIRDO!" over the roar when suddenly the ground stopped shaking and we were surrounded by silence.

For a brief second, us and the deputies looked at each other, not as hunter and prey, but as scared and lost children in the deep dark forest. Then Eddie shouted:

"GET DOWN!"

Green jets of flame erupted from unseen holes in the cliff face. Darby dragged me to the ground. The searing emerald torrents passed three feet over us. They were so beautiful that even though I was frightened out of my mind and the heat was burning my eyes, I couldn't look away. They writhed and wriggled like jade tentacles as thick sparks oozed off them. At the entrance of the rubble alcove, the tentacles were wrapping around each other, mixing, feeding, and growing. A form was taking shape out of the mass of flame: A giant skeletal face with tendrils of wild hair snaking off the skull. It's black, eyeless sockets were staring down at the tiny deputies who were all backing away in fear, except for Collins.

"It's just a trick! More of their weirdo crap. There's nothing to be afr-"

Suddenly, the gigantic face opened its flaming mouth and let out a shriek like a train whistle cutting through the deepest valley of Hell.

"EEEEEEEEEEEEEEEEEEEEEEEEEEEEEEHHHHHHH HHHHHHHHHHHHHHHHHHHHHH"

The force of it sent Collins flying back into the Future Deputies, knocking them down like bowling pins. They scrambled, kicked, and bit each other trying to free themselves of the pile. Once up, they scattered into the forest, several of them throwing away their sashes as if they marked them for the face's attention. Only Collins remained. He picked up his bat and launched it at the face. It instantly melted when it met the intense heat. The face, upset by his impertinence, shot out a forked tongue of flame and Collins finally began to run. A stray spark flicked off the tongue and caught Collins' rat tail on fire as he went crying into the night. The leviathan-like tongue faded away and the face arched up to the night sky and let out a triumphant wail.

"AAAAAAAAAAAAAAAAAAAAAAAAAAAAAAAHH HHHHHHHHHHHHHHHHH"

Then the jets began to grow dimmer, as if losing power. The face frowned and moaned mournfully.

"oooooooooooooooooohhhhhhhhhh......"

One by one, the jets gave out and soon the face disappeared completely. After a minute, we all sat up. My clothes were singed in several places and the smell of sulfur and burnt hair hung in the air. The rocks up on the cliff face where the jets had shot out were glowing red so that me and Darby were able to see the profound confusion in each other's eyes.

Eddie was the only one who wasn't fazed. He stood up and made a showman's gesture with his hands. "Lady, gentlemen, The Annoying One," Eddie peacocked, "I present you, The Face At Midnight!"

"What...in the heck...was it?" I had to ask because he seemed to have no intention of elaborating.

"It's a face. It appears at midnight. What part of the name was confusing you?"

"It's clearly a tormented soul forced to bathe in the fires of its own depravity," The Anointed One said.

"More likely the result of built-up gases and the strange acoustic properties of The Screaming Forest," Jason countered.

"Don't you two start," Darby chided.

"Whatever it is, I discovered it years ago. Named it too. It appears every night at midnight, like clockwork. Except during Daylight Savings. Then it's The Face At 11:00 PM which is a terrible name and if there's anything that Eddie Gone ain't, it's a terrible namer."

Eddie led us back to town. Our burnt clothes and dirty faces covered in cuts and bruises were perfect mirrors for the damage done to the town during the firework frenzy. The windows of several buildings were shattered and there were signs of small fires that had broken out everywhere.

The Anointed One and I walked back to our street in silence. We stopped in front of their house. I wanted to say something funny like, "Welp, Happy 4th of July!" but instead settled on, "I'll see you tomorrow."

I began to walk away and as I turned to go up my driveway, I saw that the Anointed One had not moved. They were still staring at their dark house, head tilted, shoulders slumped. All at once, I remembered that their parents were currently locked up and would not be released until the day after tomorrow. There was no one waiting inside for them. I walked back over.

"You can sleep at my house if you want. My dad won't mind. You can stay tomorrow too."

The Anointed One lowered their head and let out a quiet sob. "Do you think my mom and dad are ok?"

"They're going to be fine."

"Are you sure?"

"What does the snake say?" I clasped their snake hand in mine. They clenched it as if the snake tattoo were taking a bite.

"They're going to be ok," The Anointed One whispered.

I let go of their hand. Almost simultaneously, both of our stomachs rumbled. "Come on, we got a frozen pizza in the freezer."

"That is most wondrous news."

A few days later, Darby and I were walking to the corner store to buy sodas when we saw two of the former Future Deputies heading our way. They looked right through us as we passed, no shame or acknowledgement of the events that took place on the night of the 4th. It was as though nothing had happened.

"I hate this town," Darby said.

DARBY, AWAY

The house on the corner of Poplar and Ash was empty, but the laughter coming from inside was infectious. The laughter could only be heard if you were crossing the sidewalk in front of the house and nobody's description of it was ever the same. Where one person would hear an obnoxious guffaw, another would swear it was a shy titter. There were those who described it as a chorus of wild children, and some who heard the solitary wheeze of an old man. One woman said that the laughter sounded like "...a naughty kitten being tickled by a devilish rainbow," but nobody liked this woman.

Regardless of what was heard, the effect was always the same: As soon as the laughter hit your ears, you would immediately join in. Within seconds, you would have a stitch in your side and tears streaming down your face. The only way to stop this sudden bout of hysteria was to step off the property at which point all laughter would cease. Once the mirth had left your body, it was soon replaced with a feeling of dread. Nothing bad had happened per se, in fact most people described the experience as quite pleasant. No, the dread came from the fact that, well, that sort of thing just shouldn't happen. Empty houses shouldn't laugh, and people shouldn't be laughing with empty houses.

Because of this phenomenon, everyone agreed that the house on Poplar and Ash was a problem and in the town of Aikman, the best way to deal with any problem is to ignore it. From birth we were told never to go down that way and if we had to, then we should cross on the other side of the street. We were never given an explanation as to why we should follow these directions, but all us kids clearly saw that the children who broke the rules and came back with wild tales of a laughing house were met with severe and often violent punishments from their parents. This town-wide campaign of terror and silence was enough to keep everyone in line. Everyone, that is, except for Darby.

Darby had a plan.

We were hanging out in the shade of the willow tree by the creek. The terror of the 4th of July was a whole week behind us which is an eternity in child time. The Anointed One's parents had been released, the town was rebuilding, and there were no longer roving gangs of paramilitary children to watch out for. We'd returned to our own definition of normalcy and that morning found The Anointed One reading the newest Stephen King book, Jason tending the nets he set up in the creek to catch anymore errant body parts, me greedily scarfing down a melting ice cream sandwich, and Eddie just about to throw a huge mudball at my completely unaware head. Before Eddie could release his projectile, we were all blindsided by Darby's announcement.

"I need y'all to come with me to the house on Poplar and Ash," she called down from the high branches where she'd been keeping to herself all morning.

The four of us looked up to see her posed as if she were the prophet of the willow tree, skateboard held against her chest like it was a stone tablet with new rules from on-high.

"The heck you talking about, Darb?" Eddie asked, head craned, mudball dripping through his hands.

"I have a plan," Darby said as she nimbly moved down from branch to branch and landed on the banks of the creek. "It involves the laughing house. All of us need to go there. Now."

The house on Poplar and Ash was the last place I ever wanted to go. I'd often have nightmares about breaking out into a vicious, snot-bubble fit of laughter that would impede my ability to move, leaving me stranded on the sidewalk helpless until I could draw no more breath and my lungs finally exploded. At that point, the nightmare would turn into a press conference where Mayor Deer would profess his gratitude at my death and declare that my body would be left to feed the vultures and bugs so that my life would finally have a purpose.

I'd begun to breathe a little harder at the prospect of such a pathetic death and looked at the others for signs that they were not happy with Darby's suggestion. This was a bit of a mistake because Eddie's back was to me, The Anointed One wore a mask, and the only look that Jason ever had on his face was one of mild disgust.

"What are you talking about, lady?" Eddie finally said as he reached his hand back to wipe the remains of his disintegrated mudball on the sleeve of my grey t-shirt. "We were almost murdered out in the forest less than a week ago and now you expect us to go and die from a spook house giggle fit?"

"No one's going to die," Darby said.

"I have heard tales of that most cursed of Earths within this most cursed of towns and I wish to have no dealings with it," The Anointed One intoned.

"I agree!" I helpfully added.

Darby had a pained look in her eyes, like she hadn't expected this pushback. "Look, guys, this town has lied to you, to all of us. The house on Poplar and Ash won't hurt you."

"Says who?" Eddie asked.

"Says me," Darby shot back, exasperation in her voice.

"Yeah, but you ain't the expert on creepy crap, that's The Annoying One. If they're too scared to go then it's got to be a bad idea," Eddie concluded.

"You guys…seriously…what…" Darby fumbled.

"Darby, you are clearly losing," Jason offered, "and though I would love to take up your cause in the name of contrarianism, I fear that particular house's effects on my physiognomy will be so transcendentally at odds with your puny conceptions of normality that once unleashed it will cause a psychotic break within one or all of you."

"Huh?" Eddie huhed.

"He's talking about his laugh," I clarified.

Jason Human had only laughed in front of us once. We were down in a concrete ditch watching Darby do tricks on her skateboard when Jason caught sight of a butterfly. It landed in the center of his face, where a nose would normally be, and when it fluttered away, Jason began to shake. Soon his bulbous grey head deflated like a balloon, his black eyes turned blood red, and he let out a piercing whine. The sight was so frightening that we all scattered, except for Darby who jumped off her skateboard and was immediately at Jason's side trying to help. Eventually the whining stopped, his head inflated, and his eyes went back to the normal black. The rest of us came back out to see if he was ok and he told us he hadn't laughed that hard in a very long time. When we asked what was so funny, he said "You had to be there," which confused us because we had all been there.

"Oh cripes! I completely forgot!" Eddie said. "He goes anywhere near that house and people'll think a murder's going down!"

At that point, we all started talking over each other, listing all the ways that visiting the house was a terrible idea. That's when Darby screamed.

"HEY!"

We all stopped.

"You dorks don't need to worry about the laughing. I'll take you through the backyard. You can't hear the laughter from back there," she said and then added softly, lowering her eyes, "Please, you guys...I need your help."

We were all stunned. As far as we knew, Darby had never asked anyone for help. Ever. Just that past year, she took an ugly fall off her skateboard and twisted her ankle. It swelled black and blue right before our eyes, but she wouldn't let any of us help her walk. She hobbled away and told us not to follow her. At no point did she ever cry out in pain or let a wince break across her face. We all agreed that it was the toughest thing any of us had ever seen and that Darby was officially indestructible.

But, at that moment, as she stood on the banks of the creek, shoulders hunched, eyes cast to the ground, she finally looked like what she really was: A kid. The thought was so bizarre to me. Despite all the ways she looked after us and protected us, she was just a child the same as us.

"Please," she repeated.

That please was filled with sadness I don't think any of us could fully understand. It bypassed my brain and went straight to my gut where it seemed to rearrange my intestines into a balloon animal tragedy. I felt sick. I think Eddie and The Anointed One did too. We realized that we'd all asked so much of Darby, and she'd never asked for anything in return. Now the first time that she needed something from us, we'd all acted like spoiled little brats screaming Nuh-Uh. Having had no real experience with a mother, I am told that this is the kind of shame that only they can make you feel. Suddenly it didn't seem like too much of an ask to follow her to a definitely, for sure, haunted house that would most likely kill us.

It should be noted that Jason didn't feel any of these things because I don't think he was capable. But after The Anointed

One, Eddie, and I apologized for our deplorable behavior and agreed to go with her, Jason followed because there was safety in numbers.

The most surprising thing about the house, which I will now refer to as The House, was that it was lovely. The grass was freshly mowed, and the flower beds were in constant bloom. The garden gnomes were happy, and the exterior always had the shine of a fresh coat of yellow and white paint. Pristine linen curtains hung in the windows of the living room and second floor bedrooms. It wasn't until you realized that nobody maintained the house that the beauty became unsettling. In fact, the local homeowner's association had to stop awarding a prize for the most beautiful home because The House would have won every year, and no one wanted to deal with the metaphysical implications of this.

As Darby opened the rear gate of The House, we could see that the backyard was even more beautiful than the front. The lush green grass was so soft that it tickled your feet through your shoes. An apple tree stood in one corner of the yard, its glistening fruit shining like candy sapphires. An inflatable pool in the opposite corner was filled with water the color of the sky. The sunlight reflected off the water in explosions of vivid pinks, greens, and yellows that danced off the tall, chocolate brown fencing. Not that we could feel the sun at all. As soon as we crossed the gate, we left the 90-degree morning behind and were surrounded by a gentle breeze that was as cool as autumn and as fresh as spring.

Darby walked across the yard and up the steps of the enormous wooden deck that jutted from the house. She turned to see that we were all still by the gate, afraid to move. "God, will you guys stop acting like babies? Come over here, I want to show you something cool."

I personally felt that she had already shown us enough cool things for the day, and I was ready to be near uncool things where it was safe. But we all seemed to remember the power of Darby's "please" and crossed the yard and stood at the foot of the steps.

"Check this out," Darby said, and then dropped her skateboard so that she could lean down and rip a plank of wood right out of the deck.

"Holy cow, what are you doing?!" Eddie screamed. "You're gonna cheese off the giggle spooks!"

"It does seem rather dangerous to antagonize the intelligences that are behind this phenomenon, Darby," The Anointed One added.

"How are you so strong?" I genuinely wondered out loud.

"Shut up and turn around," Darby said.

Me, Eddie, and Jason exchanged worried glances. The Anointed One might have been joining in but it was impossible to tell under the mask.

"Turn around!" Darby commanded.

As I turned, I fully expected to feel the wrath of a vengeful spirit or a bonk on the back of the head from Darby who may have been playing an incredibly elaborate haunted house-based prank this whole time.

"Ok, turn back."

When we did, Darby was still holding the plank of wood, but we could see that the deck was now fully repaired like nothing had happened.

"Intriguing!" Jason Human declared as he quickly ripped the plank out of Darby's hand to examine it.

"I know a lot about this place. It's pretty rad. I made my skateboard from the wood of this deck," she said, as she lined her board up with the new plank to show that they were the same width.

"No wonder you twisted your ankle that time," Eddie said. "You've been tooling around on a haunted skateboard."

"Not haunted. Death has nothing to do with it. This house, my skateboard, they're alive," Darby said, smiling.

"A completely isolated atmosphere and running contrary to the laws of thermodynamics," Jason said as he began to drool. "This could be the key to unlimited resources. Ultimate Power. COSMIC DOMINATION!"

Darby tore the plank from his hands and threw it back on the deck. "It's not unlimited," she said. "The House decides what you can have and how much. That's why I brought you guys here. The House wants us to do something."

Again, there was a sharing of worried glances. Even Eddie didn't know what to say to this, so I stepped forward. "What does the house want us to do?"

"The House wants us to build a half-pipe," Darby said.

A half-pipe, for those unaware, is basically a device which enables skaters to perform recklessly dangerous aerial maneuvers because they feel that life isn't scary enough already. Darby was one of these people but until then had satisfied her craving for danger by dropping into ditches, launching off benches, and grinding the railing of any stairway she could find. If there were any authority figures around to scream at her for her trashy and unladylike behavior, so much the better.

Darby told Jason the dimensions of the half-pipe and asked him to make a blueprint along with a list of materials we would need. He did all of this in less than 30 seconds on one of his many notepads. Darby took the blueprint and list from Jason and dropped them in between the boards of the deck. There was a sound of rushing air and a flash of light from underneath.

"Okay," she said, "everything that we need should now be somewhere in The House."

I raised my hand. "Ummm, aren't you forgetting something?"

"What?" Darby asked.

"That we suck at building things."

"Yeah," said Eddie. "Don't you remember when we tried to build a clubhouse and it caught on fire? Or when we tried to build a dam in the creek and Jason caught on fire? Or that time we tried to make a fire and it floated away?"

"It's going to be different this time," Darby said as she walked through the backdoor of the house. We reluctantly followed her in.

After what we had already witnessed, I was let down by the interior of The House. The backdoor led into a perfectly normal kitchen which led out into a perfectly normal dining room and living room beyond. The only thing off about the shocking normalcy was how The House felt. It was warm. Much warmer than the breeze that swept through the yard, but not the stifling heat of summer. This was the cozy warmth of a well heated house on a winter's day. There was a fireplace crackling in the living room and when we turned around, we could see snow falling outside the windows.

"This house is messing with my head," Eddie said.

"This is a site of great power," The Anointed One declared, cloaked arms upraised as if trying to catch some of it.

"Oh really? What was your first clue?" Eddie asked sarcastically. "Was it the snow in the middle of summer or maybe it was- Oh My God!"

We all looked at what had caught Eddie's eye. Above the fireplace was a huge photographic portrait of a very odd family. Odd because the family was us. We were all wearing ugly Christmas sweaters, The Anointed One wearing theirs over their robes, and had huge, dumb smiles on our faces. Darby and Jason were posed as the mom and dad because they were the tallest and the rest of us were the children. Eddie was doing rabbit ears behind the Anointed One's head. My eyes were closed because I apparently blinked when the picture that shouldn't exist was not taken. The House sure got the details right.

"The House is just saying hello," Darby said.

She told us to search the rooms upstairs where we'd find all the materials and tools that we would need. We only set off after Darby once again assured us that The House meant us no harm. I was about to ascend the stairs with the others when I realized that Darby hadn't followed. I went back to the living room and saw her staring at the portrait. There was a half-smile on her face. She was hugging her skateboard against her chest like a teddy bear. I joined her by the fire.

"How do you know so much about this place?" I asked.

"You know how we were always told to stay away?"

"Yeah?"

"Well, I didn't listen."

"Of course," I smiled.

"It seemed to me that the more people in this town agree on something, the more likely it is to be full of crap. So, I checked it out. Started walking by it every day. Just to show them."

"Who?" I asked.

"Anyone. The neighbors, the mailman. Everyone's always staring at me all the time like I'm a murderer or got a disease, so I wanted to give them something to stare at. Show them I wasn't afraid. I would even go crazy with the laughing. Really exaggerate it like I was going insane. I remember one time this lady from across the street came out to see what was going on. I rolled my eyes back til' you could only see the whites and I began ripping my hair out. She tripped over herself when she tried running back inside her house. That was funny."

We could hear banging from upstairs. Eddie was screaming some curse words. It sounded like they had things well in hand.

"I didn't like the laughing at first, though. I mean, besides that lady falling, what's so funny? It's like when I see high school girls driving around town and they're giggling all the time; it makes me want to scream 'WHAT'S SO FUNNY?' But after a while, I realized something."

"What?"

"It felt good. It felt good to laugh. It was like The House gave me permission to feel good. Told me it was ok. I never knew that. My whole life I never...I don't know. Am I sounding like a dork? I feel like I'm not making any sense."

I assured her that she was making sense even though I had no idea what she was talking about. This was one of those times when our ages and the very different lives we lead were an insurmountable gulf. But I wanted to know more.

She told me that she gradually went from passing by to walking up to peek in the window and knock at the door. One day she grabbed some flowers from the front garden and that's how she discovered The House's ability to replenish itself. Her exploration eventually led her to the open back door.

"It's like The House knew me. All my favorite foods in the fridge. All my favorite records and books on the shelves. Teen Time was always playing on the TV."

Teen Time was a television show that came on at odd hours. Nobody knew who made it or where it was broadcast from. All we knew was that its signal was strong enough to take over any television station in town whenever it wanted. The format of the show was simple: A group of teens were gathered into a TV studio and the most popular songs of that week were counted down as the teenagers cried uncontrollably. Camera angles would alternate between a wide shot of all the teens crying and then go to a close-up of one teen in particular crying. Sometimes you could catch a glimpse of a man in a white suit walking around and collecting the tears in a jar that was labeled "Salted Wets." This was Darby's absolute favorite show, and she would often talk about how much she wanted to be one of those crying teens.

While she was listing all the wonderful things The House could do, a question began to nag at me. "Why do you ever leave this place? Like, why do you bother hanging out with us when this place is way cooler?" I asked with an extreme lack of self-esteem.

"It's The House. It doesn't let me stay long. Just a couple of hours a day. Some days, it won't even let me in. I think it doesn't want me to become, like, a junkie or something. Hooked on its powers. It knows the last thing I would ever want to be is an addict. The House is a good friend," she said, putting a loving hand on the mantelpiece above the fireplace.

I guess she could see the jealousy in my eyes because she turned to me and said, "Hey, you're a good friend too, Weirdo," and then punched me in the arm which is how she showed affection to things that weren't magical houses.

As I rubbed my arm, it finally occurred to me to ask, "Why does The House want us to build a half-pipe?"

She was quiet for a few seconds, then she spun one of the wheels on her skateboard with her left hand. "Because The House is sick of this town. And so am I."

Before I could ask what she meant, we heard a thunderous crash. We both ran to the stairs in time to see a huge cart loaded with wood barreling down the steps. It was moments away from annihilating the both of us, but luckily Darby's reflexes kicked in and she tackled me out of the path of the cart. It rushed past us and crashed into the wall of the living room causing a huge crack to serpentine its way up the ceiling. Within seconds, the crack had healed itself. We looked back up the staircase to see Eddie standing there with his hands on his hips.

"Welp, we're finished," he said as he made his way down. He pointed a finger straight at me. "Thanks for all your help, by the way. Y'know, you might be the laziest cuss I ever knew, and I once met a dead cat who was on welfare. Not that The Annoying One was much use either."

The Anointed One glided down the stairs. "I was beseeching the Great Eye to protect us on our unholy mission. It took all my concentration."

Jason Human followed carrying a large jangling sack of tools. "This palace of madness has provided all the materials we'll need to build your superfluous fun structure."

"So, what now?" I asked as Darby helped me up off the floor.

"We need to find an open space to work. A place with no one around."

We hauled everything to McKaren park. It was the perfect spot. The park was named after General James McKaren who had an absolute hatred of trees. "Trees remind me of life. A repugnant concept. A scorched, empty Earth, now there's a Heaven," he was quoted as saying when given a medal by the president of the losing side of the Civil War. When it came time to open a park to honor his memory, it was decided to make his vision of Heaven here on Earth. In addition to all the trees in the park being cut and burned, there were no benches, basketball courts or water fountains as these were monuments to leisure and fun which the General saw as the root of all sickness in our society. All of this was explained in the helpful plaque which lay at the center of the barren, sun scorched field and was the only marker that let visitors know that they were inside a park. It had already gotten up to 100 degrees, so we knew the last place anyone would want to be was that broad, lifeless expanse of baking Earth.

We couldn't feel the heat, though. Whatever power was in The House was also in the materials we gathered from it. The rays of the hateful sun didn't seem to touch us as we were bathed in a soft breeze that tousled our hair but touched nothing else. The fact that Darby's skateboard was made from The House answered a question I always had: How can she wear just a flannel shirt and jeans full of holes on both the hottest and coldest days of the year?

I had never once seen her shiver or sweat. It's possible she hadn't felt the actual temperature outside in a very long time.

We picked a spot in the middle of the park and got to work. We were all shocked when the construction went smoothly. Again, I put this down to the influence of The House. I have never since been able to hammer a nail without hurting myself or the people around me. But that day I hammered like a master carpenter, and it seemed as if we knew what to do without being told. I'm sure that The House could have produced a half-pipe on its own and it would have been grander than anything we could ever construct. But I think that The House needed us working together. It was drawing something from us, feeding off the energy we created. No, feeding sounds too predatory. It was taking nourishment, like a flower takes energy from the sun.

We completed the half-pipe in less than an hour which astonished everyone. We looked on our finished work with both pride and confusion, a look I knew all too well from my father. He always seemed amazed that he was able to make a human being, but clueless as to what to do next. Like my father, we were also amazed that we had created something from nothing but now looked at our creation wondering why we built it and what to do now. The only person who had any idea was Darby. She jumped three feet onto the end of one ramp and looked down at us.

"Dudes, this is incredible. I can't...oh man," Darby said. We could see that she was tearing up.

Eddie leaned over and whispered in my ear, "Can this day get any weirder?"

"I heard that!" Darby yelped, which shocked Eddie so much that he immediately punched me in the bruise I had already gotten when Darby punched me earlier.

"Look, sorry for acting like such a dork today, and dragging you to a not-haunted house. I've never known any other people in my life who would do this kind of thing for me. I don't think anyone has ever been friends with a bigger bunch of freaks," she laughed, and then looked out towards Aickman. "I've always hated this town and the people in it. But you guys and The House have shown me that there's good stuff too. And...I don't know...look, whatever, enough with this mushy crap, it's time to test this bad boy out!" she screamed as she held her board over her head. We hooted and hollered in response. She eased the board over the edge of the ramp, mounted it, and dropped in.

We had seen Darby skate many times. We had also seen the skating videos that Darby would bring over to my house to show us the true art of skateboarding as practiced by the professionals that she so admired. What we witnessed that day would put all the pros to shame.

At first, she was getting decent air for how small the ramps were. Every now and then she would throw in a simple handstand or kickflip. But as she got more and more into it, something began to change. Her movements became more graceful. Each time she landed back on the ramp, the sound of the impact became lighter and lighter. She was also picking up tremendous speed. Her shock of curly hair seemed to float out behind her, obeying some newly written laws of physics.

That wasn't the only thing that was changing. The gentle breeze that The House had provided was whipping up stronger and sharper, its influence spreading beyond us. The dead grass and dirt got kicked up by the phantom wind. Dust devils spouted up here and there. A tumbleweed blew in from who knows where. All at once, the sun seemed to disappear. Dark clouds filled the sky and the world turned purple momentarily as a gargantuan lightning bolt crashed overhead.

Jason whipped out one of his instruments and took some readings. The Anointed One held up their arms and began chanting. Eddie did some swears. I regretted not bringing my umbrella. The only one of us who didn't seem to notice was

Darby. She was now sailing over 12 feet into the air with each launch off the ramps. I was never very good at math, but this seemed like what the scientists would call "impossible."

It wasn't just the height she was getting either. The spins she was pulling off in midair were incredible. 360 spins at first then ramping up to 540, then 720, then 1080 and beyond. I was getting dizzy just watching. I have no idea how she didn't puke all over us.

The wind kicked up stronger and drowned out all other noise. The Anointed One put their hands over their head to stop their mask from flying off. Jason, who weighed less than nothing, got picked up by the gale and Eddie and I had to hold him down. We knew if it got any worse, we would go flying as well.

Darby, on the other hand, was surfing the wind currents, going higher and higher. She was now reaching 30 feet with each launch. She was going to get herself killed. I screamed at her to stop, but the wind tore my words to pieces, and she wasn't listening anyway.

Thunder now rang out whenever she hit the ramp and lightning flashed as she reached the heights of her arcs. I began cursing The House. It had tricked us. It had tricked Darby. It had used us to release this chaos. Pandemonium reigned and my friend was caught in the center of it. I grabbed The Anointed One and made them take my place holding down Jason. I fought against the wind, making my way to the half-pipe. My plan was to tackle Darby and drag her away from the influence of The House. Being the idiot I was, it didn't even occur to me that at the velocities she was reaching, tackling her would probably cut her in half and shatter every bone in my body.

As I got closer, I could see that sparks were now dancing off the trucks of the skateboard with every landing and intense waves of heat were shooting out. Over the wind I could hear laughter. Darby's laughter. The same senseless and frightening laughter that

I was certain had scared that woman across the street. I realized that the town had been right. The laughter wasn't harmless. It was how The House got into your mind. It doesn't get a grip on most people, but Darby had exposed herself too so much of it. It wormed its way in. It possessed her. The House was in control of my friend, and it was going to kill her.

There was no time to lose. I was right next to the half-pipe. She had reached at least 60 feet this time and was on her way down. Her descent was accompanied by a high-pitched whistle like a bomb dropping on a city. I steadied myself, ready to leap, knowing I would have less than a second to tackle my friend out of danger. As soon as the blur that was Darby entered my field of vision, I pounced.

The others would tell me later that time did not stop. They would swear that there was no moment of pause between her coming down and what happened next. But I tell you that there were 5 seconds that belonged to no one else but me and Darby. We couldn't move or say anything. There was no oxygen in that bubble of time, but I could see her eyes. Those sad brown eyes now lit by joy that I couldn't comprehend. They belonged to her. She wasn't possessed. She knew exactly what she was doing. She was giving me a look that said, "Relax, weirdo," and then the bubble burst and I was thrown back by an explosion.

I landed ten feet away, all the air knocked out of me. I was looking straight up. I could see the rocket launching into the sky. The rocket named Darby.

A trail of smoke jetted out behind and there was a second bang that I would realize later was her breaking the sound barrier. Up and up. Faster and faster. She tore through the clouds like a missile and the sky swirled and collapsed all around her. There was one last thrash of lightning and the clouds disappeared. The blistering summer day had returned as if nothing had happened.

I couldn't stop staring at the sky even as the rays of the sun burnt my eyes. The protection of The House was completely gone. So was Darby.

The others ran up to check on me. I barely noticed them as I kept looking skyward for any sign of her. In those minutes of searching, I had some peculiar thoughts. I realized that I had no idea where Darby lived. None of us had ever been to her real house or met any of her family. I had no idea if she had any brothers or sisters. It dawned on me that there were so many things I had never bothered to ask her. So many things she kept from me. She was my best friend, and I didn't know her at all

The half-pipe was in a million burnt pieces. I could hear the others saying that we had to get out of there, but I couldn't move. I looked at the sky one last time.

She really was gone.

Eventually Eddie grabbed me and drug me out of the park. I followed in a daze, not noticing, or caring where I was going.

At the corner of Poplar and Ash, the flowers began to die. The lawn turned brown. The paint peeled. The wood of the house sagged under untold years of neglect. The windows burst out and the lawn gnomes crumpled to dust. The laughter ceased. The house finally looked haunted, but the ghost was gone.

ALONE PART 3:

THE 2 KOOL 4 SKOOL KREW AND THE ROACHES OF RAMEN TOWN

2 Kool!
Rockin' Cross The USA!
2 Kool!
Everything is A-Ok!
2 Kool!
Better Not Get In Our Way!
2 Kool!
Anyone Who Tries Will Die!
2 Kool!
DIE! DIE! DIE! DIE! DIE! DIE! DIE!
KOOL!

There were 5 members of the 2 Kool 4 Skool Krew:

1.   Dak Anner: The blonde-haired leader of the Krew. He was never caught without his trusty shades and could shred a guitar like nobody's business. Though he was only 10 years old, the ladies found him irresistible.

2.   J'Aderika Wells: Bubbly lead singer and fashion icon who could rock tie dye, acid wash, and the classic black dress whether it be on stage or hunting cryptids in the Pacific northwest.

3.   Hooper T. Brathwaite: Slick and soulful, Hooper kept the beat on drums as well as being the beating heart of the Krew.

4.   Nedrick D'orkington: Bass player and brains of the Krew. He may look like a nerd, but you better shut your mouth because he isn't just Kool, he's 2 Kool.

5.   I.S.A.A.K: The Incredible Scientific Artifact And Keyboard was a robot built by Nedrick when he was five years old. He acts as the Krew's roadie, driver, muscle, and is also a self-playing synthesizer keyboard.

To be as brief as possible:

The 2 Kool 4 Skool Krew were a group of 10-year-olds who, through a series of tests administered by the federal government, were judged to be so cool that they were not legally allowed to be taught in any public or private schools. Having been stripped of any chance of an education, the only hope for the 2 Kool 4 Skool Krew to ever support themselves financially was to start a band and hit the road. Along the way, they would earn extra money by slaying monsters that happened to be burdening the towns in which they were performing.

The 2 Kool 4 Skool Krew travelled the world, fought countless beasts, and kept the dream of Rock N' Roll alive. It was a typical tv show from the early '90s and, as far as I know, I was the only person who ever saw it.

***

On the way back from McKaren park, Jason and The Anointed One argued about what they thought had happened to Darby. Jason was convinced that she'd broken through the dimensional barrier of our reality and had escaped into a new one. The Anointed One countered by saying that Darby had opened a portal to another realm and transcended through it. That they were basically saying the same thing never occurred to either of them.

"Boy," Eddie said, "you two must work at a meat rendering plant cuz you sure talk a lot of baloney. I saw the same thing you guys saw and that didn't include no realms or portals."

"Then how do you explain the phenomena we witnessed, Edward?" Jason asked, knowing that Eddie hated his full name.

"I don't know, Jasondra, and I'm not going to pretend like I do. The only thing I'm certain about is that Darby always knew what she was doing and whatever happened, she's doing okay right now." There was a tremble of uncertainty in his voice at that last part. "She's fine…she's fine." He shook his head in that usual manner of his. "She's going to be fine." He turned to look at me as I shuffled several feet behind the others. "Darby's fine, right Weirdo?"

I said nothing. I barely registered the conversation. If I had voiced my true thoughts, it would only have made things worse. A part of me knew that Jason and The Anointed One could be right. Darby could have broken free of our awful reality and found one that was so far from Aickman that the stink of the town would never bother her again. Even if she hadn't, Eddie could be right and wherever she was, she could be safe and sound.

That kind of optimism never came naturally to me, though. Part of this is down to genetics. My father's family seems to pass misery down through the blood so that none of us knew exactly how to deal with smiling people or good news. The remainder of my pessimism came from living in Aickman. Nothing good ever happened there. Not one resident, as far as I could tell, ever got a happy ending. The last thing Aickman would ever allow was Darby to be happy. It would have done anything to prevent that, including killing her.

Yes, I thought, that was the most logical explanation of the day's events.

I flinched at this certainty of Darby's fate and would probably have broken down into sobs if not for the numbness that had poured over my body. My flesh and bones felt as if they had been replaced by that thick, green cough medicine that knocks you out instantly. I trudged along behind my friends as one thought grew louder and louder in my mind: She left me. She left me behind.

I broke away from the others as we got to my house. I walked up the driveway without saying goodbye and none of them tried to follow me. Before I got inside, Eddie shouted, "Hey, do you think we'll ever see her again?"

I shut the front door without answering.

I had never lost a real friend before. Until Darby, I had never had a friend to lose. I've mentioned the pain of losing Mr. Sandwiches when I was little, but this was worse. There were no tears of outrage or threats to my dad to drink a whole bottle of sulfuric acid if he didn't bring Darby back. There was just a hole, Darby shaped, that dropped off into an abyss so dark and deep that, if not soon covered, would swallow everything.

I retreated down to the TV room in the basement. I would not leave the house, speak a word, or see any of my friends for the next seven days. On that seventh day, my TV would try to kill me.

***

(Dialogue from the 2 Kool 4 Skool Krew episode "Bigfoot Sucks" as best as I can remember it.)

The Krew stands inside the MKL (Mobile Kool Lab) while Nedrick scans info on the World Wide Web with his KoolPuter.

Dak
That Bigfoot is one seriously uncool dude.

J'Aderika
I know! So grody! He like, lives outside. Like a bum. He stinks like one too!

Hooper
He's a 10 out of 10 on the wack scale. And what's worse, he's driving property values down!

J'Aderika
OH MY GOD! NO!

J'Aderika runs into Dak's arms. He holds her tight.

Dak
I know, babe, I know.

Nedrick gets a flash of inspiration and jumps up from the Koolputer.

Nedrick
Guys! I think I know how to get rid of Bigfoot and increase property value in the area!

Hooper
Lay it on me, Drick!

Nedrick

I can program I.S.A.A.K to transform into a giant knife that will be strong enough to rip through Bigfoot's tough, smelly pectoral muscles and destroy his heart.

Dak
Sounds solid, but how will this help with property values?

J'Aderika
Seriously, Nedrick? Who would want to live in a planned community filled with ape murder?

Nedrick
If we lure him deep enough into the section of woods that's about to be destroyed to make way for that rad new golf course and kill him there, then the golf course itself can become an international attraction where people can come see Bigfoot's final resting place under the 18th hole!

Dak
A thriving tourism trade? Now that's cool!

I.S.A.A.K enters, half transformed into a giant knife.

I.S.A.A.K
Kill. The. Bum. Kill. The. Bum. Kill. The. Bum.

The 2 Kool 4 Skool Krew laugh and high five.

***

Our basement housed the ancient, wood paneled television set that my grandfather had bought years before I was born. We had a newer TV upstairs in the living room, but I rarely used it. There was something about that clunky, chunky outdated box in the basement that fascinated me. It was a black and white set that was always a bit snowy no matter how you moved the antennae. There was no remote so you had to walk up to the box and crank the huge round knobs that would roll over with an ever so satisfying CA-CHUNK every time you changed the channel. The set generated so much heat that it raised the temperature in the basement by ten degrees and let off a low-pitched hum that in tandem with the heat, much like the bitter taste of medicine, let you know that something was happening. To me, the glow that came off that cathode-ray relic was a kind of magic that newer, flatter, flashier sets could never equal.

Not that I felt any of that magic. When I got home that day, I simply descended the stairs, cranked on the set, and then flopped onto the lumpy, scratchy orange-brown synthetic material that made up the couch. I let one arm flop down to the rough, yellow carpet that felt like the newly shorn hair on the back of your neck after visiting the barber. I rubbed my fingers back and forth on the coarse fabric and zoned out.

This is how I would spend the next week of my life: lying on that couch and letting TV happen to me. I did not bathe or engage in any other form of hygiene, save for using the toilet without much enthusiasm or attention to detail. When I got hungry, I would go upstairs and make a bowl of ramen noodles, which is all we seemed to have in the house. Whenever I finished, or half-finished with a bowl, I would place it on the ground and then get a new one. The frequency of my trips to get ramen coupled with my indifference to cleanliness meant that the basement had soon become a city of half-filled noodle bowls that I arranged only to create two avenues: One that would allow me access to the TV to change the channel, and the other for a footpath to the stairs to make more ramen. The smell was horrendous. The heat was oppressive. Nothing good was on TV. I had no idea where my father was. None of that mattered to me. Nothing mattered to me.

It wasn't until the morning of the second day that I finally noticed the roaches.

***

(Extract of dialogue from the 2 Kool 4 Skool Krew episode titled "Loch Ness Loser" as best as I can remember it.)

The Kool Jet soars high above the skies of Scotland. I.S.A.A.K. is at the controls of the cockpit. He reaches over a mechanical claw and hovers it above a red button.

I.S.A.A.K.
In. The. Name. Of. Kool.

I.S.A.A.K presses the red button. The middle of the Kool Jet opens and out falls a gigantic bomb. Right before it strikes, a single, oily tear falls from I.S.A.A.K.'s left optic sensor. The bomb hits. Scotland is instantly vaporized. It crumbles like dust into the sea. Back at the Kool Kommand Center, the human members of the Krew cheer and high five each other…except for Hooper.

J'Aderika
BABE! WE DID IT!

Dak
Sure did, babe. The Loch Ness Monster won't be causing trouble for anybody ever again.

Nedrick

And with Scotland gone, England will have access to vast new underwater oil repositories that will make them an economic powerhouse in the new millennium!

Dak
High five, Hoop!

Dak holds his hand up. Hooper does not Five it.

Hooper
We just destroyed a whole country.

Dak looks up at his unrequited hand.

Dak
Sure did. Come on, Hoop, don't leave me hanging, bro!

Hooper
We just killed millions of people.

J'Aderika
Uh, yeah, Scottish people.

Nedrick
With a high unemployment rate.

Hooper
We just committed genocide!

Dak
Hoop?

Dak indicates his hanging hand with a nod of his head. Hooper backs away.

Hooper
I'm sorry, bro. I...I gotta leave you hanging.

J'Aderika and Nedrick gasp.

Dak
Hanging...

Hooper
I can't be a part of this anymore.

Dak
Leave...me...hanging?

Hooper
I just want to go home! I want to see my family! I don't want to be 2 Kool anymore!

Dak
Do you know what happens when you leave a bro hanging?

Everyone looks up at Dak's hanging hand. It begins to blister and crack. Dak screams in pain. The hand bulges, the fingernails extend into sharp yellow claws. Hooper lets out a wail of terror. With a roar, Dak swipes his claw at Hooper's head, decapitating him. The head smashes through a window and rolls away. Hooper's headless body falls to the ground. Dak looks down at his hand. It begins to absorb Hooper's blood and returns to normal.

J'Aderika

Are…are you ok, babe?

Dak

Ok?

J'Aderika and Nedrick freeze, terror in their eyes.

Dak

We just killed the Loch Ness Monster. Of course I'm ok. Why do you ask?

J'Aderika

Oh…uh…no reason.

Dak

Nedrick?

Nedrick

Y…yes boss?

Dak

I need you to make a want ad. It should say the following: Wanted: A stylish and slick drummer who not only knows how to keep the beat but is also the beating heart of the group. Must never leave a bro hanging. Got that?

Nedrick

Yes, boss.

Dak

And Nedrick?

Nedrick

Yes, boss?

Dak

Bring up that video of Scotland exploding again.

Nedrick

You got it!

Nedrick goes back to the KoolPuter to carry out his orders. J'Aderika hugs Dak from behind.

Dak

Feel like making me some popcorn, babe?

J'Aderika

You're so kool, Dak!

Dak looks directly into the camera.

Dak

2 Kool.

***

The easiest way to become the god of cockroaches is to stop caring.

The main quality that roaches are looking for in a god is indifference. They want a god who lets food fall from his mouth. They want a god who sits and does nothing as the trash piles higher and higher creating a new world, a heaven on Earth, where they can skitter and chitter and mate and birth and die and the cycle goes on and on and on…..

Such a nirvana was realized in my basement over that terrible week after Darby disappeared into the sky. All the bowls I had left out filled with ramen water and stray noodles had drawn out the formerly invisible inhabitants of our walls to come gorge themselves on a feast unlike any they had ever known. A few at first, but then little by little, Ramen Town was filled to burst with tiny, six-legged demons from the dawn of time.

I hate roaches. Completely. Totally. They make my skin crawl right off my body. If this had been any other time of my life and I had been confronted with the gathering of roaches that slurped and sipped out of the ramen bowls, that used the noodles to reenact hellish versions of Lady and the Tramp, that seemed to be forming a new society right in front of my eyes, I would have simply burned down our house.

But I felt nothing. The Darby shaped hole had somehow bypassed my most primal impulses and sucked the terror out of me. As ways to conquer fear go, having an all-consuming abyss open inside of you is incredibly effective.

So, I just lay there while the roaches played. Splashing in and out of the bowls. Chasing each other. Rubbing their antenna, their chitinous exo-skeletons bouncing and scraping, making sounds like a field of Rice Krispies in milk or Pop Rocks hitting your tongue. Every now and then a bloom of babies would explode and head out into the fetid pleasures of Ramen Town and learn their lessons about The Indifferent God that lay on the couch above them.

Yes, I am certain they were taught about me. They all knew not to come too close lest they move the god to action. There was always a respectful distance that the swarm kept from me. Even the little ones. This went beyond a roach's usual inclination to avoid humans. There was a reverence in the way they left me alone.

Except for one roach who I will refer to as The Heretic.

On the fourth day, I was laying in my stupor watching a rerun of a show from the 1970s about a racist yelling at people. As I watched the racist rant and rave, The Heretic crawled up the couch right where my head was laying. It stared at me, its alien antennae taking in signals that I would never understand. Its mandibles opened and closed as its shiny carapace gleamed like a chocolate wrong on spiked legs.

It moved closer and closer.

I remained indifferent.

Closer to my face. Even closer. It's hesitant steps a testament to the sin it was committing.

Closer. Closer.

One quivering leg probed my cheek.

I didn't move.

Another leg.

Still, I did not move.

With a heave and a leap, The Heretic was on my face. I probably would have let it explore whatever part of my body it wanted, and it would have run back to the others to tell its mad tale about touching the face of their god. No doubt this would have opened the floodgates, and my subjects would have swarmed all over me as they yearned to also lay hands on The Indifferent.

But before any of that could happen, one of The Heretic's antennae lashed at my right eyeball causing me to reflexively blink which so affrighted The Heretic that it dropped dead off my face and bounced from the couch to the floor.

At the exact moment that The Heretic died, the black and white set went to snow, and then suddenly exploded into vivid color. The opening surf-rock guitar strings of a theme song I had never heard before began to blast forth and I was formally introduced to the show that would take up all my attention for the next three days and nights: The 2 Kool 4 Skool Krew.

***

(Dialogue from a sermon by Father Roach, spiritual leader of the Roaches of Ramen Town, to the newly born roachlings concerning The Indifferent God. This is complete fiction on my part, but I can assure you that the fact that it never happened doesn't stop it from being true.)

On the outskirts of Ramen Town, at the foot of Mount Filth (The Sofa), wizened old Father Roach stands before the roachlings as he preaches.

Father Roach
ALL PRAISE THE INDIFFERENT GOD!

Roachlings
ALL PRAISE THE INDIFFERENT GOD!

Father Roach
OR DON'T!

Roachlings
OR DON'T!

Father Roach
HE DOESN'T CARE ONE WAY OR ANOTHER!

Roachlings
HE DOESN'T CARE ONE W-

Father Roach
SILENCE!

The roachlings fall silent. Father Roach points up at The Indifferent God.

Father Roach

See him up there, perched atop the filth mountain? Do you not recognize the majesty? Do you not understand the miracle of Indifference? It is through Indifference that we have Ramen Town!

Father Roach sweeps a spiked leg to encompass the majesty of the bowls of Ramen Town.

Father Roach
It is through Indifference that we have the pools of HEAVENLY MOIST! (Ramen water)

Roachlings
HEAVENLY MOIST!

Father Roach
It is through Indifference that we have the STRINGLING YUM-YUMS! (Ramen Noodles)

Roachlings
STRINGLING YUM-YUMS!

Father Roach
It is through Indifference that we are allowed to be who we are! The other fleshy gods, the putrid giants that tower over us, they smash and crush our kind. They dream up terrible potions that burn our insides or choke our crunchy skeletons leaving us prone on our backs, legs flailing helplessly as we die horrible deaths!

The roachlings wail in despair. Father Roach turns towards The Indifferent God and gets on what would be his knees if roaches had knees.

Father Roach

But then we found one that doesn't care. That neither loves nor hates us. CAN YOU FEEL THE ABSENCE OF EMOTION CHILDREN?!

Roachlings

WE FEEL NOTHING!

Father Roach

THAT IS A BLESSING MY CHILDREN! His blessing! And all he asks in return is that we leave him alone, that we return The Indifference in kind and stay away. But there are those who do not heed The Indifference.

Two roach priests drag the body of The Heretic and drop it in front of Father Roach.

Father Roach

This is The Heretic. This is the one who climbed Filth Mountain. The one who dared to touch The Indifference!

The roachlings gasp in shock.

Father Roach

His hubris has not only cost him his life, but perhaps all our lives! See The Flickering Monolith!

Father Roach points to the television.

Father Roach

Where it once shone in monochrome, it now flickers with color! We can sense with our antennae that this is an unnatural signal. The burning at the tips, the itch in our brain, this signal is evil and will soon mean the end of Indifference! TRIBULATION! REVELATION! JUDGEMENT DAY IS UPON US!

The roachlings cry in fear.

Father Roach

Soak up the pleasures of Ramen Town while it lasts! The evil is here and there is nothing to be done. The Heretic has doomed us all! So take The Heretic's body, children, take up his body and bathe it in the Heavenly Moist and feast on his flesh!

The roachlings cheer as they scoop up The Heretic's body, dunk it in a ramen bowl, and then greedily devour the flesh of the sinner.

***

By definition, nothing can surprise The Indifferent One. So, when The 2 Kool 4 Skool Krew began blaring out of my black and white television in liquid color, I took it in my stride, or lack thereof.

This wasn't entirely down to my mental state. We Aickmaniacs, the official name for residents of Aickman, were used to all kinds of TV based shenanigans. Apart from the mysterious crying teen music show that would invade our airwaves and which Darby was such a fan, there were the almost daily commercials for Mike Diamond's Used Car Lot. These always featured a manic and sweaty Mike Diamond who would implore the townspeople to take advantage of his insane deals. These commercials were remarkable for 2 Reasons:

1. Mike Diamond's Used Car Lot had been destroyed by a mysterious explosion in 1979.
2. Mike Diamond had perished in the same explosion.

The most alarming TV-based incident had occurred that past year. A kid in our class named Mike Fonseca had come to school one day with bloodshot eyes and his light brown hair turned a shocking grey. When asked what had happened to him, Mike said that he had been watching KAIC channel 29 when the signal had been replaced by something else. A new channel. Channel Eternity: We Show You Everything. He said that the channel had shown him the totality of creation in one night. The beginning, end, and beyond our universe.

"I know how all of you die," he announced at recess.

He pointed at different kids and revealed to them how they would exit this Earth. He had just finished telling Rebecca Lozano that she would perish in a completely avoidable blimp accident when his finger of fate fell on me. I was so terrified at the prospect of my own death that I blurted out, "How do you die, Mike?"

Mike's finger dropped and he stared out into space for a few seconds before declaring, "I don't. Ever. I am the endless one." He then began to cry as a grey beard grew across his face. The teacher on duty, who had been enjoying the show up to that point, rolled her eyes and escorted Mike back into the school. We never saw him again.

So, as the adventures of Dak, J'Aderika, Hooper, Nedrick, and I.S.A.A.C.K. began to unspool over a roach ocean, I just let it happen like I was letting everything else happen.

Over the course of the next three days, I would witness The Krew travel from town to town destroying all monsters that dared to go against the forces of Kool. There were aliens in Roswell, New Mexico who were trying to convince the local people to give up their relentless accumulation of money and instead live in peace with each other. Dak had the aliens tied up and set on fire. I.S.A.A.K. filmed the Krew performing their song "Alien Fuel" in front of the burning extraterrestrials, and this would become the Krew's breakout hit music video.

In another episode, the Krew travelled to San Antonio, Tx and dealt with a local monster named The Donkey Lady. She was a disfigured woman who had been so vilified and teased that she had taken to cutting off people's heads with an axe and stuffing them in a pillowcase she dragged around everywhere. She was eventually stopped when J'Aderika gave her a fab makeover, turning the Donkey Lady into a total babe who eventually hooked up with a local stud named Roth. J'Aderika centered episodes usually had happier endings.

Then there was a special Valentine's episode where Cupid used an arrow to make J'Aderika fall in love with I.S.A.A.K. She forced Nedrick to program I.S.A.A.K to take her out on a date. Dak became so enraged by this that he beat Cupid to death with his bare hands. When Dak stormed into the restaurant where J'Aderika and I.S.A.A.K were having their date and dropped Cupid's corpse into I.S.A.A.K's soup, the spell was broken. J'Aderika and Dak became an item again; Dak had Nedrick remove I.S.A.A.K.'s capacity for love.

Every episode ended with a song about the adventures they just had. Some of the most memorable included:

"Sayanora, La Llorona"

"Hey, Chupacabra, get away from that goat, sucker!"

"Only Losers Can't Murder A Ghost"

"Polterguess what, We're Gonna Rock!"

"Carving 'Wolf Man' On a Silver Bullet"

"The Loveland Frog Man Does Not Exist (because we killed him)"

"The Devil Is Afraid of Us"

Perhaps the strangest thing about the show was that the character of Dak Anner looked exactly like me. Well, maybe not exactly. He was a bit taller, much skinnier, had platinum blonde hair, wore sunglasses, rocked a leather jacket, was brave, could play guitar, people seemed to like him, and his teeth weren't as crooked as mine, but, other than those very minor differences, it was like looking in a mirror.

Dak had a habit of breaking the fourth wall to deliver monologues, mainly about how cool he was. But sometimes the monologues would be nothing more than short phrases that had little to do with the episode. He would interrupt conversations to say things like, "This town hates you," and "She left because you suck," and "Misery is your fate," directly to the camera. Several times on the sixth day, he looked out from the TV and simply said, "This could all be yours."

It wasn't until my last night on the couch that me and Dak would have a proper conversation.

**

(A meeting that took place on my porch on the seventh night that I was not present for but would learn the details of later.)

The narrator's childhood porch. The Anointed One sits on a jet-black rocking chair that they brought from home. The squeak and creak of the chair is joined by the jangle of nearby porch chimes that rustle in the hot evening wind. These are the only sounds in an empty world. Back and forth, back and forth The Anointed One rocks, like a grandma at the end of everything. The reverie is broken by thunderous and clumsy footfalls that mark the arrival of Eddie Gone and Jason Human.

Eddie Gone
Weirdo still hasn't come out?

The Anointed One
He is not ready.

Eddie Gone
How do you know?

The Anointed One
He dreams loud. He thinks loud. He hurts loud.

Eddie Gone
You make him sound like an extremely crappy superhero.

Jason Human
Typical nonsense. Too much mercy and coddling. I say we break in there and drag our weakling friend out here. Rough him up a bit. A few smacks to his lackluster and oftentimes upsetting kisser will toughen him right up.

Eddie Gone
You want to punch the pain away, bubble brain?

Jason Human
Replace the pain. A perfectly logical solution. No one has time to be sad when they're getting kicked in the face.

Eddie Gone
Yeah, great plan except for YOU'RE the only person on Earth that HE can actually beat up.

Jason Human

Of course, when I said "we" I meant that you could rough him up. Or the messiah over there could. Or a child smaller than us. Much smaller. A toddler perhaps. Or a newborn with ambitions.

Eddie Gone

Look, I ain't giving him no knuckle sandwiches just cuz he's sad but I'm tired of leaving him on his own. Who knows what coulda happened to him? For all we know, he could be dead and rotting.

The Anointed One

He's not dead but he is rotting.

Eddie Gone

What?

The Anointed One

He has transcended hygiene. Transcended most things. Attained a vulgar godhood. The worm told me so.

Eddie Gone

Worm?

The Anointed One

A traveler in the dream realm. It visited me last night speaking in visions and nightmares. Most are not capable of interpreting the signs, but I could.

Jason Human

What are you babbling about? He's probably down in that disgusting basement watching television and stuffing his face. Not even in your incoherent superstitions or worm filled dreams can a tubby child achieve godhood in a dank rec room.

The Anointed One

Depends on what you're the god of. But that is the least of his problems. Something is coming for him. Tonight.

Eddie Gone

The worm tell you that?

Jason Human

SO WHAT IF IT DID?! Who could possibly care what a dream worm had to say?

Eddie Gone

Worms are the most trustworthy animals on this planet, stretch, and if it says danger's coming, then I believe it.

The Anointed One

The worm was vague about the nature of the danger, as if some force stopped it from speaking the whole truth. But what was clear is that the danger is pure evil, and it will try to claim our friend.

Eddie Gone

Then we got to do something! Why are we just standing here?!

The Anointed One

It is up to him. There is nothing we can do.

Jason Human

Maybe there's nothing you can do, besides rock on your creepy little chair and rattle off prophecies like a depressed talking doll, but I'm going to break in and get him. I've broken in countless times before. Often to steal food or scrape specimens off their walls and laugh at the way they live their lives. I would have gone in long before now if it hadn't been for all your hippy-dippy "We've got to give him space" nonsense. YOU KNOW NOTHING OF SPACE!

Jason Human walks up to the front door. He pulls a metal rod from his pocket that seems to be made of a dancing liquid that constantly shifts its shape. He sticks the rod into the keyhole and is immediately blown across the porch by an electric shock. As he lays smoking against the rails of the porch, a mouth made of greenish television static erupts out of the keyhole. The mouth turns from Eddie to Jason to The Anointed One and lets out a fierce snarl before retreating back into the keyhole.

Eddie Gone
Holy Cow! What the heck was that!

The Anointed One
I do not know. It got me earlier when I tried to break in.

The Anointed One holds up their snake hand to reveal a fresh burn on their palm. Smoke still rises from Jason Human as he lays prone against the railing.

Jason Human
Why….didn't….you….warn…me.

The Anointed One
I wanted to see if it had gone. Obviously, it hasn't.

Eddie Gone
Look, we got to do something! Weirdo can't handle this. Not on his own.

The Anointed One
He's stronger than any of us give him credit for.

Eddie Gone

Strong or not, I can't stand by while it happens again. I can't stand by and lose another friend!

Eddie's lips quiver. The Anointed One rises from their chair and places their snake hand on Eddie's shoulder.

The Anointed One

I miss Darby, too.

Jason Human rises from the ground.

Jason Human

If anybody could have saved him, it was her. Whatever that force was that ejected me, she would have grabbed it by the throat and made it drink garbage juice. Delicious garbage juice.

Eddie Gone

Yeah, she would have knocked it into the middle of next week where she would have been waiting to really kick its butt.

The Anointed One

She would have unleashed Hell on Earth to protect any one of us.

The Anointed One suddenly has a thought and holds out their hands.

The Anointed One

Join hands with me.

Eddie and Jason give each other a look.

The Anointed One
DO IT!

The two are so startled by the outburst that they immediately follow the direction.

The Anointed One
Now think of him and think of Darby. Concentrate. Think about what Darby would do. Concentrate. Concentrate. What Would Darby Do? Concentrate. What Would Darby Do? Say it. What Would Darby Do? SAY IT!

Jason and Eddie
What Would Darby Do? What Would Darby Do? What Would Darby Do?

They remain standing in the circle holding hands, chanting their refrain, uncertain if anything good will ever happen again.

***

When I awoke on that last day, night had already fallen. The rustling of the roaches was louder than usual. They were agitated, not touching any of the ramen bowls. They were facing the television and, despite not being a variety of roach that could possibly do this, were hissing. For the first time in a week, I had the faintest glimmer of surprise.

The week had taken a toll on my body. I shifted so that the parts of my skin that had broken out in rashes from prolonged contact with the coarse fabric were no longer touching the couch. My fingernails were crammed with thick black dirt and the sweat in my hair had plastered it to my forehead and cheeks. The skin on the back of my neck, ignored even when I was washing regularly, had begun to flake and peel and was suspiciously wet and oozy in places. My feet felt as though I had been soaking them in olive oil and the nail on my right big toe was cutting into the flesh.

On TV, the 2 Kool 4 Skool Krew were in the middle of what would turn out to be their final adventure. In it, God had kickstarted Armageddon and was bringing the world to an end. The President of the United States personally asked the Krew to get involved because God's actions had sent the stock market plummeting and people were losing a lot of money. After successfully capturing an angel, Nedrick was able to experiment on it and develop a virus that wiped out God's army in a matter of days. But Dak knew that this wouldn't solve the problem completely, so he got Nedrick to invent a gun that could kill God. He, Nedrik, J'Aderika, I.S.A.A.K, and Bravo (Hooper's cousin who replaced him as drummer after Dak decapitated him) went to Heaven and in the ensuing battle, every member of the Krew, except Dak, was killed. Just when it looked like God finally had the upper hand, Dak was able to get one shot off with the special gun and send God to Hell.

Upon the death of the creator of all things, the stock market recovered almost overnight, and America entered a new golden age. The sitting president was executed for negligence and was replaced by Dak Anner. His inauguration took place in Heaven which had just been annexed as the 51st state. He addressed all life in the Universe from God's recently vacated throne.

"My fellow Americans," Dak announced, "I am honored and privileged to be your new lord and master. I have proven, time and time again, that I am, without a doubt, the coolest guy in the Universe. I have slain all my enemies. I have put the uncool to the sword, the flame, the rope, the gun, and even these bare hands to protect everything that we hold dear as a country. And I have always looked good doing it."

There was the sound of young girls screaming in adoration for two minutes as Dak strutted up and down the Presidential catwalk he had specially built for the occasion.

"You have seen me do all of this and more, so isn't it time that you got off that couch and reaped your reward?" Dak was looking straight in the camera as if he was expecting an answer. I lay there with my mouth open and a line of saliva dripping from my lips. "Yeah, you, on the couch, smelling of crap and surrounded by roaches. The tubby little baby who looks exactly like me if every decision I had ever made had been bad. HEY!"

Dak reached down and took off one of his Air Jordan sneakers. He threw it directly at the camera where it sailed right through my tv screen. It hit me on the forehead, bounced off my face, and landed on some ramen bowls sending the dirty, salty water flooding into the carpet. The hiss of the roaches grew louder, and, despite myself, I sat up.

"Yeah, that's right," Dak sneered, "I'm talking to you. I've been talking to you for days, trying to cut through all that disgusting self-pity. See all this?" He was waving his arms around the Kingdom of Heaven. "This whole show, all these adventures? It was all for you. Why do you think we look alike? My life, my wonderful, awesome, rad life, could all be yours. You can literally rule the universe! Ultimate power in your hands!"

I obviously didn't respond in the way he thought I should, which is to say that I had no response at all. This caused Dak a bit of consternation.

"Ok. That's it. I'm coming through," and with that, Dak Anner stepped out of the television. As soon as his foot hit the floor of the basement, reality seemed to bend around him. The basement itself transformed from the grubby dungeon it was into something off a TV show. Everything was nicer and cleaner than it had ever been. There was no longer filth on the walls or clouds of dust kicked up by every little movement. Up above, I could see studio lights shining down on me. The half full ramen bowls were now filled to the brim with steaming piles of noodles that had a shine to them like you would only find in a commercial. Even the roaches had become more presentable. Their carapaces had a glow that was impossible to find in nature.

I could feel myself changed as well. I was no longer covered in dirt and grime. I felt as clean as if I had just walked out of a shower. I had trouble seeing, so I reached my hand to my face to discover that I was now wearing sunglasses. I removed the glasses to look down at the rest of me: Leather Jacket, white t-shirt, blue jeans, and Air Jordan's. Me and Dak were finally identical twins.

"Looking good, bro," Dak smirked. "And you can always look good. Forever. If you just switch places with me, you get my life and I get yours. You've already seen how wonderful my existence is. I do what I want when I want, and nobody can tell me no. In fact, they love me for it. Everyone loves me. I can't be beaten. I can't be hurt. It's a life free of pain and misery. It can all be yours. All it takes is one high five." Dak raised his hand into the air and lowered his sunglasses with the other hand to look directly at me. "What do you say?" he winked.

I looked up at his raised hand that I knew could only be quenched by a return five or by blood. I looked at his face, my own face, which even I admit was very punchable and even more so with Dak's sneer plastered across it. With sunglasses lowered, I finally saw his eyes for the first time. They didn't belong to me, but I recognized them. They were the same dead eyes that I had seen twice before that summer: Behind the car wash and then in front of Mr. Garcia's house.

For the first time in a week, I started thinking. I briefly thought of Mr. Garcia. Was this how it happened to him? Was this the battle he waged every month? Was he offered the same promises or did his doppelganger have a different line of attack? But mostly I thought about Darby. Not of her as a person or as my friend but only as the hole she had left. I thought about how I'd been falling down that hole for an entire week and there seemed to be no bottom in sight. All I had to look forward to was a lifetime of pain in that disgusting basement with an army of roaches. That was my reward for finally making a friend.

"Come on, bro," Dak said, a snarl starting to overtake his sneer. "Don't leave me hanging. You know what happens when you leave me hanging."

In my mind I turned away from the Darby shaped hole and I thought to myself…why not? No more pain? No more misery? Just one little obnoxious hand gesture and I no longer had to feel the way I felt? Mr. Garcia had been a fool to fight this fate for as long as he did. A measly high five and I could live in the TV where everything was perfect, and your best friend never leaves you behind? That sure beat being the unfeeling lord of vermin. That sure beat a lot of things. In fact, it sounded like quite the bargain.

I stood up from the couch and raised my hand. The hissing of the roaches grew deafening. The studio lights above shone brighter and brighter. An unseen audience somewhere began hooting and hollering. Dak smiled. I just had to walk the few feet over and the high five would become inevitable.

"Welcome to Kool, bro," Dak whispered as we both started the swing of the most momentous high five in history.

Just as our hands were about to collide, an invisible bullet shot into my brain. I reeled back from the unseen force, the five failing to connect. The bullet lodged into the center of my cerebral cortex and shrapnel exploded all around my skull. The shrapnel was information. Information from outside myself. A plea. No. A message in the form of a simple question: What Would Darby Do?

All around my brain, the shrapnel of that psychic bullet danced.

What Would Darby Do?

Pirouetting over my medulla oblongata.

What Would Darby Do?

Hot Stepping over the divide between the hemispheres.

What Would Darby Do?

Tap dancing right where the spinal column connects so the message reverberated up and down my body.

What Would Darby Do?

Below me I could hear tiny voices chanting. The cute enough for television roaches had been granted the power of speech by the spell in the basement. They were using their voices to say one thing:

WHAT WOULD DARBY DO?! WHAT WOULD DARBY DO!? WHAT WOULD DARBY DO!?

Suddenly, the Darby shaped hole inside me grew flesh and bone. Blood and oxygen circulated through it and what had once been an endless abyss was now the living memory of my best friend. I could feel the memory's unbelieving eyes staring daggers into me as it tried to comprehend what I was about to do. The memory was so perfect that it said exactly what Darby would have said in that situation, "You're not actually going to listen to this dork, are you?"

In tandem with the memory's stabbing stare, scenes from episodes of The 2 Kool 4 Skool Krew began to flash in my mind. In them, all the monsters were replaced by Darby. Instead of being brutally slaughtered, she slaughtered back. I saw an 8-foot hairy Darby-Sasquatch crushing Dak's skull between her two huge hands. I saw the Loch Ness Darby chasing a screaming Dak across the highlands of Scotland until he tripped over a rock and fell. Loch Ness Darby brought her huge jaws down and bit him in half. Over and over, I saw the hated and despised monsters of each episode turn the tables on their tormentor and save the world from the forces of Kool. At that moment, I knew exactly what Darby would do.

Dak, hand still in the air, had turned his attention from me and was now staring at the roaches who were continuing their refrain.

"WHAT WOULD DARBY DO?! WHAT WOULD DARBY DO?! WHAT WOULD DARBY DO?!"

"Shut up, you pieces of filth!" Dak roared as he lifted his foot to crush them.

"HEY!" I shouted.

His foot stopped. He looked at me.

"Leave them alone. We're the ones that got business," I said, raising my hand.

"You finally ready?" Dak asked, lowering his foot to the roach free path.

"Yep. I want to live in the TV forever. I want to be kool. Kool like you, Dak."

The sneer returned to his face. We began moving towards each other once more. We moved like mirror images, every movement matched. As we once again drew our arms back for the high five, I shot my right foot out and kicked Dak right between the legs. His sunglasses went flying off and his dead eyes crossed in agony. He fell to his knees. The unseen studio audience broke out into waves of laughter and cheers.

"God, you're a dork," I said.

Dak, sputtering and coughing, looked up at me, his face bright red. "I'm not a dork! I'm Kool! I'm 2 Kool! Everybody loves me!"

"The TV is always trying to tell me that people like you are cool. Screw that. I know what cool is. I've met her. You're nothing in comparison."

Suddenly, the audience burst into wild applause. Dak rose from his knees and bellowed, "SHUT UP!" The unseen audience immediately stopped. Dak looked at me. He smiled. "If she was so cool, why did she leave you behind?"

"Because she had too!" I fired back, realization finally dawning on me. "Aickman was going to destroy her, like you're trying to destroy me now. She got out while she could. I have no idea if she's alive or dead, but she's not here anymore and for that, I am so happy. I am so happy for my friend! I am happy Darby escaped!"

A growl emanated from Dak's throat. The flesh on his hanging hand splintered and split. Within a few seconds, he would come swiping and I would be dead. Beneath me, I could still hear the chanting of the roaches. Without thinking, I reached down and picked up two bowls of ramen and tossed them at Dak. He was covered in the heavenly moist and stringling yum-yums. I looked down at my subjects and gave my first and only command: "EAT!"

In an instant, the roaches swarmed Dak. They covered every inch of his body. He tried knocking them off, but there were just too many. With each swipe of his monstrous hand, he cut into his own television flesh. I could hear their little mandibles digging into him, taking chunks out of the ramen-stained TV-mass. Dak's skin began to flicker with the changing of channels. One channel static. Then a cooking show. The news. A rerun. A commercial where an old woman had fallen and could not get up. Soon he was just a twitching mound of television helpless against the onslaught of The Roaches Of Ramen Town. Dak was just able to peer out of an opening left by the roaches. He let out a scream in a very familiar voice, "I WILL DEVOUR YOU!" before his mouth was filled with insects. The TV-mass let out one final, choking cry and then exploded in a burst of static.

The force of the explosion sent me flying across the room, over the couch, and into the back wall. When I stood up, I could see that the basement was back to its usual disgusting self, and so was I. I walked over to the couch and surveyed the carnage. Every single one of those devout, brave, disgusting, wonderful, repellent roaches had perished in the blast. Their upside-down corpses lay scattered around the basement.

The TV screen had burst. Sticking out of the fried wooden frame were plant stalks, scorched and dead. They were the same stalks I had seen hypnotically waving back and forth at the start of the summer. The Tall Grass Beyond the Car Wash.

I immediately went running up the stairs, across the living room and out the front door where I took the first gulp of fresh air that I had had in a week. As I sucked in the sweet, sweet taste of a world beyond television, I turned to see Jason, Eddie, and The Anointed One holding hands and chanting.

"What would Darby Do?! What would Darby Do?! What Would Darby Do?!"

"I know what she would do," I shouted. "And I did it."

They stopped their chanting and looked at me. I smiled at them, but the smile quickly twisted into a pout and soon the tears were falling.

"I miss her," I sobbed.

THREE
QUESTIONS

We held a funeral for the roaches in my backyard. Eddie and Jason gathered the corpses. The Anointed One and I dug a long trench to a set of specifications that Jason provided.

"I have a lot of experience with mass graves," Jason assured us.

I had to look away as Eddie and Jason placed the roaches in the trench. The sight of them had caused me to hyperventilate, but I was heartened by the return of my fear for it signaled that I had once again joined the ranks of the living. Jason dumped his load of corpses without ceremony and observed that this was proper etiquette for such a burial. Eddie chose to place them in one at a time, taking a moment to give each fallen roach a name.

"Here lies Oreo Jackson," Eddie respectfully intoned. "Here lies Dolores Howyabeen. Here lies Fast Freddy Spaghetti. Here lies Uncle Geometry Cunningham. Here lies 'The Big Man' Texas Richard Applewhite…"

In all, it took Eddie an hour to name the dead, a process that greatly annoyed Jason but which I felt was an honor they had more than earned. After the trench was filled with dirt and the roaches began their eternal slumber, I approached the grave and cleared my throat:

"I don't know what happened. I never know what happens. Nothing ever makes sense. Then one day, your TV tries to kill you and roaches save your life. Thank you, roaches. I hope my nightmares about you will someday turn into dreams."

"Amen," The Anointed One concluded.

***

The increasingly disastrous events within this chapter are unique for the simple fact that they were entirely my fault. Well, mine and a third party whose actions in a time long before I was born set in motion a possibly endless cycle of pain the ramifications of which are, at the very least, soul shattering. Some of the blame must be given to them. But I mostly blame myself.

It all stemmed from the fact that I had no idea where Darby lived. I couldn't understand how the basic details of the life of someone I held so dear could be a complete mystery to me. It was my first taste of real failure. It wasn't the kind of failure assigned by the disapproving looks of teachers or doled out by the taunts of strangers you share a classroom with, but pure, raw disappointment in myself. My incuriosity and negligence I was certain played no small part in Darby's decision to leave and I promised myself that I would not let it happen again. I was determined not to lose one more friend. So, I started asking questions. That was a mistake.

The first catastrophe happened on one sweltering July afternoon as I was helping Jason monitor some storm drains. I was on one side of Plum Street and Jason on the other. He had become convinced that there was an ostrich loose in the Aickman sewage system when, during one of his weekly sifts through the run-off from the pipes out by the dunes, he'd discovered a fragment of an egg shell that could only belong to an ostrich or a dinosaur.

"Couldn't be dinosaur, though. We made sure of that," he said with a distant look in his eyes.

He didn't want to commit to a full exploration of the sewer system because he had observed what the people of Aickman liked to eat and surmised that the contents of the wastewater below us would most likely burn his skin off. Aside from that consideration, fighting an ostrich in close quarters would be difficult and physical confrontation would be an inevitability because the ostrich would want to get at his eyes.

"My eyes are a delicacy to flightless birds. It's why I scream when any of you mention penguins."

So, he decided to observe the sewers from a distance, an activity that most of us declined to join him in but which I felt would be the perfect opportunity to really get to know my friend.

"Any sign?" Jason called over his shoulder.

"Not yet," I called back.

"This avian is cunning. A long-necked ninja. Stinky feathers in a shadow world. It cannot hide forever. I will prove this town is rife with subterranean African fauna," he declared.

"Why does it matter to you so much? It's just a sewer bird," I called over my shoulder.

"A sewer bird keeping secrets."

"So?"

"Secrets are power," he stated matter of factly.

The mention of secrets seemed like my perfect opportunity. "Jason?" I asked.

"YOU'VE FOUND HIM?!" He'd turned to look at me expectantly.

"No, I just wanted to ask you a question."

His face fell and he turned back to his drain. "Oh. The answer is yes."

"What?"

"Yes, your head is too big for your body. I would say you'd grow into it but by my calculations your head will always be twice the mass of the rest of you. You will need the help of an elaborate pulley system to move you around your house by the time you are twenty."

"That wasn't what I was going to ask," I said, tentatively squeezing my head between my hands.

"Of course it was. But if you feel the need to perform some sort of charade to mask how absolutely predictable you are, then, by all means, make up another question."

"Where do you live, Jason?" I asked. "Where do you go when we're not hanging out?" There was silence. I didn't hear him move, but when I turned my head from the drain, I was startled to see Jason towering over me.

"Who wants to know?" Jason hissed.

I stood up, but still only came up to Jason's chest. I knew perfectly well that he couldn't physically harm me because he had the strength of spaghetti flailing in the wind, but he had drawn himself up to his full height and there was a look of menace in his eyes I had never seen before.

"I...I want...to know," I stammered.

He craned his massive head over me. "Why?" he whispered.

"Because...you're my friend and I want to know things about you," I said, trembling.

His head drew closer. "Did the MIBs contact you? Is that it? Are you working for them? Are you a government stooge now? One of J. Edgar's boys?!"

"No, Jason, I'm not working for anybody." My fear was being replaced by annoyance in the same way a German shepherd grows weary of the yappings of a chihuahua. "It's just that when Darby left, I realized that I didn't know anything about her life outside of us."

He leaned back and his tiny mouth twisted into a snarl. "You would have me believe that trauma has turned you into some kind of truth-finder general? That the most incurious boy in the world is now the seeker of knowledge? That you have no ulterior motives?" he spat.

"I just want to know where you live." I was getting genuinely angry.

"A likely story. No, I think the truth is simpler than that. The trauma has changed you, yes, but it's twisted you. Turned you into a tiny Machiavelli, an information gatherer who will use these secrets to hurt others before they can hurt you. That's the lesson our dearly departed Darby taught you. You will no longer be the victim but the victimizer! Well, know this: I WILL NOT BE YOUR VICTIM!"

The sheer volume and annoying pitch of his voice exploded so close to my face that my anger boiled over, and I did something I'd never done to anyone: I shoved him.

For perhaps the first time ever, Jason was lost for words. The situation didn't require words, however. Jason and I had entered The Boy Zone. In The Boy Zone, words are meaningless. Action is all that matters.

Following the proper etiquette of The Boy Zone, Jason shoved me back.

I returned the shove.

He shoved.

I shoved.

He shoved.

I shoved.

This went on for a while because neither of us had any experience with The Boy Zone, but, eventually, we were rolling on the ground weakly jabbing and slapping at each other with our eyes closed. If there had been any witnesses to this sad, pathetic display, they would have reported back to their friends that they had seen what could only be described as a cluster of pool noodles wrestling with an undercooked ham in shorts and a t-shirt.

"How had that ham angered those noodles?" their friends would ask.

"Ham is a controversial meat. It promotes strong feelings," the witness would reply.

"Well, I do prefer ham sandwiches to turkey," one of the friends would say.

"You bastard!" the witness would retort, and the cycle of violence would continue.

Luckily, nobody saw our lackluster facsimile of a Real Boy Brawl and it was soon put out of its misery by the neatly timed appearance of an ostrich head sticking out of the storm drain. We stopped our tussling and stared in amazement at the creature.

It blinked.

We blinked.

It blinked.

We bl-

"GET HIM!" Jason shouted.

What followed was an adventure that I refuse to include in this book because it is too gross and embarrassing. I have written the story, however, and have safely hidden it away, to only be released to the public in the event of my death. When you do finally read about what happened in the sewers of Aickman on that July day in 1993, please do not think any less of me nor hold any grudge towards the people and government of Luxembourg.

My questioning of The Anointed One was less physically painful, but, as with most things involving them, was much more spiritually upsetting.

I was on The Anointed One's porch taking a dancing lesson. This was not something that I had any interest in doing, but it was a notion that had captured The Anointed One's imagination. They often got these notions. They referred to me as a "…blank sheet of paper…" and that "If you aren't going to write your own story, then someone else must."

Past notions had included dying my hair bright green which Darby had a hand in and resulted in me having to shave my head. Then there was the day they showed up at my doorstep with an ill-fitting suit that they told me to put on and which made me look exactly like a ventriloquist dummy. They told me it would be good for job interviews or making speeches about the coming darkness in the town square. They also made me try Feta cheese for the first time. That might not seem like a big deal to you, but that cheese blew my tiny mind.

Whenever they were seized by one of these notions, I let them do whatever they wanted because I truly had no better idea about what to do with my life. So, when they announced that it was time that I learned to dance, I did not fight my fate.

The lesson consisted of The Anointed One playing discordant notes on their fiddle made of the bones of either a long extinct animal or a creature that had never existed. They were very vague on this point. The closest I can come to approximating the sound of the bone fiddle is to ask you to visualize a baby robot crying for a mother that will never come. Now, the sound isn't the cry of the baby robot, but rather the upsetting emotions you are experiencing from that thought experiment turned into a noise.

Above the din of the bone fiddle, The Anointed One would bark instructions as I grappled with their most recent life-sized birthday doll which served as my dancing partner. I've never had an affinity or talent for rhythmic movement and the lifeless doll coupled with the hellish caterwaul of the bone fiddle made it a less than successful lesson. Finally, at about the fifth time I managed to get the doll to kick me in the face while trying to do a waltz, The Anointed One ended the lesson by declaring, "You are the anti-dancer, the one who will end the boogie forever."

I dropped the doll to the ground and rubbed my chin where I had been kicked. The Anointed One had not yet tired of playing the fiddle and started up a new dirge which they were making up on the spot. It was from a genre of music called "Tears of the Future" which were very popular in their religion. The idea was that these songs would be matched with an as yet to happen calamity and provide comfort for the people of the future during their tribulations. The Anointed One was certain that the song they were currently improvising would bring solace to the victims of a moon-based cataclysm some hundred years hence. As I sat there listening and contemplating those poor people and their moon trauma, I was struck with a notion of my own and blurted out another disastrous question.

"What do you look like under that mask?"

The Anointed One stopped playing and slowly let the bone fiddle drop to the ground. I immediately regretted asking.

This was something that we never talked about. The Anointed One had gotten permission to remain covered in school on religious grounds and whenever other students would inquire about what was under the mask, The Anointed One would ignore them or chase them off with their snake hand.

Darby had made it a point to tell me, Eddie, and Jason not to mention it until The Anointed One did, which never happened. One day, I brought the subject up to Darby while she was reading comic books in my basement.

"Do you think they're a boy or a girl?" I asked Darby.

"Doesn't matter," Darby replied.

"Doesn't it?"

"Why should it?"

"Well, because…." I couldn't think of a reason.

"See."

"Okay," I continued, "but what do you think they look like under the mask?"

"That's none of my business," Darby again replied.

"Aren't you curious? I know I am. Like, are they blonde or bald or like you know how their hand has a drawing of a snake on it? Like, what if their head is just a big hand but with a human face painted on it?"

"I mean, that would be rad," Darby reasoned, "but until they choose to show us, it's none of our business."

"I don't know if I agree with you."

At that, Darby lowered the issue of Sandman she was reading and snapped, "Show me your butt!"

"WHAT?!" I panicked.

"You heard me. Show me your butt. I'm curious about what your butt looks like. Pull down your pants and show me your butt."

"NO WAY! Nobody gets to see my butt!" I protested.

"What about people talking about your butt? Making guesses about your butt? Is that okay?"

"NO!"

"Why not?"

"Because my butt is private!"

"Exactly," Darby concluded and went back to reading her comic book.

Looking at the way that The Anointed One's head was hanging, I realized I should have heeded what Darby had to say.

"Hey, I'm sorry," I said, "I didn't mean to-"

"I don't fault you for your curiosity," they said. "Jason told me about the incident with the ostrich."

"He...did?" My face turned red.

"Yes, and I don't know if I can ever forgive the government or the people of Luxembourg, but he also mentioned what you said about Darby."

"Oh."

"I feel the same way. Darby was such a force that her very existence was all we needed to know about her. Even with everything I have seen in my life, Darby was the closest thing to a legend I have ever met. In my mind, I put her amongst the Gods. Untouchable. Beyond even the Serpent." Their snake hand spasmed a few times as if recoiling at that heresy. "Her leaving taught me one thing: Don't put your friends where you can't reach them."

My mouth had completely dried. I'd never heard another person voice the exact thoughts that had been ricocheting around my mind.

"I understand your need to know. You feel that if we shared that secret, we would become closer. A bond would be formed. But I need you to understand that this isn't a mask. It is me. It is who I am. Whatever else is physically underneath has no bearing on the reality of me. Is that clear?"

I nodded.

"I'm going to go inside now. I will see you tomorrow."

After they went in, I stood on the porch thinking about what had just happened. Suddenly, I heard a voice call out, "You can take my mask off if you want." I looked down to see the life-sized doll tilt its head up as it let out a giggle. I ran back to my house and gave my father strict instructions not to let any living dolls inside.

But neither of those encounters went as spectacularly wrong as it did with Eddie Gone.

Two weeks had passed since Darby's leaving. July was about to become August and we could feel the freedom of summer dying around us. Eddie had wanted to show everyone a cool rock that he had found after a large section of the Screaming Forest had collapsed into a sinkhole. The Anointed One and Jason said they were busy, so it was just me and Eddie.

"What makes it so cool?" I asked as we trudged through the blistering heat of the forest.

"No coming attractions, buddy boy. This thing is best seen blind. You're gonna flip!"

Along the way, Eddie pointed out many interesting examples of the flora and fauna of Aickman's accursed forest. They were mostly things that Eddie had already told me about numerous times before, but he so loved talking about these strange wonders that I didn't interrupt him.

"Over there's a Cubed Owl. A perfectly equal six sides of feather and meat. They can't fly, they can't walk, and I have no idea how they live. Good for stacking though on account of cubes being top 10, geometry wise. That pond over there? That's fool's water. It's like fool's gold but liquid and it'll kill you. Don't get involved. See that thing up in the tree there? Way up there? You see it? That thing? See it? Yeah, I don't know what the heck that is. Let's get out of here before it notices us."

He was a few feet in front of me with his head turned slightly to explain why a particular squirrel was carrying around a knife, when the angle of his head caused his face to be dappled by a sunbeam which broke through the trees. This spotlight fell perfectly on the three scars which tore across his cheek. It reminded me that the scars were the first things I ever noticed about him. Those, and his eternal black eye.

"Eddie, how did you get those scars?"

Eddie stopped walking and put a hand up to his face, tracing the scars with his index finger. "I've already told you."

"Yeah, but you always tell different stories."

"No, I don't. I ain't no E.B White. I ain't spinning Charlotte's Web here. Truth and nothing but, that's what I'm all about."

This was patently false. The first time we asked about the scars, he said a koala did it, which none of us believed. His story changed constantly and at various points had blamed his scars on:

1. A koala
2. A cat he rescued from a fire
3. A group of rowdy bikers who were up to no good
4. A bald eagle that had lost its patriotism
5. A sandwich that got out of control

When I pointed this out to him, he quickly countered with the classic, "You calling me a liar?"

To which I returned, "Yes. Yes I am."

The bluntness so blindsided him that he opened his mouth as if to scream, then closed it, raised a fist as if to strike me, dropped it, then finally threw his hands in the air. "Ok, ya got me! I was lying. I lie sometimes. I never said I wasn't a liar. Not once."

"So, how did you get those scars? And why does your eye never heal?" I said, pointing at his eternal shiner.

His hand moved away from the scars and he began to trace the outline of the bruised eye like those people who play music off wine glasses. "Why do you think it never heals?" he asked, not looking at me.

"How would I know?"

"It's been on your mind so much; you must have thought of some reasons? Come on, morning glory, what's the story?"

He was right, of course. I had often thought about possible explanations for his forever wounds. From what Darby had shown me of punk rockers in magazines, I thought he might have been making a fashion statement, punching his eye every day, and recutting the scars every week to make sure they looked as fresh and vital as they did. Or maybe it was a genetic condition. His body just didn't heal right, and the causes were more mundane and embarrassing than he wanted to admit. Or possibly they were just birthmarks, plain and simple. Every one of these explanations had that tacky feel of unbelievability as they fell out of my mouth.

"Huh, yeah, well, I guess those could explain it." he said, finally.

"But what's the truth?"

Eddie gave a shrug so big that his shoulders went over his head, "I have no idea, sport."

"What do you mean? How can you not know?"

"Not knowing things is easy. You just do it. You don't even need to practice."

I wasn't convinced. "Why don't you want to tell me?"

"BECAUSE I DON'T KNOW!" he shouted, sending flocks of birds screaming from the trees above. "I don't know how I got this," he pointed at his eye, "or these," he pointed to his cheek, "or these." He lifted his shirt and for the first time I saw his pale torso. There were three parallel scars across his chest that bulged out like huge, chalky slugs.

"Holy crap," I whispered in astonishment. He lowered his shirt and turned away from me.

"One day I just woke up in the forest with them. I don't like to talk about them or think about them. When I think about them, it feels like there's an icicle inside of me that just gets colder and colder. I hate the feeling. It hurts. So yeah, I lied about it so I don't have to think about it. Sorry the mystery bothered you so much, but I'm the one who has to live with it."

I apologized to Eddie, who accepted it with a nod. He suggested that we forget about the rock and just head back. I knew how excited he had been to show us and how disappointed he was that Jason and The Anointed One hadn't come. I figured the best way to cheer him up was to insist we see the rock and I put on an act of atypical enthusiasm, assuring him how excited I was to see it. I've always been a terrible actor and Eddie was clearly not convinced but agreed to go on.

We came to the sinkhole that had unearthed the rock about twenty minutes later. The perimeter of the hole had to have been about a quarter of a mile and right in the center was the rock. The rock turned out to be a 20-foot marble statue atop a 10-foot plinth covered in indecipherable writing. The statue was of a muscular giant in a loincloth. The body was grotesquely human with the head of a screaming, savage ram that had massive horns exploding from its skull. The goat man was wielding an axe in its six-fingered right hand that was so massive that it would have been comical if it wasn't for the look of absolute murder emanating from the statue's hellishly black eyes. It was such an impressive sight that I let slip several words that you are not supposed to say in polite company, but which didn't matter because Eddie did not fit that description. I realized that, in classic Eddie fashion, he had undersold his rock to maximize the effect of what we would see. If he had told us exactly what it was from the start, Jason and the Anointed One might have come, but that would have ruined the surprise. I hoped that my stream of swear words was enough to show him how grateful I was, but Eddie ended up only muttering, "Yeah, it's alright. I guess."

We stood at the edge of the sinkhole for a few more minutes. Eddie just looked at the ground and kicked little pebbles into the chasm. The talk of the scars had really hurt him. On the way back, I told him that we should definitely bring Jason and The Anointed One to see the statue. He just shrugged. Eddie's silence was making me panic and I began to wildly point out different sights like he did at the start of the journey.

"Hey, look at that…uh…tree," I fumbled, "boy that's a big tree, man. Has to be 30….yards maybe. Oh wow, check out that deer! It's pooping! That's cool. Everybody poops. I know I do. Check out that snake! Oh, wait, it's a stick. Cool stick though, huh?" As we reached the edge of the forest I was soaked in both heat and flop sweat.

"See ya," Eddie said, and began to walk away. I didn't want to leave it like that. There were so many times that Darby walked away with that dark look in her eyes, and I figured if I had done or said something, maybe she wouldn't have been as sad as she was. So, I was determined not to leave Eddie alone until he felt better.

"Hey," I said, "why don't we go and hang out at your house?"

"Huh?" This idea seemed to shock Eddie.

"We always hang out at my house or the creek or the forest. Why don't we go over to your house and play?"

Eddie got a confused look on his face. His hand went up to trace his scars and then he quickly shook his head like a dog trying to dry itself. "My...house?"

"Yeah, I can finally meet your sisters. You said you have two sisters, right?"

The confusion on his face began to melt away as his mind seemed to focus on something. "Sisters...yeah." A smile took hold of the corners of his mouth. "Penelope and Irma." He let out a little laugh. "Pen and Irm. Sure, my older and younger sis. That's right, ol' Eddie Gone's a middle child, the best kind of child!"

He began walking swiftly towards town, turning every once and awhile making sure I was still behind him. "Come on, the house is down on Durant. 331 Durant. Home sweet home. Don't know why I've never had you over before. Well, I know why, you're one of those undesirables, bring down the whole tone of the neighborhood. But I'll just explain you're from the wrong side of the tracks and I'm teaching you how not to be a bozo your whole life." He was almost running, like he couldn't wait to get home.

He breathlessly told me about his sisters who he'd only mentioned once or twice before in passing. "Penelope's five. A real firecracker. You think I'm crazy, wait till you check that little girl out!" He laughed. "Irma's 15 but something happened when she was born so she don't act like a teenager. She's more like Pen, which is great because teenagers suck. She likes to pick me up and throw me up and down like I'm her dolly! She gets real nervous when I'm not around. Come on, you'll love 'em!"

We were running at full force now. "My mom had to go away for a while, she'll be back but we're being watched by Aunt Delia." Suddenly, Eddie stopped in his tracks, and I almost ran into him. "Aunt Delia…" he said and began to rub at his scars.

"Are you okay?" I asked, out of breath from the run.

Eddie opened his mouth as if to say something, but then quickly shook his head again. "Yeah, I'm fine. Aunt Delia…behaves in front of guests. Besides, I think she's out playing canasta with some old ladies, so she won't even be there." His hand went down to his chest, and he began to trace the scars under his shirt. "She shouldn't leave Irm in charge of Pen like that, though. Come on, we're almost there."

We tore off and were at Durant Street in minutes. When we reached 331, Eddie stopped, and his confusion returned. "What the heck?" he said.

"What's wrong?"

"It's…it's blue." He was pointing at the house, which was a ground level with a yard filled with dead, yellowing grass, painted in a very faded royal blue.

"So?"

"Our house is red. We live in a red house. When I left the house this morning with Aunt Delia, the house was red." He had begun pacing back and forth.

"Maybe they painted it when you were gone?" I said, not believing that at all.

"THE GRASS WAS GREEN!" he shouted, pointing at the dead lawn. "You telling me that my sisters painted the house and killed the lawn in 8 hours?!"

"Maybe it's the wrong house?"

"331 Durant!" He was pointing at the number on the black mailbox. "This is my home! But something's wrong. This isn't even our mailbox!" he said as he punched the mailbox hard enough to knock it off the support post.

Suddenly, a scream came from within the house. We both turned in time to see the front door burst open and a large woman in her late forties come running out. She wore thick framed glasses, a long denim skirt and a yellow t-shirt. She stopped on the porch, her hands on her belly scrunching up the shirt. She was making squeaking noises and her face became redder and redder. After a few seconds, she shouted "EDDIE HERE! EDDIE HERE!"

Eddie began to back away and I followed his lead. The woman kept excitedly jumping up and down on the porch screaming "EDDIE HERE! EDDIE HERE!" At that point, Eddie turned on his heels and began to run, and again, I followed. The woman gave chase, changing her cry to "Eddie, wait! Eddie, wait!" but it was clear she wouldn't be able to catch us, and she gave up halfway down the block. As we turned the corner, I could see her running back to 331 Durant.

Eddie didn't stop running until we reached the steps of the Aickman library where I screamed that I couldn't go any further. I collapsed onto the steps, huffing and wheezing. My nose started bleeding, as it often did when I got overheated, and I used my t-shirt to staunch the flow. I looked up at Eddie who, as usual, showed no sign of physical exertion. He just stood by the steps, expressionless, staring out at the distance.

"Who was that?" I asked. He didn't answer. He began to trace the scars again and his whole body started to tremble. I stood up and put my free hand on his shoulder. "Eddie, what's going on?"

Eddie turned to face me and the look in his eyes sent a chill up my spine. "You know what's going on," he whispered.

I slowly lifted my hand off his shoulder and backed away. His eyes were burning into me. They looked so much older than they had just a few seconds ago. I didn't know how to respond to his accusation. "Eddie..."

"It's like you said at the roach funeral. 'I don't know what happened. Nothing ever makes sense.' You said it perfectly." His eyes were growing wider and wider. "One day you wake up in this town with scars you don't remember getting and the next you're being chased by kids with baseball bats. Maybe one day your friend disappears into the sky? Huh? How about that? Aickman, where your home isn't your home anymore. It's craziness. We live in craziness. You get through it cuz you have to, but eventually the craziness gets you." Tears began to well up in his eyes. "What's happening? Where are my sisters? Where's my mom? Where are you taking me Aunt Delia?!"

I had become so entranced by the panic in his eyes that I didn't notice the woman from Durant Street coming up behind him. She picked Eddie up in her huge arms and hugged him close. "Eddie, here! Eddie, here!" she screamed again.

Eddie wriggled his way out of her arms and fell to the sidewalk. "GET AWAY FROM ME!" he bellowed as the woman reached down to try to pick him up. She backed away, visibly hurt and equally as confused as Eddie.

I stood there with my t-shirt over my bloody nose looking around for help, but the streets were empty on that hot Sunday afternoon. If there was one thing you could count on the town of Aickman for, it was making sure that hope and comfort never felt welcome.

The woman stood over Eddie, hands scrunching at her t-shirt, her weight shifting from foot to foot as if she had to go to the bathroom. Eddie just lay on the ground, the gravity of Aickman crushing him. He looked like he just wanted to go to sleep right there on the pavement. His nightmares couldn't possibly be any worse.

"Who are you?" he asked the woman. "What did you do to my sisters?"

Suddenly the woman lit up and began nodding. "Sister! Sister!" she shouted while reaching into a green bag she now had slung around her right shoulder. She pulled out an ancient, yellowing rolled up poster. She unfurled it and held it out to us. "Eddie, gone! Eddie, gone!"

I couldn't believe what the poster was showing me. There seemed to be no bottom to the craziness that day. The sinkhole in the forest was nothing compared to what me and Eddie had fallen into. On the poster was a black and white picture. It was Eddie. There were no scars on his face and both eyes were perfectly fine. He was holding a kickball in the crook of his left arm and waving. Above the picture was the word MISSING in bold black letters. Below the picture was printed the following:

Have You Seen Edward Cartwright?
Last Seen on May 15th
DOB: March 21st, 1952 Age: 10 Height: 4'5" Weight: 75 Pounds
Last Seen Wearing a White T-shirt, blue jeans, and red sneakers
If you have any information about his whereabouts, please contact Sheriff Burlington

"Eddie, found! Eddie, found!" the woman trumpeted.

I was so dumbstruck that I let my shirt drop and my nose started bleeding again. Eddie slowly got up off the ground and approached the woman. He took the poster out of her hands and studied it. He looked up into the woman's face and cocked his head to the side. He reached out a hand and put it on the woman's cheek.

"Irma?" he said in a shaky voice. The woman nodded her head frantically and once again picked Eddie up in her arms. "IRMA!" Eddie shouted as he wrapped his arms around her neck, letting go of the poster which was carried away by the wind.

I could feel the blood dripping from my chin, so I returned the shirt to my nose. My brain could not process what was happening, but I felt a warmth spreading in my stomach. It was a warmth that I felt with Mr. Sandwiches and Darby and, sometimes, my grandfather before he died. It was the hope and comfort that Aickman seemed hell bent on extinguishing, that the craziness sought to suffocate.

Irma was kissing Eddie repeatedly, and Eddie was gripping her neck tight, eyes closed. "I missed you," Eddie cooed, "and I didn't even know it."

Suddenly, the warmth fled from my stomach, replaced by the feeling that Eddie had described earlier: An icicle deep inside of me, getting colder and colder. The heat of the day disappeared and was replaced by a chill wind like the kind that only seems to exist in your fantasies of October. Irma and Eddie could feel the change. Irma got a worried look on her face and Eddie released his hug.

"You got to put me down now, Irm," Eddie said. "Just like the last time."

"Eddie, go?"

"Yep. I gotta go. I don't know when I'll be back."

"Eddie, stay! Eddie, stay!" Irma pleaded.

"I wish I could, Irm. But I don't know how it works. Come on, put me down." Irma slowly lowered Eddie and he turned to me. "Guess the Annoying One and Bubble Brain really missed out today, huh?"

"What's happening, Eddie?" I asked, frightened because I knew the answer. Not the specifics, not the mechanics, just the outcome. I had made it my mission to never lose another friend and I had failed miserably.

"I don't know, Weirdo, but whatever it is, it's happening again. It was nice knowing you."

"Eddie, please!" was all I could get out. The icicle in my stomach choked off any further words.

Eddie turned to the weeping Irma. "I missed Pen this time. Tell her I said hi." Irma nodded and said "Promise, Eddie. Promise."

He turned back to me, changed now. He was less substantial, the color draining from him. I could see through him. This was worse than Darby. Darby had left in a blaze of glory. It fit her. Eddie was fading away. It was a betrayal of who that boy I met in the forest was. That boy who was so proud of the toes he caught, whose knowledge saved our lives over and over, and was always willing to help a friend. All of that was disappearing right before my eyes.

"What was that thing Darby said before she left?" the fading Eddie asked.

My voice trembled, "Relax, Weirdo."

"That Darby, always with the good advice. Relax, Weirdo. Say hi to Darby if you ever see her again." Going. "Tell bubble brain and the Annoying One that they'll never get to see my cool rock." Going. "At least I remember how I got these scars now." Gone.

"Eddie, gone. Eddie, gone," Irma sobbed.

I wanted to offer Irma some comfort, but just then, a woman with curly red hair approached. Irma quickly ran to her, smothering her in her arms.

"PEN! PEN! Eddie! Eddie!" Irma repeated this over and over as the woman tried calming her with rhythmic pats and soft shushes.

"Thank you for telling me, Irma. It's always nice to hear from him," the woman said in between shushes.

Irma began to cry. "Eddie, gone! Eddie, gone!" The woman led Irma to the library steps, and they sat down. She began to rock Irma whose sobs grew softer and softer.

Once Irma was calmed, the woman looked up at me. "Your face is covered in blood." The woman took a blue handkerchief from her pocket and held it out to me. "Here, run this under the water fountain and clean yourself off. Don't worry, hasn't been used." I took the handkerchief and ran it under the water of the nearby fountain and cleaned my face off. I walked back to hand it to her.

"Keep it," she said.

"Are you Penelope?" I asked.

"I was watching. Saw most of it. I didn't want to intrude this time," she smiled. "You must have been a friend of Eddie's. You seemed close. Were you?" I nodded. "That's good," she said. "He needs friends. Everyone does."

I stood there in silence, watching Eddie's sisters, my mind picking out all the ways they were like him and trying to piece together what the man he would never become would have looked like.

"He's gone, sorry to tell you," Penelope said, breaking the silence. "He'll be back, but not for a while."

"How long?" I asked, with a trace of hope in my voice.

"Ten years, at least. Disappeared in '62. Our Aunt Delia took him out one day and he never came back. They found her a week later in Arkansas. She never told anybody what she did with him." Irma started sobbing and Penelope began rocking her again. "I was five when it happened, so I don't remember much. But every ten years he comes back. Happened in '72 and again in '82. Each time, me and Irm find him, try to talk to him. Every time we do, though, it's like he remembers whatever it was that happened, and he gets called back. I suppose it takes him ten years to forget. I can't imagine what was so awful it would take ten years." Dark thoughts seemed to cross her mind and she shook her head in the way I saw Eddie do many times before.

"He showed up last year, didn't he?" she asked, and I nodded. "I tried to stay clear. Kept Irma away too. Away from the forest and the creek. That's where we usually find him. I thought he was better off not remembering. I just wanted him to have fun. Did he have fun?"

"He did," I was finally able to croak out.

"Did he have other friends?"

"Yes."

"Did he run and play? Did he laugh?"

"All the time."

"Good. That's good. Thank you for being my brother's friend." Penelope whispered into Irma's ear, "You ready to go, Irm?" Irma nodded, and the two rose from the steps. Before they went, Penelope turned to me and said, "If you're still here in ten years, just let him be, okay? Seeing you could remind him like we remind him. Let him play. Let him make new friends. Will you do that?"

"I will," I promised.

Eddie's sisters walked away, and I was left alone. The wind kicked up again and out of nowhere, Eddie's MISSING poster came flying into my face. I ripped it off and stared at it. Eddie stared back. No black eye, no scars. Aickman's lost boy.

JASON HUMAN:

RADIO STAR

A few days after the initial shock, The Anointed One insisted that we go to The Screaming Forest to pay our respects to Eddie.

"It is his home. He is out there, somewhere, waiting to return. He may hear our words and take comfort in them."

I had expected Jason to go on one of his Science Boy rants about these metaphysical assertions, but he had been oddly quiet since I related the details of Eddie's fate. For the entire journey out to the woods he said nothing but kept looking all around and flinched at every little cough and nearby footfall.

The Anointed One had wanted to find the rock wall where the Face At Midnight had saved our lives. Without Eddie, however, we didn't dare travel much past the bridge that led into the forest. It was strange to realize that the secrets of Eddie's playground were all but forbidden to us now. If we ventured too far, there would no longer be a smile in the wilderness to lead us home. There was only danger.

Of course, at that point, danger seemed to be everywhere. We'd lost two friends in a matter of weeks and what protection we'd had in both the forest and Aickman proper had gone with them. The three of us had become easy prey of the beasts of the wild and the beasts of civilization.

Even before Eddie's leaving, we had to take extra care to avoid Griffin Collins. It hadn't taken Collins long to realize that Darby was gone and without her he wouldn't need the law or his goons to get revenge on us. We made sure to hide when we saw him prowling the streets. In the glimpses I caught, I could see that the dull cruelty in his face was replaced by a manic hatred. He had taken to wearing a large winter hat, presumably to cover the burns on his head from our last encounter, which caused sweat to streak down his pink, puffy face. He looked so odd that he could have easily fit in with us. I had put Jason's edginess down to Collins' inevitable attack, but the real source of his fear would be revealed at Eddie's improvised wake.

The Anointed One had decided to give Eddie the full funereal rights of their people. This entailed them singing a poem in a language whose intonations caused visual hallucinations in the listener. I clearly saw the sun split like an egg to reveal a putrid white heart barely beating as if the universe itself was dying. I also saw a hippo standing on its hind legs in a yellow dress winking and blowing kisses at me. Even now I cannot tell you which filled me with more fear.

After the poem, The Anointed One danced the Dance of the Unfound. It was a highly technical affair involving precise flips and spins. The movements were hypnotic and sad. The Anointed One, decked in deep blue mourning robes, twirled and whirled through the air with an otherworldly grace that, more than their religion or manner of dress, marked them as a stranger to Aickman. The performance would have had me in tears if not for the smile that cracked across my face as I thought about Eddie's reaction to The Anointed One's display.

"This supposed to be a funeral or a talent show? Where are my score cards at? I want to give them a ten out of ten for goofiness. What, is Jason going to do some freestyle yodeling next? What's your talent, by the way? Not helping? Being useless? Taking up space? Boy oh boy, only freaks like you could turn a funeral into a ballet recital. I'll tell you this for free: the dead hate ballet. You know how I know? Cuz I'm dead!"

I shivered. I wasn't sure how to feel. My friend was dead, but he'd been dead the entire time I knew him. He was gone, but he would be back. I was never going to see him again but that was only to ensure his future happiness. Being friends with a ghost is very, very confusing.

As The Anointed One's dance reached its climax, they climbed up the nearest tree, walked out onto the highest branch, and screamed out to the forest, "I MOURN YOU, LOST BOY! I SWEAR THAT WITH ALL THE POWERS AT MY COMMAND I WILL ONE DAY FREE YOU OF YOUR PRISON OF TIME!" They then leapt off the branch. I ran over to try and catch them, but their robes caught the wind and they gently floated to the ground.

"Do you want to say anything?" they asked, looking up at me.

"I mourn you, Lost Boy. I swear that with all the powers at my command I will one day free you of your prison of time," was all I could think to say. We both looked over at Jason.

"Jason, would you like to make your feelings known?" The Anointed One asked.

But Jason wasn't paying attention. He was looking far into the distance, shaking. Just then there was the sound of a twig snap and Jason let out a scream. A bull frog hopped by. Jason immediately pounced on the amphibian and grabbed it up in his long fingers. He held it up to his face and shouted, "WHO ARE YOU WORKING FOR? THE FBI?! CIA?! THE GOONS AT THE DMV?! SPEAK, UNDERCOVER FROG!"

As an answer to Jason's questions, the frog shot his tongue out at Jason's left eye, causing him to fall back in pain and drop the frog, who languidly hopped away, no worse for wear from his minor inconvenience.

"Jason, why are you screaming at frogs?" I asked.

"SPIES! SPIES EVERYWHERE! The forest is filled with eyes and they're all on me. The Americans send their bullfrogs, the Chinese send their bats, and the Russians, the most dangerous of all humans, they've turned the lady bugs against me!"

"Jason Human, there is no right way to mourn," The Anointed One intoned. "But accusing the animals of the forest of being spies for former and current communist nations is not something Eddie would have appreciated."

"He might have, actually," I said. "I once saw him accuse a roly-poly of being a democrat."

"You tiny fools," Jason countered, spittle forming on the edges of his mouth. "You can't see the spider for the web. You think it's a coincidence that first Darby and now Eddie are gone? Do you think people just disappear? NO! This is a carefully orchestrated operation coordinated by the various superpowers of this pitiful planet!"

"What are you talking about?" I asked. "You're saying that China built a spook house for Darby and Russia killed Eddie over 30 years ago just to get at us?"

"Not us! Me!" Jason began to pace back and forth. "I thought I had chosen the perfect camouflage, but they must have seen through my impeccable disguise. They've been watching me, studying me, quietly becoming fascinated and obsessed with me. Some have even fallen in love. It's only natural. I cannot help how alluring I am. Surely that love has cost them their lives."

Jason seemed to space out contemplating his imaginary admirers until a string of drool fell from his mouth and splashed on his sneaker. He twirled towards us; eyes wider than I'd ever seen. "The point is, they've seen enough of me in action to know that when I am at the top of my game, I am indestructible. If they came at me head on, I could easily defeat their best minds and strongest agents. But they're sideswiping. THEY'RE SIDESWIPERS! Coming at me through my peer group, taking you out one by one, the strongest to the weakest. First Darby, then Eddie. Next will be The Anointed One, then Carl at the corner store who always lets me take an extra pickle followed by that woman who waves at everybody on the corner of Primrose Street. After them, they'll come for the secret mouse that I keep in my pocket and feel nothing for. Then, finally, it will be you!" he screeched, pointing at me.

I had no idea what he was going on about, but he was obviously in distress. I wanted to calm him down, but just then a ladybug landed on a nearby leaf which caused him to scream "THE RUSSIANS!" and he tore off across the bridge.

The Anointed One and I stood on the edge of the forest for a few silent moments until they finally declared, "I think Eddie would have enjoyed his funeral."

Later that night I had a nightmare. I was on an old-timey riverboat being chased by a giant, bloody open-wound that had somehow become detached from the upper thigh of an immense used car salesman.

"Say boy, you got them chicken bones a body just loves to crunch!" the wound slobbered as it chased me around the deck to the amusement of cowboys, gamblers, and a group of pink dolphins in tuxedos. As I was doing my 300th lap trying to stay out of the gory maw of the ambulatory wound, I tripped and fell between the boat and the wheel that propelled it. Each slat of the wheel slapped my head over and over until I finally woke up to find Jason standing on my bed slapping me over and over. I screamed and tumbled to the ground. Jason looked down at me.

"Finally! Get dressed and meet me at The Anointed One's house. HURRY!" he declared while he skittered out of my room.

I looked at my clock. It was past midnight. I remember thinking that I was probably better off being swallowed by the wound, but I got dressed and headed down.

Jason was pacing back and forth on The Anointed One's lawn. There was a long pole with numerous wires sticking out of it laying against The Anointed One's parent's minivan. There was no sign of The Anointed One.

"Jason, what the heck is going on?" I whispered, trying not to wake the neighborhood.

"HOW CAN I POSSIBLY ANSWER A QUESTION AS ALL ENCOMPASSING AS THAT! I AM UNDER ENOUGH STRESS!" he shouted and flailed his arms. I shushed him and rephrased my question.

"Okay, why did you slap me awake and make me meet you here?"

"Because they wanted you to come along. I was against the idea, but they insisted."

Having no idea what he was talking about, I was going to ask a series of follow up questions when I heard a loud thud behind me. I turned and, with the help of the dim glow of the streetlight, saw The Anointed One crumpled in a pile by the house. As I ran over to see what had happened, I noticed that their bedroom window on the second floor was open. They weren't moving.

"Jason, I think they fell! We should get help!" I shout whispered as quietly as I could.

"Why?" was his only response.

Jason Human was one of the most infuriatingly slappable individuals I had ever met in my life, but even I was taken aback by the level of his callousness. I wanted to punch him in his huge head for his indifference to a friend in need, but there was no time. I kneeled and shook The Anointed One. No response. Because my only frame of reference for life in general was television and movies, I decided to check their pulse. I had no idea how to do this, but I knew it had something to do with the wrist and as soon as my hand touched their flesh, I jumped back.

It was that damn doll again. It lay there, motionless, mocking me.

Just then, a voice from above whispered, "Coming down." I looked up and saw The Anointed One leap from their window, the air catching their robes as they floated to the ground.

"That doll is going to give me a heart attack someday," I said as The Anointed One gathered up their doppelganger.

"No, that won't be why you have any of your heart attacks," The Anointed One said as they headed for the minivan.

I chose to ignore that fresh jolt of future fear and decided to stick with more pressing matters. "Jason won't tell me, so can you explain what the heck is going on?"

"Yes. Jason is going back to Ohio and we're going to help him," The Anointed One said.

Shock at this revelation got the better of me as I shouted, "WHAT!?"

Jason put a hand over my mouth and shushed me. "Do you want to wake up the entire neighborhood?!" He turned to the Anointed One who had produced a set of car keys and unlocked the passenger door of the minivan. "See! He's a total liability! He can in no way help us!"

The Anointed One heaved the doll into the passenger seat and unlocked the mini-van's sliding side door. "Jason Human, he has to come with us because he has already come with us," The Anointed One said flatly.

"Stop trying to blow my mind you tiny little mystic and explain yourself," Jason harrumphed.

"In the future he will write about everything that is going to happen tonight and the only way that is possible is if he comes with us. With that being the case, I invoke your god, Logic, and conclude that he must come with us."

Jason was starting to shake. "You are claiming to be able to see the future?"

"It is not a claim, but a fact."

Jason's left eye began to twitch. "If you can see into the future then how does tonight end?"

"I don't know. I haven't seen it."

The twitch now encompassed the entire left side of Jason's face. "You don't know what will happen tonight, but you know that he will write the story about what will happen tonight?"

"That is correct."

Jason covered his face with his hands and was trembling uncontrollably. "Then how does the story end?"

"How would I know? I haven't bought the book yet."

Jason sent one of his fists flying into the side of the minivan where his knuckles collapsed like rubber causing his fist to bounce back and smack himself in the face. He hit the lawn with a soft thud and laid there for a few seconds before taking a deep breath and getting to his feet. Without saying a word, he grabbed the strange pole and got into the back of the minivan.

I stood there, dumbstruck, my face contorted by confusion to such a degree that when The Anointed One looked at me, they flinched.

"You seem confused," they said. "We'll fill in the details on the way, but right now just understand that we are stealing my parent's car to drive twenty miles outside of town to radio station KAIC: Aickman's Home of Classic Rock to aid Jason in committing further crimes for his personal benefit. Please, get in the van."

I got in the back of the minivan and buckled my seatbelt. The Anointed One slid the sliding door closed and then walked around to the driver side door, opened it, and got behind the steering wheel.

"Why did you bring that doll?" I asked.

"So they could work the pedals," they said as they dragged the doll over and plopped it on the floor of the driver seat. "My legs aren't long enough."

It was at this point that I realized that either one of two things was going to happen:

1. We weren't going to get the minivan moving because The Anointed One's driving system couldn't possibly work.
2. The Anointed One's driving system would work, and we were all about to die in a fiery car crash.

I was about to bring up my reservations about this doll-based system, but then I realized something: To Heck With It. Being the voice of reason hadn't gotten me anywhere. It seemed like no matter what happened that summer, danger and loss had my number and there was nothing I could do about it. I had already lost two friends and I was apparently about to lose a third. So instead of looking at the situation as a prelude to a horrible death, I instead saw it as one last hangout. Thinking of it like that calmed me down immeasurably, but there was something I had been meaning to ask The Anointed One for some time.

"Is that doll alive?"

"How do you define alive?"

"Something is alive when it can move around and plan to hurt me," I said.

"By that definition...yes, it is alive." The Anointed One then turned the key in the ignition, put the minivan in reverse and proceeded to back over their mailbox and the mailbox that belonged to the Taylor's across the street before we tore off into the night.

For somebody who had never driven in their life and was depending on a system whereby they kicked a life-sized doll of themselves in the head once to accelerate and twice to break, The

Anointed One did a pretty good job. Certainly, the dollar amount in both public and private property damage was only somewhere in the low thousands.

As the minivan careened through the mercifully empty midnight streets of Aickman, Jason brought me up to speed.

"I am not waiting around to be captured by some ridiculous world power that wants to harvest my body and mind to attain the ultimate truth. I need to flee to save my flesh and sanity. They cannot reach me in Ohio so I must return there. To get back to Ohio, I must contact my family."

At this point, The Anointed One hopped a curb and plowed through a newspaper box filled with the previous day's issue of The Aickman Truth. I could read the front-page headline as multiple copies flew by the window: "If you don't vote for me, you will burn in Hell." proclaims Mayor Deer

"Unfortunately, the only way I can contact my family is with this transmitter." He held up the pole. "But its signal strength was weakened in an explosion the details of which I will not share and arising from circumstances I refuse to elaborate on that directly resulted in me ending up in this town and were in no way my fault. I should have fixed it and called them a long time ago, but I got drawn into the tawdry dramas of small-town life and the lure of Aickman's myriad anomalies." He then kicked the back of the driver's seat as he screamed, "DAMN MY CURIOSITY! DAMN MY GENIUS!"

"Please stop doing that," said the Anointed One. "It's hard enough driving when you don't know how and are wearing a mask that limits your vision by up to 50 percent."

As if to underline this point, they then ran two red lights and cut through town square, barely missing the gazebo, but absolutely destroying the rose garden. After a few more near misses and The Anointed One clarifying the kick to the head system to the doll, we were soon on the road that was a straight shot out to the radio station. It was a moonless night and the hungry darkness looked ready to pounce on three idiots and a doll who were foolish enough to enter its hunting ground.

Once my heart rate had gone down from all the near crashes, it finally occurred to me to ask why we needed to go to the radio station.

"I need their tower. If I hook my transmitter up to theirs it will give me the power I need to reach my family who will then come get me."

"Then why do you need us?" I was still very heavy with ignorance.

"I don't. Not you, anyway. I went to the Anointed One's house, woke them up-"

"He threw a garbage can at my window," The Anointed One interrupted.

"Whereupon I asked them to steal their parent's car and drive me out here."

"Why?"

"Because I didn't want to walk. It's very far."

"And you just agreed to this?" I asked The Anointed One.

"Immediately," they nodded.

"Why"

"Because it sounded fun."

"But then they made me grab you so I did and here we are and so can I please stop explaining things?!" Jason screamed, throwing his hands in the air.

"You forgot to mention your promise, Jason Human," The Anointed One said.

"What are you babbling about? What promise?" Jason looked genuinely puzzled.

"The promise I made you make before I agreed to help."

"Oh yes, that. Right, sure, whatever."

The Minivan came to a sudden and violent stop. Jason flew face first into the back of the front seat. I was unharmed because I was wearing a seat belt like a good boy.

"What are you doing! The Feds could be on us any second!" Jason spat as he scrambled back into his seat.

The Anointed One turned around and stared directly at Jason. "You WILL honor your promise."

"Yes, okay, fine," Jason sputtered as he discreetly clicked his seat belt into place. "I will honor my promise, you diminutive blackmailer."

"What was the promise?" I asked. Jason just crossed his arms and looked out the window. The Anointed One turned to me.

"I made him promise to say goodbye to both of us before he goes." They turned around and put the minivan into gear. "I don't know who taught you Aickmaniacs manners, but none of you seem to be able to say goodbye properly."

KAIC was the home of classic rock in Aickman and was also the only local radio station. This made it very popular because it was the only station that acknowledged Aickman's existence. All other stations were based out in the big cities that were at the very least an hour away and they seemed to never have heard of the town that was "The Smile At The End Of Everything" which was our official motto.

Being a classic rock station, they played the same 37 songs from the 1960s and '70s over and over again. The people of Aickman didn't seem to mind this repetition at all. They found comfort in the old, danger in the new, and were always wary of the present for it was the knife edge between the two.

The overnight DJ was a man called "Coyote" Dan Blackmoor who had a habit of saying the most distressing things in the calmest and friendliest voice on the airwaves. We turned on the radio to hear what was going on at the station.

"All right Aickman, we are firmly in the midnight hour, and it is still hot and muggy out there with a temperature hovering at 89 degrees. I tell ya, the government's weather satellites must be working overtime superheating the planet. The endgame, of course, is to drive the population, that being you and me, into a frenzy and thus instigate an armed uprising they foolishly feel they can quash with little resistance and thus institute eternal martial law. Well, we'll just see how easy they find it when they try to mark me with the sign of the beast. I am not now, nor do I ever plan to be cattle for the New World Order. Also, don't forget that the 20th annual Aickman Jelly and Jam Jamboree and Assorted Preserves Prom is this Saturday and I think that Mrs. Cottonwood is in for some stiff competition this year. Can't wait to taste some of that blackberry jam, yum yum, my favorite. Course if any government agents are listening, you'll be tasting something else if you try to come on my property. Anyway, let's get back to rocking as your friend The Coyote plays you the only music that matters. AWOOOOOOOOOO!"

"I've always found The Coyote to be the most level-headed person in Aickman," Jason said as The Anointed One clicked off the radio.

"Level-headed or not, what do we do if he catches us messing with the tower?" I asked.

"There's no if about it," Jason said. "The modifications I need to do are not limited to the tower. I'll have to go into the control room. That's the other reason I brought The Anointed One along."

"I don't feel very comfortable about that part," The Anointed One said.

"We both have promises to keep, don't we?" said Jason.

"What do you have to do?" I asked.

"They will sneak up on The Coyote, as well as anyone else who gets in our way, and do one of their hand snake tricks to stun them long enough to do what needs to be done," Jason said.

The carefree attitude I'd had about this final hangout had begun to wane, and I got a bad feeling in the pit of my stomach.

We arrived at the KAIC building a few minutes later. It was a small, box-like wooden structure that resembled five shacks glued together rather than the home of anything, let alone classic rock. The dull neon letters that designated the building as KAIC barely illuminated the broadcast tower which stretched up into the night sky. Everything else around was flat darkness.

The Anointed One stopped the car away from the building to avoid being spotted. The three of us got out, Jason dragging the transmitter, and headed for the entrance. The parking lot was made of loose pebbles that crunched and popped under foot. The evening was still, save for an occasional wind gust that brought the scent of dying things that were rotting somewhere out in the night.

When we were halfway between the minivan and the building, the minivan sprung to life and rushed past us. As it went, we could see The Anointed Doll in the driver seat, its fake snake hand waving at us. The minivan then turned onto the road and headed away from Aickman. Me and Jason looked at The Anointed One who tilted their head and said simply, "God Speed, fake me."

We peaked in through the glass door of the main entrance. There was a small, deserted reception area and a main desk with no one behind it. The door was unlocked, so we walked in and were greeted with a sweltering room that stank of stale cigarettes.

We could hear The Coyote's voice coming from behind a door next to the main desk. We tip-toed towards it and found that it too was not locked. We opened it slowly and saw The Coyote. He was sitting at the far end of a long, thin room covered in peeling, faded posters of the 10 bands that were featured regularly on the station. In front of him was a chaotic collection of audio equipment that looked like it was from a time before Rock N Roll even existed. His back was towards us, so all we could see of him was long, grey hair which cascaded greasily over a bleached out Hawaiian shirt. The On Air sign above him was glowing red and he was busy talking about the best way to remove microchips from your body at home.

"Some people say the best way to deactivate a chip inside of you without cutting yourself open is with a microwave oven. Now, while it is possible to set up a microwave to function with the door open, doing that is just going to cause more problems than it could possibly fix."

He hadn't noticed us. As he went on with further tips about home based self-surgery, Jason looked down at The Anointed One and mouthed the word "Now". The Anointed One reluctantly raised their snake hand and crept up to The Coyote. Just before they could strike, The Coyote stopped talking and flipped a switch causing the On Air light above the mic to go off. He then wheeled around in his chair and pointed an AR-15 machine gun right at the Anointed One's face.

"You two at the door, get in here," The Coyote said. Jason tried to run, but I grabbed his arm and pulled him into the room.

"Who sent you?" The Coyote asked, grip tightening on the machine gun trigger. "FBI? CIA? The goons from the Department of Agriculture?"

"We're not with the government," I said. "Please, we can explain."

"I sure hope you can," the Coyote said, not lowering the machine gun.

I looked up at Jason and down at The Anointed One and then cleared my throat. "Sir, we are on the run from the government, and we need your help."

Having a machine gun pointed at your face is a great aid to mental dexterity. I don't think my brain has ever moved that fast ever again. Within five minutes I had spun a tale of a secret underground government laboratory just outside of Aickman being run by a group called Agency Zero. The purpose of Agency Zero was to enact Operation Zero Hour where genetically modified child super soldiers would be unleashed on America to take away people's freedoms and liberties.

I explained how we were all experiments: Jason had his intelligence expanded which explained his huge head and The Anointed One was so mutated that if they were to take off their mask, the ugliness underneath would drive people insane. For myself, I was a failed experiment who had manifested no powers and as punishment had to cook and clean for the special kids. Tired of our treatment and hoping to warn the rest of the world of the existence of Agency Zero, we escaped. The reason we had come to KAIC was to use one of Jason's inventions to increase the power of the KAIC tower to transmit worldwide where we could unmask the agency and finally get the truth to the people.

The Coyote, still pointing the machine gun at us, mulled over all the lies I had just spewed and finally declared, "That sounds about right." He then lowered the machine gun, turned back to the mic, and flipped the switch that put him back on air.

"All right Aickman, looks like The Coyote has fallen in with a group of child soldiers who are finally going to reveal the truth to the world so stay tuned because we are about to peer through the looking glass, and nothing will ever be the same again. Speaking of nothing ever being the same again, if you're looking to change up your hair do or just looking for a whole new you, Dorothea's Hair Salon on Cherrywood and Smith is offering specials on permanents, dye Jobs, updos, downdos, and Scooby Dooby Doos all week so head on down to Dorothea's where she'll make a new woman out of you. Right now, I can't think of a better way to ring in the revolution than with some of that classic Rock & Roll that they just don't seem to make anymore. AWOOOOOOOO!"

He lowered the needle on one of the record turntables in front of him and flipped off the On Air switch. He then turned back to us, laid the machine gun against the wall, and smiled. "So, we just got to connect that thingamagig in big head's hand to the tower and we bring the government to its knees or what's going on?" The Coyote asked, his actual speaking voice much less refined than his radio voice.

"You're going to help us?" I asked, disbelieving.

"Hell yeah, The Coyote's going to help you. The Coyote'd do anything to make the government pay for what they did to him."

"What do you think the government did to you?" Jason asked.

"Think, nothing. I'm just like you kids. An experiment. Only I didn't have no fancy schmancy Agency Zero or nothing like that. Nope, The Coyote got himself abducted by aliens."

"You don't say?" Jason said, looking incredibly sketchy.

"I do say. I say what happened cuz it's the truth. I say what's true is that The Coyote had himself a little smoke break outside the studio one night almost two years ago." At the mention of a smoke break, The Coyote pulled a cigarette out of his pocket, lit it with a cheap blue plastic lighter, and began puffing with abandon. "There I was, sucking on a lil' cancer stick, oh you kids shouldn't smoke by the way," he said while blowing a huge cloud in our faces. "And I was just about to head inside, when all of a sudden, I'm surrounded by a bright light, and I can hear someone calling my name. It was my grandma's voice. That's the grandma on my mother's side, not my daddy's momma who we called MeeMaw cuz she was married to PeePaw. So here I am thinking my long dead grandma is calling me from heaven and then I realize that there is no way that awful old woman made it to heaven, so I start to panic and all of a sudden, I'm floating up to the light." He had sucked down the first cigarette so quickly that he lit another and recommenced puffing. "So, as I am going up and up, I see the light is coming from this huge ship and I'm all like 'Oh crap, it's aliens' and the next thing I know, I wake up two days later naked in The Screaming Forest with a chip in my right arm and my life destroyed."

"Why was your life destroyed?" I asked.

"Because I wouldn't shut the hell up about aliens," The Coyote puffed.

"But if it was aliens, why blame the government?" Jason asked.

"Heck kid, everyone knows the government and the aliens work hand in hand. The government lets the aliens do experiments on us to make gizmos and doodads which the aliens give back to the government so they can sell them to us. Like feeding hamburgers to cows. You can't trust them! You can't trust any of them!" The Coyote sprang out of his chair and picked up the AR-15. "So if we're going to do this, then let's do this. COME ON!" and with that, he ran out of the room screaming.

"I thought he looked familiar," Jason said, before following The Coyote outside. The Anointed One and I were left alone in the tiny studio.

"Why do you think most people can't tell that Jason is an alien from outer space?" The Anointed One asked.

"I don't know," I said. "Why do you think we can?"

"Hmmmm, it is puzzling." The Anointed One was stroking the chin of their mask. "I would have asked Jason a long time ago, but I don't think I could have handled the hissy fit he would have thrown."

"Yeah, it would really hurt his feelings if he knew that he never fooled us," I said.

"Now that he's leaving, I have to admit that as much affection as I have for Jason, I don't ever want to go to space."

"Being around him has definitely made me less interested in the cosmos," I confessed.

The Anointed One looked at the tangle of equipment that made up the KAIC studio. They walked towards the Coyote's chair and sat in it.

"With just this chaos of wires, The Coyote can reach everyone in Aickman," they said.

"Not everyone," I said. "Most people are asleep."

"Everyone in Aickman. What power. What awesome responsibility." The Anointed One purred as they lifted the needle off the record and flipped the broadcast switch. The red On Air sign seared to life.

"What are-" I quickly covered my mouth as I realized that everyone currently listening in Aickman could hear me.

"Good evening, Aickman," The Anointed One whispered into the mic. "It is after midnight. We now find ourselves on the dark side of the witching hour. A time when the borders of sanity collapse under the weight of the unthinkable and we are left at the mercy of the unimaginable. Brave travelers of the twilight highway, let my voice guide you through the darkness, through the fear, and deliver you to the promised land that awaits beyond the forever night."

They then took a deep breath and made a loud, wet farting noise with their mouth. "Pbbbbbbbbbbbbbbtttttttttttt. That's right, brothers and sisters, welcome to The Farting Hour."

I was, understandably, aghast at this development, but The Anointed One took no notice of my shock as they proceeded to vocally reproduce every type of fart imaginable. To aid in listener comprehension, they made sure to always precede the fart with a backstory that gave listeners insight into the unique emotional makeup of each fart. They would say things like: "This fart fancies itself a lady's man," or, "This fart misses it's dad," or, "This fart is bad. Not in the ways a fart is usually bad. There is darkness in this fart's heart. Pain. This fart will have its vengeance."

It was when they were about to introduce the "Fart that will always be there for you" that we heard machine gun fire coming from outside. I froze immediately, but The Anointed One leapt from The Coyote's chair and ran out of the studio. As quickly as I could, I overrode every one of my instincts and followed them.

We both peaked through the glass door of the main entrance and could see The Coyote firing his gun at the tower. At once, I realized it was a mistake to have left Jason alone with The Coyote. Even if he couldn't tell that Jason was an extraterrestrial, Jason's personality and people with machine guns do not mix.

As my brain was busy listing all the ways that we could not hope to stop a man with an automatic weapon, The Anointed One burst through the front door and screamed, "HALT, DOG MAN! DO NOT MURDER OUR FRIEND!"

"Murder him? I'm trying to help him. Look!" The Coyote said as he pointed to the tower.

The Anointed One turned to the tower and then immediately started running towards it. I walked out to get a better look and I could see Jason hanging by his neck. He had somehow gotten one of the wires from his transmitter wrapped around his throat and was swinging like a condemned outlaw in the old west.

"I was trying to shoot the wire to get him down," The Coyote said to me.

The Anointed One had gotten to the tower and scrambled up it in no time. They reached Jason in seconds and was able to lift him up enough that he could grab onto the tower and unwrap the wire from his neck.

"Boy, that ugly kid sure is fast. I thought that other ugly kid was a goner." The Coyote said.

After they both had come down, Jason led everyone back into the control room and used a screwdriver and a strange implement to refit the ancient technology of the studio. He worked so quick that the whole process took less than three minutes.

"Dang, that Agency Zero sure knows their stuff," The Coyote marveled.

"It is done," Jason said. "We are ready."

The Coyote had a huge grin on his face as Jason switched the broadcast live. There was a scream of feedback as Jason adjusted various knobs and switches. When the feedback stopped, Jason brought the microphone to his tiny lips and said, "Attention, what you are about to hear is dangerous. It is recommended that the elderly and pregnant women turn off their radios now." Then Jason leaned his head back at a 90-degree angle and began to make a series of piercingly shrill ululations that sounded like robotic hyenas ripping each other to pieces. The sound was so sharp that I could feel my ear drums twitch in agony. Just as I thought that blood was about to burst from my eyes, the ululations ended and Jason capped them with, "And hurry!" before switching the mic off.

"Wait, was that it?" The Coyote shouted, hands over his ears.

Jason thought about this for a second and then said, "Actually, no." He switched the mic back on. "Attention people of Aickman. You don't know me, at least not the real me, but I have been watching you for the better part of two years. In that time, I have observed you to be a vicious, small-minded, thoroughly unlikeable lot of lower order beings save for Carl at the corner store and the lady who waves at everybody. I have also been keeping track of all the various lies, double crosses, and shady dealings you've all tried to hide from each other and, while I wait for my ride, I will now list them."

In his book, "Divided: America's Unknown and Much Smaller Civil War" journalist Edwin Donaldson wrote about how a completely unknown American town erupted into what can only be described as open warfare amongst its citizenry in the winter of 1994. The book details the carnage that led to at least half the town being destroyed and the arrest and imprisonment of the deer that had for so long been the mayor. Though Donaldson was able to work out that the violence sprang from a series of small grudges that had been festering in the preceding months, he was never able to determine the root cause of all the troubles. Even though it has been over 25 years since the book's publication, and subsequent financial failure due to the public not believing any of the events described in said book, I would now like to put Donaldson's mind at ease: The seeds of the Aickman Civil War were planted by a petty alien airing dirty laundry on a classic rock radio station.

As Jason rounded off his list of outrages by accusing the town dogcatcher of working with the dogs to overthrow humanity, he signed off on his residency in Aickman by proclaiming, "So Aickman, it has been your absolute pleasure to know me, and I hope to never see any of you ever again."

"What in the Hell was that?" The Coyote shouted. "Why didn't you say anything about Agency Zero or that Zero Hour stuff?"

"Because all of that was a lie. We were lying to you because you are a very gullible person," Jason said.

"Friend, you just said the absolute wrong thing." The Coyote raised his gun and pointed it at Jason's head.

"Then allow me to say one more thing. Snake Hand."

"What?" The Coyote said.

"Snake Hand. NOW!"

"Boy, you have gone loco in that huge cabez…" The Coyote trailed off and then crumpled to the floor. The Anointed One's hand was still raised from where they had just "bit" him.

"Thank you for taking so long," Jason said.

"I fulfilled my promise, Jason. Now fulfill yours," The Anointed One warned.

Jason sighed. "Fine. I have prepared a goodbye speech and will now dazzle you with it." He cleared his throat. "Genius is a word that gets thrown around a lot, but you have surely been in the presence-"

"What in the hellfire is going on in here?" a gruff voice interrupted.

We turned to see the doorway of the studio being filled by the gigantic frame of Sheriff Little Veal Burlington.

It was my first ride in the back of a police car. I didn't think much of the accommodations but was glad of the company as I sat between The Anointed One and Jason. The Anointed One and I exchanged glances while Sherriff Burlington raged about the terrible night he'd been having.

"There I was, sound asleep, when I get a phone call from a deputy telling me that some sort of terrorist attack had happened. I get up, get dressed, and head out to find a trail of destruction cut through the middle of town like a tornado had just torn through and while we're trying to figure that out, we get another call from somebody saying their radio is farting. When I finally get around to turning on KAIC, I hear somebody accusing me and my brother Big Beef of embezzling money from the town!"

He rattled on and on about the various laws we had broken and how we were going to do hard time and how he and his brother eat gophers like us for breakfast. It was difficult for me to work up my usual level of fear because I was worried about Jason. He was staring out of the car window, saying nothing.

"Will your family still be able to find you?" I asked. He stayed silent as Burlington's rant continued.

"Big Beef's already working on amending the law. We're bringing back corporal punishment!"

"Jason?" I asked. Nothing.

"Big Beef and me got big plans!" Burlington shouted. "We're making the Deputies of America year-round. Future Deputies of

America too. And they ain't just going to have baseball bats, no sir!"

I reached a hand to Jason's shoulder and shook him. He slowly turned his head but did not look at me. Instead, he stared at Sheriff Burlington.

"Justice!" Burlington slobbered. "Real, actual justice! Like back in my granddaddy's day, before this country went to Hell!"

"Sheriff Burlington?" Jason asked.

"What is it? Gonna plead for mercy?" Burlington snorted.

"No. I was just going to ask you to shut your big, fat wet mouth because you're giving me a headache."

I could feel The Anointed One tense up just as I was doing the same. Jason continued to sit as languidly as he had been. It took Burlington a few seconds to register what had just been said.

"What did you say, punk?" Burlington was looking at Jason in the rearview mirror. Jason leaned forward, his face inches away from the metal grill that separated the front and back seats.

"I said, did your father meet the hippo that birthed you and your brother while on safari or during a trip to the zoo?"

Burlington slammed on the brakes. The Anointed One stretched out one protective hand to my chest to keep me from flying forward just as I had done to Jason. Burlington turned to face Jason, his face nearly touching the grill.

"Why don't you say that again?" Burlington hissed, fury in his eyes.

Jason leaned back and put his hands behind his head. "Sheriff Burlington, I am going to strap you to an exam table, stick needles in your eyes and shove a scoop up your nose to remove what little there is of that miniscule brain of yours."

"Son, you just threatened an officer of the law." Burlington smiled, then quickly removed his keys from the ignition and threw open his door. He took his nightstick out and was looking at Jason through the window.

"Jason!" I screamed. "What do you think you're-"

I didn't get to finish my sentence because at the exact moment that Burlington put his hand on the door handle to get at Jason, a perfect cylinder of light shot down from the sky and enveloped Burlington.

"What in the world?!" Burlington shouted. Jason tapped at the window. Burlington looked down at him. Jason gave a small wave to Burlington and the very next second, Burlington shot straight up into the sky. Jason then turned to me and The Anointed One.

"Oh, by the way, I'm not really from Ohio," Jason said as a beam of light surrounded the car, and we were lifted into the air. A smile broke across Jason's face as his eyes went bright red and his head deflated. The last thing I heard before losing consciousness was the horrible, horrible sound of my alien friend's laughter.

I woke up the next day in my bed. From what I could gather later, the sheriff's office had declared that the damage to the town was caused by a small tornado that had struck Aickman in the middle of the night. The authorities would also blame the disturbances at the local radio station on political agitators from outside the area. These proclamations came directly from Sheriff Burlington right before he announced that he was stepping down as sheriff to concentrate on a new career in crystal healing. Many people took note of the sheriff's near constant nose bleeds on that last day and a vacancy in the eyes that was more pronounced than usual.

When asked for a comment about his brother's actions, Big Beef Burlington was quoted as saying, "My baby brother...a gopher," through streams of large, salty tears.

Later that morning, when I went over to The Anointed One's house, the first thing they said to me was, "That cosmic jerk didn't say goodbye."

THE SERPENT

The Anointed One and I watched the willow tree burn. A breeze carried the ash and still burning leaves in every direction. I could no longer see the carved heart or the multiple "liars" that made me fall in love with the tree the first time I set eyes on it.

As I stared, the flames became windows and within them I saw happier times. I saw all of us together, and we were made of fire and we danced and laughed and played. Well, Flame Eddie, Flame Jason, Flame Darby, and the Flaming Anointed One were playing, but my fire-ganger was staring back at me. He was smiling a smile that, for obvious and not so obvious reasons, was brighter than anything I was capable of. He beckoned, inviting me to crawl into the burning window and join them. I had no intention of following, but it still felt good when The Anointed One put their hand on my arm to hold me back and whispered, "Sometimes your mind is the enemy."

Though the tree dying in such a horrible way was barely a surprise based on the trajectory of the summer, it was extra painful because we had come to say goodbye. Or rather, The Anointed One had come to say goodbye.

They'd delivered the news earlier that week.

"We're moving. Back to Antarctica. My parents feel it is safer there," they said, sitting on the railing of my porch.

In the course of about a minute I burst out laughing, punched the wall, broke down into sobs and then got myself under control. If nothing else, the summer had taught me how to be economical with my emotions and I was oddly proud of the compact nature of my mini-breakdown.

They said that their parents had been talking about moving ever since being arrested by the Deputies of America on the 4th of July. Then when their minivan had been sucked up by a tornado, their minds had pretty much been made up.

"You didn't tell them that your doll stole the car?" I asked.

"Confessing to vehicular theft and flagrant property damage as well as negligence that resulted in a false me committing further vehicular theft would only have strengthened their resolve to leave. The outcome would have been the same, so I remained silent to escape punishment."

"Sometimes I worry about the lessons you'll teach your followers."

"So do I."

After being told of their parents' decision, The Anointed One made a list of things that they and I were to do before they left. It was written on ancient parchment in their own blood which added a rather unearned solemnity to such items on the list as "Throw a toilet off a bridge."

"Eddie and Darby always talked about throwing toilets off a bridge, but they never got to. I think this would be a nice way to honor them," they explained.

Among the items on the list, there was one that stuck out immediately: Make peace with Griffin Collins.

"Make peace with Collins?" I asked.

"Is that so strange?" The Anointed One countered.

"YES!" I shouted. "Very strange. Incredibly strange. In fact, I can safely say that making peace with Griffin Collins is the strangest idea you've ever had."

The Anointed One seemed taken aback by my statement, but I was serious. When it comes to things like ghosts, aliens, soul-eaters, and religious roaches, those were all just part of life. Everybody deals with that stuff at some point. What they were suggesting, however, was unthinkable. Unknowable. Like trying to picture what there was before the universe. There are just some things the mind cannot contemplate.

"Is this because you're a messiah?" I asked.

"What has that to do with anything?"

"Miracles and stuff, right? When they write books about you, it's supposed to be filled with all the impossible things you've done. I think the only reason you want to make peace with Collins is because you need to get some miracles under your belt before you go back to Antarctica."

The Anointed One lowered their masked face into their hands. "How is it that as an actual human being you have a worse grasp of spirituality than Jason?"

"It doesn't make sense," I said. "Collins once hawked a loogie in my mouth and made me swallow it. Another time, I saw him pour gasoline on an anthill and light it on fire and then he saw me see him and chased me with the gas can screaming that he was going barbecue my head. You can't make peace with that. Why would you even try?"

"Because I worry," they said. "You're going to be left here all on your own. Defenseless. At the mercy of Collins. It's either peace or destruction. I must do this. A part of me still feels as though I failed Eddie and Darby. I don't want to fail you as well."

"You don't have to worry about me," I said. "You're always telling me how when I get older, I'm going to write a book about everything that happened here, so obviously I survive."

"Survive, yes, but there are worse things than death."

Their peace plan meant a great deal to them and, as much as I hated the idea, I agreed to it on the condition that it would be the last thing we do. They were happy with that, and I was certain that with less than a week before they were set to depart, we wouldn't get around to it. My certainty was due to the general tendency of things not getting accomplished once I'm involved and the fact that Griffin Collins was, at that point, in the hospital.

Two days after Jason left, Collins, for reasons that no one has ever understood, decided to attack the bronze statue of Mayor Deer in town square with a chainsaw. He did this in broad daylight in front of several eyewitnesses. He managed to hack off one of the statue's antlers and maul a hoof before the deputies arrived. When they tried to talk Collins down, he rushed them with the saw, but tripped on an untied shoelace sending the saw out of control. Collins ended up with chunks being taken out of his right arm and leg. He was rushed to the hospital and the story spread around town quickly. Most everybody thought that this was one of the funniest things to happen in some time. You could see everyone from children to the elderly mime Collins' self-mauling for days afterwards. When I first heard the story from my dad, I burst out laughing. When I told The Anointed One about it, they were not amused. I guess you had to be from Aickman to see the funny side of it.

So, with Collins in the hospital, I figured that he wasn't going to be a problem and we were free to cross everything else off The Anointed One's list.

In those last days together, The Anointed One and I made up for a summer that had been stolen from us. We rose early each morning, always with a plan for the things we were going to cross off the list that day, and then we accomplished those things without a hint of tragedy or thoughts of our inevitable separation.

It turned out that throwing a toilet off a bridge was exactly as fun as Darby and Eddie had always claimed it was. We were lucky that the abandoned toilet they had mentioned in June before the disastrous game of tag was still on the side of the road. We were luckier still that it was near Moth Woman Bridge, so named because of a legend about a half-moth half-woman who was said to decapitate teenagers on the bridge at midnight. This turned out to be utter nonsense and the spate of decapitations that plagued the bridge in the 1970s were down to nothing more than a garden variety maniac.

Another item on the list was one last visit to the railroad tracks. Every Thursday at 3:15, an unmarked locomotive would come through town hauling 5 train cars. Through the windows of these cars, you could see shirtless old men with wild looks in their eyes. They seemed to be screaming and biting each other, possibly to establish who the dominant old man was. The strangest thing about the train was that it was never the same old men. Every week would see a new group of about 50 old, shirtless biting men slowly gliding through our town. That's over 2500 old, shirtless biting men a year. Where did they come from? Where did they go? Like many things in Aickman, it was just a mystery we learned to live with. On that final visit, me and The Anointed One waved, wished the old men well, and hoped that their bite wounds would be free of infection.

One of the more inscrutable items on the list simply said, "Lick Cake." This referred to a very specific cake in a very specific place: The Peach Street Bus Stop. There were two notable things about the Peach Street Bus Stop:

1. It served no purpose because the town had never had a bus service.

2. On the bus stop bench perpetually sat a tall, white wedding cake that was not affected by rainfall, snow, or the schemes of those who feared the cake.

In a lot of ways, The Cake was like Darby's Laughing House. The House, however, was far more infamous due to its effect on people and because the pointless bus stop on which The Cake sat was out by the abandoned brick factory where few lived. The Cake bothered no one and most people in town returned the courtesy.

Children are not people, however, and this subspecies of humanity would often dare each other to lick The Cake. It had to be a lick because, like the sword in the stone, The Cake could not be moved or otherwise broken down. Those who had licked The Cake reported no side effects apart from a coppery aftertaste, though one kid was rumored to have swallowed his twin brother two hours after taking a lick.

Neither of us had ever licked it and it seemed like a fun, if unhygienic, thing to do. When we got to The Peach Street Bus Stop, though, The Anointed One let out a yelp of pain.

"What is it?" I asked.

"Something in my head. A voice. Pleading. Begging."

"What's the voice saying?"

"Don't lick me," they said. "It's The Cake. It hates being licked."

"Oh. Well, that makes sense," I said. "I'd hate it if I was constantly being licked too."

"It is also begging to die."

"Okay. I mean, I guess that makes sense. It would be awful if food wanted to live and we still ate it anyway, I suppose."

"It cannot die."

"This cake has got problems," I concluded.

In the end, we did not lick The Cake. Instead, we went to the drug store and purchased supplies to make a sign that we attached to the bus stop bench that read:

Please Do Not Lick, Cake Hates Being Licked
p.s.
If anyone knows how to kill immortal cakes, please act on this knowledge

Most of the rest of the list wasn't very noteworthy but the completion of each one was like a needle to my heart.

On the night before The Anointed One was set to say goodbye to the willow tree, Aickman, and me, we took a trip up to Miller's Peak which was a high cliff that offered a great view of the Southern Lights. The Southern Lights were a phenomenon like the Aurora Borealis but were created by the pollution that seeped out of a nearby petrochemical facility. Instead of purples and blues, the Southern Lights were made of violent reds and sickly yellows. As the waves of light undulated and pulsed, they were sliced by cracks of thick black lightning that never made a sound. It was, by far, the most beautiful sight in all of Aickman.

As we sat and watched the dance of the splendid pollution, the weight of The Anointed One's impending departure began to bear down on me.

"What's Antarctica like?" I asked.

"Cold," they said.

"Duh," I duhed. "I know it's cold. But what's it like living in such a cold place?"

"Actually, it's only cold in the known Arctic. We'll be living in the unknown Arctic which lies just beyond the mountains."

"Which mountains?"

"Do you know the names of any Antarctic mountain ranges?"

"Well, no," I admitted.

"If I were to tell you the name of the mountains, would that make it any clearer where they were located?"

"No."

"Then I could just make up a mountain range and you would never know, would you?"

"I guess so."

"In fact, I could be making everything up. My religion, my purpose. That suicidal cake. It could all be a lie. I could just be a regular kid who got their parents to play an elaborate prank on you, couldn't I?"

I didn't know how to respond. There was a fragility in their voice I'd only ever heard before on the 4th of July.

"Wouldn't that be nice?" they said. "I'd just scream April Fools and then Darby, Eddie, and Jason would come out of their hiding places and have a good laugh at you. Then I could take off this mask and these robes and I'd be free. I'd be a regular kid and you could call me a regular kid name like Jonathan or Jessica. All I would have to worry about is growing up and getting a job. I could be an accountant or an astronomer or a birthday party clown. It would be entirely up to me, and I could choose where I wanted to go and what I wanted to do. If all of this were just one big joke, wouldn't that be nice?"

They'd begun tracing a finger around their snake tattoo as their body trembled. I was about to put my hand on their shoulder when they quickly said, "They don't have a name."

"What?"

"The mountains. They're simply called The Mountains. In the same way that the city where we'll be living is just called The City."

"Did your people build The City?"

"No. It was built long before The Book of the Never. Some say it was built long before The Serpent even began telling the lie that is this universe. The City is the only truth in the world, and it will still be here when The Serpent finishes this lie and everything we know disappears. The City will then be the bedrock of The Serpent's next lie. It is an eternal place, meant for giants who walk in the infinite. I hate it there. I don't want to go back."

"Can't you guys move somewhere else?"

They didn't answer. After a few minutes of silence, I asked, "What if I came to visit you?"

"What?"

"Yeah, I mean, it's not like outer space or ten years in the future. It's Antarctica. People go there all the time. I'm people, so why can't I visit?"

"It is forbidden."

"Who says?"

"It's one of our most sacred laws. No outsiders are allowed in The City."

"Yeah, but you're The Messiah, right?"

"There's a limit to-"

"Who puts limits on The Messiah?"

"It's not as simple as-"

"Look, when you get to that forever city of yours, just say that instead of the universe being the lie of a serpent, it's actually the burp of a monkey and if that monkey ever stops burping then that's good because monkeys shouldn't be burping like that. And then while everyone is busy freaking out, just sorta mention that your friend from Aickman is visiting for a bit. They won't even notice."

"You want me to make a mockery of my most sacred beliefs, turn my back on everything I have ever been taught, imperil an ancient and beautiful religion, and in doing so endanger the very Universe by risking the wrath of The Serpent just so you and I could hang out?"

"Yep."

"I'll have to think about it."

That next morning, we headed out to the willow tree. There were dark clouds in the sky, a sight that hadn't been seen since the game of tag in June which marked the last day the town had seen any rain. Most houses had dead lawns and dying trees and over those dry two months we lived in a world painted in corpse grass yellow and a dirt brown bleached by the blazing white of the sun.

When we were halfway to the willow, The Anointed One talked about getting a ride to the hospital to visit Collins.

"I am certain he will be more open to peace talks in his weakened state."

I was annoyed. I had somehow convinced myself that they had forgotten all about their idiotic peace plan. In my head I had been trying to concoct different excuses as to why we couldn't possibly visit the hospital and the best I could come up with was lying on the ground, screaming, "I DON'T WANNA!" until they gave up. But before I could humiliate myself in that fashion, The Anointed One spotted smoke coming from the direction of the willow and ran towards it. There was a peel of thunder from above as I followed.

After The Anointed One's calming hand had dispelled the flaming visions in my mind, I was able to clearly see that the burning debris blowing in the wind was catching the dead grass that lay further off from the tree. The banks of God Help Us, They're Killing Us Creek on which the willow lay were muddy and green because the drought had seemed to have no effect on the creek at all. It was still flowing with the same lifeless water that had brought the toes into our lives. Regardless of what power had kept the creek filled, the fact was that once enough of the dead grass got burning, it didn't matter how wet and muddy the banks were. The fire would eat up everything in its path.

"Come on, we got to get out of here," I said, grabbing The Anointed One's arm. They didn't move.

"Poor willow," they whispered.

"The fire's spreading. If we don't go, we'll die. Come on!" I yelled. They still didn't move.

"You didn't deserve this."

"God Damnit, Anointed One, we have got to-"

My vision exploded white, and I was dimly aware of a sound like THUNK going through my mind as my skull vibrated. I spun and then fell onto my back. After shaking my head to get the world to stop spinning, I looked up to see The Anointed One holding a rock with a spatter of blood on it. My hand went to the pain that was growing above my left eyebrow. When I pulled my hand away, I saw the fingers were coated with blood.

"You hit me with a rock?" I yelled.

"No, not me. It bounced off your skull and into my hand," they said.

"Then who-" and then I froze as I heard a familiar laugh coming from across the creek.

I looked over and on the other side was Griffin Collins. His right arm was completely bandaged and, as he slowly made his way towards us through the creek, I could see he now had a terrible limp. His face was covered in sweat that oozed down from the huge winter hat he was wearing. In his left hand dangled a red, plastic gasoline can and out of the opening of the can hung a dirty, limp rag.

"Hell Yeah!" he screamed. "Got the little piglet in his fat head. Don't worry, piggy, I'm coming to finish you."

A bolt of adrenaline shot straight to my heart as I registered the limping maniac with his gas can. I forgot all about the blood and possible brain damage and sprung immediately to my feet. I grabbed The Anointed One's arm with every intention of dragging them all the way home.

"HOLD IT!" Collins shouted. "You run and I'll light this rag and turn the gas can into a Molotov cocktail." He was holding a lit lighter close to the rag. "I'll chuck it right at your fat head. Make you sizzle, pig."

There was every chance that he would just as likely blow himself up by doing something so stupid, but luck was never on my side, so I stayed put. The Anointed One shook off my hand and took a step towards the bank.

"This is fortuitous, Griffin Collins, we were just about to visit you in the hospital," they said.

"Bull," Collins said, his slow limp making it so that he was only halfway across the creek. "If any of you freaks came to the hospital to laugh at me, I'd have gutted you with a scalpel and fed your guts to the burn victims."

Collins' evocative image made me painfully aware that the fires were growing stronger and closer.

"Anyways, I'm out now," he said, now on the same bank as us. "Sprung myself so the cops couldn't get me and put me in juvie. It's not fair. It was just a dumbass statue. Whole town acting like I killed the mayor. Why is everyone so stupid?" He limped closer and closer, the gasoline sloshing in the can. "I've already suffered enough. Doctor said I almost died on the operating table. Now I got to go to kiddie jail too? For a deer? Not even! A statue of a deer. Naw, if I'm going down, it's going to be for something legendary." A cruel smile broke across his lips as he surveyed the spreading fires all around us.

"I didn't realize your wounds were that bad," The Anointed One said. "I'm so sorry that happened to you. It must have been frightening being that close to death."

The smile fell away from Collins' lips, and he got a faraway look in his eyes. It was the same look I would often see in Eddie's eyes. Like Eddie, he quickly shook his head to banish the unwanted thoughts and turned an evil scowl towards The Anointed One.

"I ain't a God Damn baby. What? Do you think I was bitching and crying for myself like the little piggy here is always doing? Naw, I started making plans. One night one of my stitches came undone and I was bleeding out. You think I called for help? I don't need help! I took that blood on my fingers and wrote a list on my pillowcase. It was a list of all the things I was going to do before the cops took me to juvie. Know what was at the top of that list, you little freak?"

"Make peace with your enemies?" The Anointed One asked.

This seemed to catch Collins off guard and, not able to express his disgust with words, he quickly hawked a loogie right on to The Anointed One's eye plate. The green blob slowly slid down their mask. The Anointed One never acknowledged it.

"You think I burned down you and the other freak's favorite tree because I want peace? Naw, number one on my list was to make you pay for what you did to me," Collins growled.

"WHAT!? WHY?! WHAT THE HECK?!" I finally snapped. "We are about to burn to death and one of you is talking peace and the other revenge!? For what? What did we do to you Collins!? What did anybody ever do to you?!"

As an answer, Collins ripped the winter hat off to reveal a shock of matted, sweaty bright green hair. It was the same shade of green as the flames The Face at Midnight had used to burn off his rat tail.

"This! Look at this! You punks ruined my life. I was an officer of the law, and you did this to me! All my friends laughed at me. All of them! When I tried to punish them for laughing, they ganged up on me and beat me like the cowards they are. You had no right to do what you did. I was an officer of the law!"

"I think it looks very cool, Griffin Collins," The Anointed One said.

Collins' eyes grew wide and his face flushed red. His bandaged right arm shot out and he grabbed The Anointed One by the throat. Not thinking, I jumped at the arm, trying to squeeze at the parts where I thought the chainsaw had got him. He let out a scream, dropped the gas can, and in moments, his left hand was around my throat. It tightened and I couldn't breathe.

Collins leaned closer to The Anointed One's mask. "Now why don't you tell me how scary it is to be close to death," he hissed through gritted teeth.

I was punching and scratching as hard as I could against Collins' arm, but his grip was too tight. My panic was such that I had begun spitting and trying to maneuver my mouth to bite him. Collins just laughed. The Anointed One showed no outward signs of panic nor anything else. Their only reaction was to gently place one hand on Collins' wrist and the other hand on my shoulder.

"Now…you will both…see," The Anointed One croaked, and with a gentle squeeze to my shoulder, everything went black.

The next thing I knew, I was on the floor of a strange living room looking up at the furniture, walls, and windows which all looked massive. I was a toddler. I was a toddler making a connection in my mind. It was the first complex thought I had ever had. I realized that the two large beings who carried me around and fed me seemed to not like the messes that I made in my diaper. The way their faces twisted when dealing with these messes made me laugh. I liked laughing. Those faces made me laugh. I just so happened to have a mess in my diaper at that moment. What if I…what if I just reach in there, wrap my little fingers around the mess, pull it out. So squishy, so smelly. What if I just took this squishy smelly mess and rubbed it all over the couch? There we go. Cover as much as I can. Get under the cushions and- Oh, there's one of the big ones now. They can see what I did and- HOORAY! There's that face. That funny, funny face. I like it when they make that face.

The next moment I was at my fifth birthday party. There were no other kids there because they're all so stupid and annoying.

They'd wanna touch my stuff and do dumb things like pin the tail on the donkey or other baby crap. I stared up into the faces of my parents. They were smiling. Good. I hope that meant they learned their lesson from last year. I have my suspicions but, as I hungrily tear through my presents, it seems like they're on the right track. These two idiots usually don't get anything right but everything I've asked for is here so maybe- Wait…I've just opened the last present. Where the hell is the big yellow Tonka truck? I asked for a BIG. YELLOW. TONKA. TRUCK! DID THESE IDIOTS FORGET?! WHY ARE THEY SO STUPID?! WHY IS EVERYONE SO STUPID!? DO THEY LIKE IT WHEN I BREAK THINGS?! DO THEY ENJOY IT WHEN I BITE THEM?! WHY DO THEY LIKE TO HEAR ME SCREAM????!!!! WHY WHY WHY WHY WHY WHY W

I was standing over an ant hill covering it in gasoline that I'd stolen from the garage. I'd just seen in a book how an ant hill is made from all these tunnels and there are millions of ants inside that go to and fro. Those little idiots. They think they're safe underground. They never once considered that somebody far smarter and bigger could do whatever he wants to them and there is nothing they could do to stop him. Even though I can't see it, I imagine their confusion as the tunnels fill with gasoline and they begin to choke on it, gasping for breath. But I am merciful, and I end that suffering when I light the hill on fire. Instead of choking, they quickly fry and pop and burn. Hoo boy, if this isn't one of the best days of my life then I don't know-Hey, wait a minute. That chubby kid from school is looking at me. I always see him crying in the playground. Makes me sick. Why's he looking at me? What's his problem? Why do people insist on ruining my good time? I'm going to teach him a lesson. Look, the piggy's running. Get back here piggy, I'm gonna barbecue your head!

On and on I lived this short, mean life. I felt all the slights of every human being I had ever known cut me deep and the only thing that ever healed those wounds was revenge. But revenge could only quiet my rage for so long and soon it would build up and up. It was a rage that came from living in a world that does not understand how special I am. This world surrounds me with idiots and weaklings, from my parents who were afraid of me, to the kids at school who were utterly worthless and needed reminding of that fact. The worst part about it is that they walked around thinking they were my equals. If they were my equals, why did I hold the power to hurt them? Why were the weak and pathetic allowed to live? Why? WHY? WHY WHY WHY WHY WHY WHY WHY WHY WHY WHY WHY

"WHHHHHHHHHHHYYYYYYYYYYYYYYYYYYYYY!!!! !!!!!!!!!!!" I screamed as I came back to the banks of the creek. Collins' hand was still on my throat, but there was no force in the grip. Collins was staring at me, just as I was staring at him. He took his hand from my throat. I knew in that moment that he had just experienced the same thing as I. He had lived my life. Somehow, The Anointed One had made us walk in the other's shoes. In my heart weighed all of Collins' deepest secrets and fears. I could feel his passions and joys inside of me. I could still sense how hamburgers and hot dogs and cakes tasted differently on his tongue. I also knew that he now carried everything that was me inside of him. We now understood the other more completely than any friend, brother, sister, or true love ever could.

"What have you both to say now?" The Anointed One said as Collins' hand fell from their throat.

We looked into each other's eyes.

"You," I sputtered. "You are a completely awful person."

"You," he sputtered back. "You are a whiny little piss baby."

Then, with the complete knowledge of everything thing that I was, Collins kicked me in between my legs, and I collapsed. The Anointed One lifted their snake hand, ready to strike, but Collins quickly grabbed their wrist.

"Naw, I don't think so," Collins said. "Jesus, I can't believe how dumb you are. You just made me live piggy's whole life. I know exactly what you can do with this hand. God, so stupid. Was your plan really to make us see life through the other's eyes? To make us understand each other. That's how you were going to make peace?"

The Anointed One was now struggling to get out of Collins' grip. I tried to get up to help but I was barely able to suck in any air and what air there was available was thick with smoke.

"Didn't work," Collins laughed. "All you did was make me hate that piece of crap even more. But I was laughing my ass off at all the bad stuff that happened to him. You're going to have to show me that again some time."

"Please, Griffin Collins," The Anointed One pleaded. "Life doesn't have to be this way."

Collins lifted The Anointed One off the ground by the arm and dangled them in mid-air. "Naw, it does. I like it this way."

I knew what Collins was about to do before he did it, and I so wished I could have stopped it. But my legs gave way as I tried to stand and I could barely get out a "No!" as Collins lowered The Anointed One, took their right arm in both hands and then snapped the bone on his leg like he was breaking a stick. He then ripped off their mask, partly because he'd always wanted to do it, but mainly so that he could see the tears.

I will not describe what The Anointed One looked like under the mask. That was something they had never offered to show me and neither Collins nor I had any right to see it. It was a complete violation, and I am sick to my stomach for having been there to witness it.

What I will say though, is that if Collins was expecting to find tears under the mask, he was sorely disappointed. All that lay under it was rage. A rage so incandescent that it made the lifelong hissy fit that had fueled Collins look like the pathetic, drawn-out tantrum that it was. Collins was not prepared for that look of anger, or the fact that the breaking of bone had seemingly caused no pain. He let go of the shattered arm which fell limply to The Anointed One's side.

"What…what are you doing?" Collins said as he slowly backed away. "Why are you looking at me like that? What's wrong with you?"

The anger in The Anointed One's eyes suddenly gave way to an emptiness and they started to chant. I recognized the language from poetry they had shared but could not discern the meaning of the words. Slowly, The Anointed One raised the shattered limb. The upper forearm hung at a 45-degree angle to the rest of the arm. The chanting grew louder.

"Stop it!" Collins screamed, still backing away. "Stop it or I'll kill you! I WILL KI-" he stumbled over a large rock in the bank and fell on his back.

The Anointed One stopped chanting. Neither I nor Collins were breathing.

Suddenly, The Anointed One's broken arm snapped back into place with a sickening crunch. Collins screamed, got to his feet, and began to limp away as fast as he could.

I watched mesmerized as huge fangs sprouted from The Anointed One's fingers and the snake tattoo seemed to come to life, its scales popping out of their skin. The snake grew and swallowed their arm until what I had always referred to as their snake hand had become a giant living serpent. A bright purple liquid dripped from its fangs, and it had blazing red eyes like the rubies in the stone altar. Those terrible eyes were fixed on the retreating Collins.

"Help! Help me!" Collins bleated as his limp barely covered any ground.

The serpent opened its mouth wide and let out a venomous hiss. With one fluid motion, the snake whipped back and then shot forward, stretching at least 30 feet to catch Collins' left shoulder in its jaws. Collins let out a scream of agony as the snake lifted him in the air and shook him violently. He started making panicked, animal sounds like a rabbit caught in a trap when the jaws clenched tighter, and he was no longer able to make any noise. Soon, his body grew limp, and he hung like a rag doll from the serpent's maw. After a couple more shakes, the serpent dropped Collins with a wet thud into the creek. The serpent's head hovered over the prone body looking for signs of life.

The combination of heat, smoke, kick to the groin, and absolute terror conspired to make me vomit which was lucky because it broke me out of the stupor the serpent's arrival had put me under. I crawled towards The Anointed One, keeping an eye on the head of the monster that extended from their arm. It paid me no attention.

"Are you okay? Can you hear me?" I whispered into their exposed ear. Their eyes were empty. "Can you hear me, Anointed One?" Still nothing. I could see that the fire would be on top of us in minutes and, regardless of the serpent, I had to save my friend. I wrapped my arms around their tiny waist and lifted them. The hiss from behind was loud and immediate. I turned and the serpent had its terrible eyes fixed on me, fangs bared. I lowered The Anointed One back to the ground and, just as I let them go, the massive head flew right at me and sent me flying five feet back.

I landed hard on my left knee, but that pain was overshadowed by the one in my right arm. The source of the pain was a huge gash that had the same purplish fluid from the snake's fangs seeping from it. A fang must have grazed the arm when it rammed me. I felt woozy, my head was spinning. I was dimly aware of the unbearable heat of the fire growing closer and of the serpent's face hovering above me. The fangs glinted in the firelight and the blistering red of the eyes shone like the blood of Hell. I could see the muscles tighten as it got ready to strike. The venom was making my head spin, and I had no wish to see what was about to happen, so I closed my eyes and involuntarily spoke what I was sure would be my last words, the only thought swirling around my brain at that moment.

"What would Darby do?"

The bite never came. I opened my eyes. My vision was swimming, but I could just make out the serpent's head which was inches from my face. The ruby red murderousness had been replaced by something else. Someone else. The Anointed One. I gave my friend inside the serpent a weak smile.

Suddenly, there was a loud bang. I couldn't be sure what it was as I was too weak to move my head and look, but it must have been Collins' gas can which had finally alighted. The fire was on top of us and for the second time that day I closed my eyes and waited for death. I was dimly aware of the serpent's jaw gently closing around my waist and there seemed to be a great rush of wind and the sense of soaring and I thought to myself that death didn't feel so bad before losing consciousness.

The rain woke me up. The clouds had finally unleashed their torrent. The serpent's head hovered over my injured arm. Even in the rain I could see bright yellow liquid falling from its fangs. This new poison fell on the gash, and I tensed as the wound sizzled. The wound began to close, and a bright green scab was forming over it. The nausea and wooziness left my body. When the last of the yellow liquid fell, the serpent looked at me, smiled, and then slowly lowered its head to lie next to me.

I sat up. We were easily two miles down from where the willow tree once stood, still on the banks of the creek. The smoke from the fires was far off and in the deluge that was falling, it didn't seem like they had much chance of lasting.

I turned to the serpent. Its eyes were closed. I reached out my hand to touch it, but it began to shrink and recede. As it got smaller and further away, I finally noticed The Anointed One lying flat on the bank at the other end of the serpent. Soon the serpent shrank completely back into their arm and was once again just a tattoo.

I got up and ran to The Anointed One. I tried to rouse them. Nothing. They were still breathing but whatever had just happened had taken so much out of them. I knew that the only people that could possibly help them were their parents, so I gathered them into my arms. As I did this, in the now swelling and rushing waters of the creek, I could see Griffin Collins float by. There was purple smoke streaming out of the wounds around his shoulder. He was, astonishingly, still alive. He was looking straight into the sky, his mouth moved but no words came out. He floated on and that was the last time I saw the worst person I ever knew.

I ran back as fast as my pitiful body would allow me. I got The Anointed One back to their home and told their parents everything that happened. I asked if we should take them to the hospital and they said no. They quickly bundled up The Anointed One into their remaining car and told me that everything would be fine once they got them back to Antarctica. They pulled out and drove off. I stood in their driveway for a few moments, the rain still coming down, and then waved at nobody.

"Goodbye," I said.

I sat up in my room in my wet clothes and thought about what had happened. The scab on my arm pulsed and I could feel the arm swell. A sort of bright purple luminescence peaked through the cracks in the scab with every beat of my heart. I paid it no attention. I didn't care about my arm because the enormity of my situation hit me.

My friends were gone.

All of them.

I had no idea if they were happy or safe.

I was probably never going to see any of them again, regardless.

I was alone.

Just like before.

I laid in my bed. I didn't move. I didn't sleep. I simply existed.

At midnight, I heard the laughter. It floated through the window, and I knew it was meant for me. It was a mocking laugh, coming from somewhere in the distance.

I sat up. I don't know how I knew, but I was certain that the laughter was coming from the other side of town. I walked downstairs and opened the front door. The laughter grew louder and the pain in my arm increased. I stepped out into the night and headed for the car wash.

ALONE PART 4:

RETURN TO THE TALL GRASS BEYOND THE CAR WASH

The rain had stopped, and the air was thick and close. The empty, midnight avenues and alleyways of the town I grew up in seemed to take no notice of the maniacal laughter that was drawing me closer and closer to my doom. I soon realized that the cackling was only inside my head and the good people of Aickman were left unbothered as they dreamt their little dreams while yet another child was about to disappear forever.

I never told my friends about The Tall Grass Beyond The Car Wash because I wanted to protect them. If I had mentioned the hungry, brain invading grass that waved against the wind, they would have wanted to check it out and possibly been devoured. Even after it tried to take me into the TV, I still said nothing because I was the target, and they were safer not knowing. Like Darby's house, Eddie's death, and Jason's origins, The Tall Grass had become my secret.

Now, with everyone gone, my secret was calling.

As I made my way across town, I found myself taking little detours. I stopped by the tree from which I witnessed Chad Pennington's disastrous game of tag. I thought about Chad and how he was the first kid to disappear from Aickman that summer. I so wished that I could have taken the burden of "It" from him that day. I didn't like Chad, but he didn't deserve what happened. Like my friends, I had no idea where he was or if he was okay, but I hoped that he and his family had found help in a place far from Aickman.

I went to the town square to look at the desecrated statue of Mayor Deer and acknowledge the one good thing that Griffin Collins had ever done in his life.

I passed by Darby's laughing house. Part of me took some joy in the rotted wreckage of the creature that took my friend from me. But I also recognized that The House was just one of many souls that this town never wanted and would never mourn. As far as secrets went, Darby's was much better than mine.

Really, though, I was just stalling. But the time for stalling was over.

By the time I reached the car wash, the laughter had stopped. My entire body was numb save for my right arm which had now swelled to twice it's normal size from the serpent's poison. The green scab resembled a giant leech and the cracks in it were growing bigger, the purple light underneath peeking out more and more. I was certain that this magical infection was going to kill me, but that didn't seem like it would be an issue for much longer.

In the light of the moon, I could see that the car wash was littered with garbage. The broken glass of soda and beer bottles carpeted the lot, and the bays were covered in graffiti. Water poured out of the first bay and the sickly yellow light within revealed that one of the hoses had been ripped out and nobody had bothered to stop the leak.

I crunched over the broken glass and made my way past the bays.

The Tall Grass Beyond The Car Wash was beautiful in the moonlight. The brilliant emerald was now a liquid silver, and the undersea swaying of the metallic seeming blades was even more mesmerizing than I'd remembered. Again, I was filled with visions of all the incredible things that must lay within that miraculous jungle: Mile high water falls that empty into crystal clear pools where you can see deep, deep into the Earth. (Darby) Lost cities filled with people who knew nothing of the rest of the world and where the laws of reality and nature held no sway. (Eddie) Glittering palaces filled with pizza rolls and basements crammed with videotapes that you could spend endless weekends watching. (Jason) A tall and gloomy willow tree on the banks of a lifeless creek where the wait for one of your friends to arrive was never very long. (The Anoin-

I shook my head to banish the thoughts. That's when I noticed Garvey Towne.

The car wash attendant seemed to have lost a considerable amount of weight since I saw him last. His clothes were loose, and he now gave off the impression of an abandoned tent rather than a walking garbage heap. He was maybe ten feet from The Tall Grass, staring at it. His bulging bags of tokens were hanging limply from his right hand which rested by his side.

"Mr. Towne?" I called. He didn't notice. "Garvey Towne?" I tried again. He didn't move. Remembering his use of boots during our last encounter but being mindful of the sea of glass all around, I picked up a crumpled can of coke and hurled it at his head with my injured arm which caused me to cry out in pain and the scab to writhe. The can caught him squarely in the back of the head and his orange baseball cap slid off. Still no response.

I walked towards the man who had never admitted to saving my life at the start of the summer. When I got next to him, I could see a glazed look in his eyes. I tugged on the sleeve of his work shirt and pleaded with him to wake up. I pulled on his arm and screamed in his face, but nothing roused him. Finally, I grabbed the bag of tokens. I pulled a fistful of them out and launched them at the silvery fronds of the grass. I could hear a little chuckle inside my head.

"Tokens don't work anymore," the voice next to me whispered. "It's been a bad summer." I looked up to see that life had returned to his eyes, but his attention was still taken up by the grass.

"Mr. Towne, are you okay?"

"Oh yeah, sure. I'm always okay. Never got a care in the world does old Garvey."

"Mr. Towne, what happened here? Why is the car wash trashed?" I asked.

"That's how the people like it," he said.

"What do you mean?"

"What do you think I mean?" he asked, now swaying with the grass. "The people trash the car wash so that means they like it that way. They like broken glass everywhere and garbage piling up or else why would they do it? I was the sap cleaning it up for so long. When you clean up one mess, another's waiting. It never stops. Why fight it? The customer is always right."

"Mr. Towne, I think you need to get out of here. You need to go home."

"Why?" He finally looked down at me. "What's there? A big broken chair and a tv with nothing on? Home is the last place Garvey Towne needs to be. It's time for a change of scenery. I was thinking of a place. I think I visited there once when I was little. I remember the grass being so tall. A hundred feet tall. It went on forever and you just knew there was something amazing waiting for you inside. You ever hear of a place like that?" he asked, looking back at The Tall Grass.

"Please, Mr. Towne, whatever it's showing you, whatever it's telling you, it's not true, not real. Don't listen to it."

He looked down at me. "Remember when I told you about the punks?"

"Yes, Mr. Towne."

"I forgot to mention one thing."

"What's that?"

"The punks win, kid. They always do," he whispered as he began shuffling towards the grass. I held onto his arm, pleading with him to stop, but he just dragged me along. As he reached the edge of The Grass, the stalks parted and I pulled with all my might, but my injured arm spasmed and I let him go. He stepped through the stalks which closed behind him as he passed. I expected to hear a scream, but it never came. Instead, the laughter started again.

"WHAT'S SO FUNNY?!" I screamed at The Tall Grass.

(You had to be there.)

"I am here."

(And I can't thank you enough for visiting. I had worried that I hadn't made a big enough impression. The worst thing that anybody could ever do is forget all about you. But I don't have to tell you that.)

"What happened to Garvey Towne? Why was he acting like that?"

(I believe the syndrome that Garvey Towne was suffering from is referred to as being a big stupid crybaby who couldn't take it anymore. It's a condition I think you're very familiar with.)

"Mr. Towne wasn't a crybaby, and neither am I."

(Really? How do you come by that incredibly erroneous conclusion? Do you actually believe you've grown over your wonderfully horrid summer? Are you a big boy now? Have you developed that callus on the soul that humanity mistakes for maturity? Please. That armor is as thin and brittle as lottery scratchings.)

"What do you know about my summer?"

(Absolutely everything! I saw it all. My roots run through the entirety of this town. They stretch from the scrublands in the south to the Screaming Forest in the north. They bathe in the pollution neath The Southern Lights and sip the dead waters of God Help Us, They're Killing Us Creek. I have buds flowering in every yard, garden, and sidewalk crack throughout this wonderful, wonderful Aickman.)

"So, it's you, then? It's always been you? You're the reason Aickman is the way it is?"

(You give me too much credit. I'm no ancient evil from the dawn of time manipulating destinies. I'm just a hungry plant looking for my next meal. I have no idea why Aickman is the way it is. This town often shocks me more than anyone. For example, those roaches in your basement that ate my delightful avatar Dak Anner, what in the world was that about?)

"They were probably just mad because that tv show you made sucked so bad," I said. At that, the stalks of The Tall Grass tensed and shook with fury. It was a seething I would come to recognize later as that of an artist who can't handle criticism. After a few seconds, the stalks relaxed and resumed their hypnotic swaying.

(Regardless, my only certainty about Aickman is that it makes everyone miserable. It's an insidious misery that blinds the people to the wonders that surround them and leaves them willing prey to fat and sweaty clowns like Beef Burlington. It is a misery born of so little yet is so flabby and juicy. Aickman produces so much misery and, until I came, nobody was doing anything with it. That didn't seem right to me. So, I set down my roots here where my stalks could pluck it from the air and feed.)

"You eat misery?"

(Gorge on it. Stuff myself silly.)

"If Aickman makes so much misery, then why pick on me, or Mr. Garcia, or Garvey Towne? If you can just suck the misery out of the air, why do you need our bodies?"

(Because you're delicious. You're a concentrated blob of the most pathetic kind of sadness. To put it into terms you'll understand, you're like a pizza roll, but instead of small chunks of questionable meat and ooze that isn't legally cheese, you're filled with buttery, salty sorrow. Yes, I more than thrive off my diet of Aickman's airborne misery, but the pleasure of flesh marinated in tears and longing is just so...)

A series of frankly obscene noises gurgled and sloshed around my brain. "So, you're nothing more than a greedy parasite?" I said, hoping to get another rise out of it and make the noises stop.

(Takes one to know one.)

"What does that mean?"

(It means you take and never give, just like me. Why do you think we get along so well? I am this town's parasite just as you were your friend's parasite.)

"That's not true!"

(Of course it is. Those four with their incredible secrets and wonderful abilities and what did you have to offer them? Insecurity, doubt, and occasionally someone to rescue.)

"You're talking crap. I may not be anything special, but we looked out for each other."

(They looked after you, yes, but when were you ever there for them? Why did you do nothing to help Eddie, to break him out of his cycle?)

"What could I do!?"

(How about something? How about anything? How about not leaving a friend to suffer?)

I knew full well that it was only saying these things to feed off the misery stirring up in my guts, but the words stung as bad as the pain in my throbbing arm. "If I could have saved him, I would've. What's happening to Eddie is beyond me."

(What about earlier today? Was that beyond you? You're bigger than The Anointed One. It was your job to protect them, not the other way around. If you were any kind of friend, you would have stopped Collins from doing what he did. Instead, The Serpent was unleashed and The Anointed One paid the price!)

I wanted to yell something back, but I couldn't. As the events of the day replayed in my mind for the hundredth time, the sound of bone cracking echoed in my ears and tears welled in my eyes.

(And Darby...)

"Don't you talk about her!" I snapped.

(You never once asked her about her life. It was a miserable one. Compared to the house of horrors she faced, your life was a parking lot carnival. She was forced into the role of protector. Your weakness meant that she had to be the strong one and it's a role she played for so long that there was no one for her to turn to or confide in. There was no one to understand her. No one, save for my wretched sister.)

I blinked the tears out of my eyes, shocked. "Sister...The House?!"

(Yes, my dear sister. We arrived in Aickman at the same time along with our idiot brother The Cake. Always jealous of me and my beauty, my despicable sister knew how much I wanted that lost little girl. If you're a pizza roll, then Darby was Thanksgiving and Christmas dinner topped with Halloween candy. But my sister caught Darby in her web. Infected her first. If I had tried to eat her flesh after that, she would have tasted of ash and rust.)

My stomach dropped as my worst fear had been confirmed. "The House was evil?"

(Oh yes, completely. And a coward. She feared my wrath for taking Darby from me. She knew I would retaliate. That's why she used Darby as a battery to power that ridiculous escape in the guise of a skateboard.)

"So, they did escape?" I said, grabbing on to any hope that I could. "Where are they now?"

(I have no idea and could care less where my sister has gone. As for Darby, well, let's just say she went Away.)

"What does that mean?"

(I mean she went where everyone goes when they're no longer around: Away.)

"Away is not a place."

(Where do you think your mother went so soon after having you? Where do you think your grandfather is right now?)

"They're both dead."

(And who do you think lives in Away? The dead, obviously.)

"Darby's not dead," I whispered, more to myself than The Grass.

(There is a land inside of me, beyond terror and pain. A place where misery never reaches because I chew and digest it. That place is called Away. That's where Darby has gone.)

"I know you're lying. I know Darby escaped. She isn't inside of you. You've already told me that you never got to eat her."

(Alas, I never did get to taste her despairing flesh, but do you remember when she shot into that collapsing sky?)

Suddenly, a spike seemed to drill through my skull and the memory invaded my mind.

(That was my sister chewing her up, sucking her energy.)

The psychic spike took me up above the clouds on that fateful day. I saw Darby screaming in agony as she was ripped, torn, and consumed by translucent tendrils snaking out of her skateboard.

"NO!" I shouted, slapping my head to rid myself of the vision.

(When the body was gone, my sister spit out her ragged soul and it fell from the sky.)

"Shut up!" I yelled as I saw the tattered and ghostly remains of my friend's soul fall to the Earth and land right next to me as I searched the skies on that day. Her soul extended a bleeding, transparent hand to me, but I couldn't see it.

(Ignored and forgotten, it pulled its bruised and bloodied form across the Earth that no longer wanted it.)

I let out strangled cries as I saw the broken soul claw and scratch its way across the entire town for days, never finding the help it needed, until it reached The Grass.

(I was the only one that extended my stalks in friendship.)

"PLEASE!"

(Though robbed of my feast of flesh, I took pity and gave the wretched remnants of Darby entrance to the kingdom within me. A home in Away.)

I couldn't take it any longer. I put a hand around the swollen flesh of the scabbed serpent bite and squeezed. The scab cracked and warm fluid leaked onto my hand. The blinding agony pushed The Grass' psychic spike from my mind. Once the pain subsided, I reached down and picked up shards of glass and spilled tokens from the ground and launched them at The Grass, screaming the whole time.

The Grass continued to sway back and forth, unbothered.

(I understand that the truth can be difficult. I think what you need right now is to see a friendly face.)

Suddenly, the stalks parted and the horror that walked out of The Grass stopped my screaming. The shattered glass and tokens fell from my now bleeding hands.

It was Darby. She was the same moonlight silver as The Grass. Her flannel and blue jeans were shredded and torn. There were gashes in the flesh of her face and arms from which thick black fluid was leaking. She looked every bit like the chewed-up soul I saw in my head.

But the worst part were the eyes. They weren't empty and dead like I'd expected. Like I'd hoped. No, they were very much alive.

"Hey, Weirdo," the ghoulish vision waved.

Struck dumb with terror, I could do nothing but wave back.

"Cool arm. Rocking the Popeye look? Bold," said the thing with my friend's face.

"You're…. you're not Darby," I finally managed to hiss.

"I wish. Sucks to be me, huh?" the being shrugged.

"Darby's not dead," I again whispered to myself.

"You're just going to have to trust me on this, Weirdo. I was an idiot who was murdered by a house. It sucks but then so does everything. We just have to live with it. Or, I guess, die with it in my case."

I turned away from the creature and started repeating "Darby's not dead" over and over like a chant or prayer. "Darby's not dead Darby's not dead Darby's not dead Darby's not-"

"I'll prove it," the being said. "I'll tell you things that only I would know."

"-dead Darby's not dead Darby's not dead Darby's-"

"There was the time I made you stand as look out while I stole eye shadow at Sanderson's grocery-"

"-not dead Darby's not dead Darby's-"

"-and you got so nervous you puked all over the shampoos and then begged Mr. Sanderson to let you work for him until you paid off all the damage."

"-not dead Darby's not dead Darby's not-"

"Or the time you begged me to lend you that one run of Hellblazer comics even though I kept telling you that you couldn't handle them?"

"Dead Darby's Not Dead Darby's Not Dead-"

"So, I let you have them and then you gave them back the very next day and had nightmares for weeks after."

"Darby's Not DEAD Darby's Not DEAD-"

"Or how about every time you ever accidentally called me mom?"

"DARBY'S NOT DEAD DARBY'S NOT DEAD DARBY'S NOT DEAD-"

"You'd get so embarrassed and start to tear up."

"DARBY'S NOT DEAD! DARBY'S NOT DEAD! DARBY'S NOT DEAD!"

"I'd never make fun of you for it. I was actually kind of touched. Once or twice I even gave you a great big hug."

"THIS MEANS NOTHING!" I finally screamed at the creature. "The Tall Grass sees everything. It would know all about me and Darby. This is a trick. You're not real! Darby Is Not Dead!"

"Fair enough," it nodded. "But then ask yourself this: Based on everything else that happened this summer, what do you think is the most likely thing to have happened to me that day?"

Trying not to picture that day again only made the memory return stronger and more vivid than ever. I saw her launch into the sky. I saw the sky collapse. I knew how the scales of justice fell in Aickman. Even though The Grass was a liar, that didn't change the certainty in my heart that I'd been trying to bury under a mountain of delusional hope.

"You're…you're not," I muttered. "I…I tried…I tried to save you."

"Yeah, I know. I saw. It wouldn't have worked. That's not your fault, though. I shouldn't have made you guys build me my own personal suicide machine."

"Darby, I'm so sorry I wasn't there for you."

"A little late, but it's whatever," the being shrugged. "Actually, dying is the best thing to ever happen to me. Like, for real. All I ever wanted to do was escape Aickman, and I did. The Away is amazing. I don't have the words to describe it, but I know someone who might."

The being turned its head to the right as another section of grass parted. Out walked Eddie, the same gleaming silver as Darby. His black eye was swollen shut and the scars on his face were raw slashes leaking the black fluid.

"Eddie," I breathed.

"Hey, there he is, Doubting Thomas!" Eddie laughed. "I hope you won't be saying that Eddie Gone ain't dead, cuz, let me tell you, Eddie Gone is for sure dead."

"How…how did you get here?"

"I live here. Always have done since my aunt murdered me. My horribly violent death guaranteed that I'd become a spook doomed to roam the land forever. The Grass here was kind enough to give me a place to stay. Made a deal with me: Every ten years I get sent back out with my mind erased, make some friends, have some times, and then when I realize I'm dead, I relive said death, and get sucked back in. The Grass gets to eat all that recycled misery and I get to play in The Away for ten more years."

"That's horrible, Eddie," I said, not sure how I was still on my feet and not curled in a ball on the glass covered lot.

"Hey, there's no such thing as a free ride," Eddie said. "Eddie Gone always pays his way. I ain't no freeloader. Not like some people."

Just then, another figure walked out of the grass. It was Jason Human. He looked far worse than the other two. His once bulbous head now hung like the remains of a burst balloon from his neck. The only remaining feature on the collapsed, leaking alien meat was his mouth which rested upside down against his chest. I gagged at the sight of him.

"Please," the mouth on the meat sack said. "I know you're excited beyond belief to see me, but you must control yourself."

At this point, I lost the ability to speak or form rational thoughts. I just stood there and smiled at the three awful visions in front of me.

"Uh oh, looks like we broke Weirdo." Darby said.

"Aw man," Eddie said. "He was supposed to ask Jason what happened to his head. I love that story!"

"I don't think he's in a state to comprehend anything," Jason said.

"No way, come on, you gotta tell it," Eddie said, turning to me. "You gotta hear this, you're going to love it!" He turned back to Jason. "Come on, dangly face, tell it!"

Jason let out a wet sigh. "All right, if I must." The mouth then took a deep breath which sounded like bubbles being blown into milk. "The unfortunate circumstances of my demise can be wholly blamed-"

"So, he gets rescued, right?" Eddie cut in. "And all the way through the untold expanses of space, he's expecting to get this hero's welcome, a parade and a space key to a space city and all that. But when he gets back, the only thing he gets is a bill for the rescue operation. It's like an ungodly amount, like 50 bajillion grublacks or whatever, I don't know, I don't mess with un-American money. So, he gets this bill, and he can't possibly pay it cuz he hasn't had a job for two years cuz he's been busy hanging out with a bunch of kids. The debt is so heinous that the got dang president of the planet personally sentences him to death. They stuck a hose into his skull, filled it up and up with air until his head just went POP!" he finished, throwing his hands in the air.

"POP!" I shouted, mirroring his movement.

"Yeah! POP!" Eddie called back, both of us jumping and throwing our hands in the air at the same time.

"An ignorant if concise retelling of the end of Jason Human," Jason said. "Oh, and I don't think I ever thanked you all enough for saving my soul. Lord knows I wouldn't want to miss a second of an eternity where my head is a floppy blood sack. It was really an honor being rejected by both Heaven and Hell, two places I'd spent my life assured were complete fictions and forced to find refuge in a patch of psychotic grass whose greatest ambition, it seems, is to depress a small child to a point that he will allow himself to be consumed. THANK YOU! THANK YOU SO MUCH! I WOULDN'T WANT TO MISS A SECOND OF THIS!"

"He hasn't taken his death as well as some of us," Darby said.

"POP!" was the only thing I could think to say.

(And now, I have a surprise for all of you.)

"Whoah, I thought Weirdo over there was the only one supposed to be surprised," Eddie said.

(He was. But I didn't plan this. We've got a new arrival.)

I was still giggling as my destroyed mind kept picturing Jason's head exploding over and over again. The giggling stopped as soon as the last figure of that night stepped out of the grass.

It was The Anointed One, of course.

"Hoo boy! The gang's all here!" Eddie shouted.

"Sweet! When did you get here?" Darby asked.

"Only minutes ago," The Anointed One whispered. "My body gave out on the plane back to Antarctica. I can still feel my mother's arms around my corpse. I still sense the warmth of her tears falling on my cheeks."

"Aren't you supposed to be one with The Serpent now, or some other such nonsense?" Jason's mouth bubbled.

"I was unworthy of being The Serpent's avatar. My physical form could not handle it. I was a false prophet. Everything I had been taught was a lie."

"Yeah, death is like that," Darby said.

"Rejected by The Serpent, The Away was the only home left to me," The Anointed One said. "It is the only home for those the world does not want." The Anointed One lifted their ghostly snake hand toward me in welcome. "Won't you, my dearest friend, join us in these forever lands where you may finally wake from this summer of nightmares?"

As I stared at the four figures of my lost friends standing before me, I thought about something The Anointed One had said only the day before. "Wouldn't it be nice…" Well, wouldn't it?

A part of me was certain that everything I was witnessing was a lie, but The Tall Grass was, above all else, a salesman. A salesman's job is to make us believe in lies and though I didn't believe what I was seeing, I believed in the lie it was selling.

I believed it would be nice to be a silver and bleeding child of midnight playing in The Tall Grass just like I saw us playing in the flames of the tree. I believed that the people I cared about most in the world were gone and that this was my only chance of being with them again. I also believed that The Grass was the only creature left in Aickman that understood me and what I was going through. Even though all it wanted was to devour me, it at least wanted something from me.

I couldn't say that about anyone else in town.

As I stood there on the verge of completing the sale and purchasing the lie, my wounded arm suddenly exploded in pain. The swollen flesh began to pulse, twitch and bulge. I fell to my knees, screaming.

"What's up with Weirdo?" Darby asked.

"It's...The Serpent's venom," The Anointed One said. "I...tried to cure him, but...uh... being an imperfect vessel, it didn't work."

I flipped onto my back as another jolt of pain ripped through my arm.

"Jeez, this is almost as bad as when I was murdered," Eddie said.

"How much longer will the venom take?" Jason's mouth asked. "His screaming is very annoying."

"Uh...the pain will wrack him for hours. Days, even," The Anointed One's ghostly frame proclaimed as it floated towards me.

"Oh. So, we'll just come back later, then?" Jason said.

The Anointed One lowered one ghostly hand to my arm. The cold of their touch caused steam to rise from the heat of my flesh. The Anointed One pulled back their hand in pain. I let out another scream.

"This is the worst death imaginable!" The Anointed One shouted, raising their hands into the air. "The venom of The Serpent will destroy each of your cells one by one until you are nothing more than a writhing mass of fluids! Please, my friend, there is no need to suffer."

"Seriously, dying is the worst part of death," Darby said.

"Yeah, you're better off just doing what none of us got to and skip this part," Eddie said.

"These three won't come out and say it, so I will. JUST WALK INTO THE GRASS ALREADY!" Jason's mouth flailed.

As I twisted on the asphalt lot surrounded by voices begging me to kill myself, I felt my arm rip open. The scab had torn off completely and fell with a wet splotch to the ground. Bright, neon purple fluid sprayed from my arm as I felt something moving around beneath my flesh. I looked down in horror as I watched a slimy, solid mass wriggle out of the wound.

I recognized the being immediately: It was The Worm from my Mr. Garcia nightmares. It was now nearly a foot long and covered in a tar like slime. It oozed its way up my arm. The pain was getting worse and worse, so I kept screaming which meant I wasn't able to close my mouth when The Worm launched itself down my throat. It tasted of blood and burnt toast. I felt it wriggle its way down to my stomach and then stop moving.

"I spoke to The Anointed One in their coma," The Worm's voice rumbled from deep within my guts. "They created a bridge. I travelled from the nightmare realm into the venom. They are awake now. We have a plan."

Suddenly, the pain lessened. I could see the four phantom friends in front of me still talking, but I couldn't hear their words. I couldn't hear anything except for a low hiss that seemed to be coming from up above. I tilted my head skywards and in the center of the full moon was the face of The Serpent. It had the same eyes I saw earlier that day. The Anointed One's eyes. The real Anointed One.

The Serpent opened its mouth and from it fell my entire summer.

I saw the toe fight and all of us coming together to stand with The Anointed One on the 4th of July. I saw the sheer look of joy on Darby's face right before she rocketed up into the sky. I saw Eddie, Jason, and The Anointed One join hands on my porch to send me what help they could during The Grass' television assault. I saw all the moments of happiness buried deep within the desert of sorrow that was the summer of '93. The lie The Tall Grass was selling could not stand up to the simple truth of my memories. The frauds The Grass had presented me with could never hope to match the real thing. I knew who my friends were and what they meant to me. They were my strength, not my destruction.

The face of The Serpent disappeared from the moon, the pain returned to my arm, and a familiar voice entered my head. It had apparently been talking for some time.

(...and so you see, there is no need to die in such pain. I promise you, just walk through my stalks and the nightmare will end. You and your friends can play forever in The Away. I know you want it. It's the only reason you came here tonight.)

"HA!" I screamed through the pain.

(What's so funny?)

"You had to be there!" I yelled, wracked with another spasm from my leaking arm.

(Is this a last show of bravado before the inevitable?)

"No, it's just setting the record straight," I hissed as I rolled back onto my knees. "I didn't come here for you to eat me."

(Then why did you come?)

"Yeah, that don't make no sense," Eddie said.

"You may have finally got the eyes right on your creations, but your Eddie sucks," I taunted. "The roaches were right, you're a terrible writer. You only saw what Eddie talked like but never paid attention to what he said. He would never make a deal with a bully like you. If there was one thing Eddie Gone wasn't, it was a bully."

Darby stepped forward, "Look Weirdo, being dead means that-"

"Oh, shut up," I rounded on the ghoul. "I spent way too much time thinking about What Would Darby Do to even think that she would mention those times I called her mom. She was too cool for that. I have no idea if she's alive or dead, but I am certain she is far, far from here right noaaaaaauguugug!" I shouted as my arm sent up another flare of agony.

"Being this close to death has scrambled his brains," Jason's mouth flapped.

"As for your Jason: it's perfect. Absolutely nailed it. Makes sense that he would be the only one of us that you actually understood," I said through gritted teeth.

"The Serpent's venom-" The Anointed One started.

"Is killing me? Maybe. Maybe not," I said, as more and more of the purplish fluid flowed out of my arm. "But what I am certain of is that The Anointed One isn't dead. Wherever they are right now, they just used their mind powers to make a nightmare worm crawl out of my arm and into my mouth causing me to see a serpent in the moon who just vomited up my entire summer in the sky!"

(....what?)

"Yeah, exactly, that's how cool my friends are. They would never hang out with a loser like yooAAAAAHHHHHH!" I was cut off as the fluid was now spraying from my arm in heavy spurts.

(Really now, you're just making a mess and causing a scene.)

"Yeah, because I'm pissed off!" I said, finally getting to my feet to face The Grass. "I know you like misery, but how does anger taste? Fury?! AAAAAHHHHH, God it hurts! You stupid weeds! I didn't come here tonight to get eaten. I came here to have a good laugh. A good laugh at the most pathetic creature that lives in the crappiest little town on Earth. You tried two times to eat me. You created a whole land of fiction in my television set just to get at me, and you absolutely failed! Getting eaten tonight was the last thing I had to worry about. I just had a bad day so I came here to laugh in the face of the idiot who couldn't manage the simple task of killing and eating the biggest weakling in this God Forsaken Town!"

I then unleashed a torrent of laughter, real and deep. I laughed at The Grass that had such a high opinion of itself even though it lived behind a car wash. I laughed at how scary it thought it was even though an army of ramen addicted roaches had foiled it. I laughed at its vanity even as it was engaged in a battle of wills with a child. I even laughed at myself for being taken in for a second by a tangle of weeds whose idea of cool was to wave against the wind even though nobody ever noticed.

I laughed and laughed and laughed.

As I laughed, the four ghostly figures and the stalks of The Tall Grass stood still. This stoicism, I knew, was meant to intimidate me, but it only caused me to laugh harder. I could feel the seething it was trying to hide radiating off the stalks and it was almost as if I was feeding off it just as The Grass fed off misery. It powered me and I had every intention of laughing until dawn.

Suddenly, a great scream of wind erupted from deep within The Grass.

"GRAB HIM! STUFF HIM DOWN MY GULLET!"

The four false friends advanced on me as I continued to laugh in the wind. Eddie and Darby grabbed my legs while Jason and The Anointed One grabbed my arms. I was still laughing when they picked me up and began to march me to The Grass.

I was certain that my last thought would be of how my joyful flesh would taste bitter and stick in The Grass' throat, when the voice of The Worm rumbled in my stomach.

"When was the last time you all laughed this hard together?"

Not sure why The Worm wanted me to take a trip down memory lane, my mind instantly went back to the toe fight under the willow tree. I thought about that pile of toes and about how Eddie was probably right about them. They must travel from town to town helping people out, fixing what was broken. Such nice and helpful toes…

Above the wail of the wind, there was a loud, wet pop.

Then another.

The four false friends stopped and so did the rushing wind. The four figures and I looked around to find the source of those sounds. Suddenly my arm pulsed. There was another squelchy pop, and a neon purple glob launched into the sky to join the two other purple globs floating above us.

"What is goi-" the voice from within the grass started but immediately stopped as approximately 57 other globs machine gunned out of my arm and into the sky. The globs circled around each other 30 feet in the air. Suddenly, they began to descend, and I could see that they weren't globs, they were toes. 60 severed human toes.

"QUICK! GET HIM INSIDE MY STALKS!" the voice commanded, but the toes shot through my shadow friends like bullets. Green fluid erupted from their wounds. The four dropped me as the toes repeated their assault, ripping the goons to pieces with their high velocity impacts. Within a minute, the toes had turned them into a thick pulp that lay in puddles on the asphalt.

The toes then surrounded me, like they were waiting for an order. I said nothing, but simply looked at The Grass.

The toes rocketed in, shredding the front stalks in an instant.

"WHAT IS HAPPENING?!" The Grass cried in pain.

"Looks like you're losing again, you loser!" I laughed.

As the 60 toes shredded and tore at the grass, I realized that it would take even them quite some time to finish it off.

"It's after MIDNIGHT, who should we get to FACE The Grass?" The worm in my belly nudged.

I rolled my eyes at The Worm's lack of subtlety but raised my arm and pictured flames erupting from a cliff wall. More purple fluid launched from my arm and took the shape of that immense skull that Eddie had named The Face at Midnight. The skull turned towards The Grass and let out its terrifying shriek: "EEEEEEEEEEEEEEEEEEEEEEEEEEEEEEEEEEEEEEEEE EEEEEEHHHHHHHHHHHHHHHHH"

The Grass screamed.

The Face at Midnight unleashed a torrent of flame so hot that stalks not touched by the fire still burst from the heat. It floated on, creating avenues of destruction within The Grass.

Not waiting for further prompts from The Worm, I unleashed other figures from my arm.

A purple Dumpling O'Whiskerson shot out and ripped through the grass screaming about animal rights and firing ruby laser beams from his eyes.

I resurrected The Roaches of Ramen Town who fanned out in waves like locusts and feasted on The Grass for a second time.

The last thing I conjured was The Serpent, giant and mighty. As the last of the purple fluid drained and my arm shrunk to normal, the leviathan looked down at The Grass.

"PLEASE! NO!" The Grass pleaded.

The Serpent let out a murderous hiss and then slithered and rolled, crushing any still standing stalks and shooting acidic venom from its fangs. It joined up with the other creatures of my summer in the absolute destruction of a plant that completely deserved it.

They worked back, further and further, deeper and deeper. When only a small portion of the stalks still stood, I heard a faint whisper in my mind: (please...please)

"Don't worry," I said. "You're just going Away. I hear it's nice there."

Once the purple venom creatures had destroyed every stalk, they gathered in the center of the field. They began to conjoin and melt into each other until they were a large purple mass.

I felt a stirring in my stomach and suddenly The Worm launched itself from my mouth. It headed towards the purple mass at great speed. When it entered the blob, the fluid rearranged itself into a new shape, that of a giant worm.

The giant turned its head towards me. "It was nice working with you. Hopefully, we will never see each other again. If you'll excuse me, I must reclaim this soil from the evil that possessed it."

The giant worm then burrowed deep into the dirt and within seconds was out of sight.

It was then that I heard footsteps crunching over the decimated remains of The Grass. I could see a figure walking out of the darkness. It was Garvey Towne.

"Mr. Towne, you're alive?" I called out.

"Uh, I guess so," he said.

"Hey?"

"What?"

"Do you have a car?" I asked.

"Uh, yeah, why?"

"Can you drive me to the hospital? I've had a very rough day.

Epilogue:

Now Leaving Aickman

In the end, the summer of 1993 would succeed in ridding Aickman of five of its least wanted residents.

Garvey Towne drove me to the county hospital and waited with me until I was taken back to see the doctor. Garvey had wrapped my hands in rags to stop the bleeding and I explained to the nurse on duty that the bright, purple fluid that I was covered in had fallen from the sky after an unmarked airplane had flown overhead. Chemical dumps from mysterious aircraft were a regular occurrence in town so this didn't raise suspicions. I made up further lies to explain my injuries, which were corroborated by nods from Garvey Towne, who I had identified as my uncle.

As Garvey Towne and I waited, we sat silently in the mutual understanding that we had both taken turns saving the others' life and had achieved that state of perfection known as even. When the doctor was finally ready to see me, the nurse escorted me to the back room and before the door closed behind me, I heard Garvey Towne say, "Thanks, kid." That was the last time I ever saw him.

My hands were bandaged and where there had once been a gaping hole in my arm, there was now a serpent shaped scar. My father was contacted, and he snuck me out of the hospital before the doctor could do anything crazy like ask him how he planned to pay for my treatment.

It was on the car ride back that he informed me that we were about to lose our house.

"We have to be out by the end of the month. The bank owns it now," he said.

"How? Why?" I asked, stunned by the news.

"The thing you have to understand about our situation is that banks are filled with bad people. These bad people love to get you to sign things. Terrible things. Deceitful things. And now, well, we have nowhere to live," he helpfully explained.

So, on the Saturday before school was set to begin, we packed as much as we could into our car, and he laid out some vague plans about surprising distant relatives by showing up at their houses and throwing ourselves at their mercy.

"It's pretty much going to be up to you on this one," he said. "We got to appeal to their basic dignity. Most people, even in our family, don't want to be responsible for making a kid homeless. It's really the only ace we have to play. Actually, it's pretty lucky I got you. My family wouldn't care if it was just me."

My father spent the rest of that Saturday night redecorating the house.

"The bank's gonna have to spend a pretty penny fixing this place up before they make any money off our misery," he said as he poured Jell-O powder into the downstairs toilet. He left raw meat out on the kitchen counters and doused the carpets with bleach. He dropped several nails into the garbage disposal and let the machinery crunch until smoke began to rise out of it.

I eventually had to talk him out of setting the whole house on fire. I carefully explained that the damage he was doing, when discovered, could be blamed on vandals. But if our neighbors saw us tearing away from a smoking house that was then consumed by flames, we would be arrested. He quickly saw my point and conceded that maybe a fire was going too far. He then grabbed a wrench and proceeded to smash every mirror in the house.

After that night of destruction, the sun rose on a balmy Sunday morning in August that didn't feel all that different from any other in my life. Except, of course, that it was.

"Ready to go?" my father asked as he turned the water hose on with every intention of letting it flood the yard.

"No. But that doesn't matter," I said.

"No, it doesn't. It sure doesn't," he said with a sad smile on his face.

My dad got into the car and started it. I was about to get into the passenger seat when I noticed the mailbox. As a rule, we never really checked the mail because it was just filled with bills and advertisements.

"It's a vicious cycle," my father had explained. "All the ads do is get you to buy stuff, thus creating more bills. Mail is just a scam for bill creation so that the post office doesn't go out of business."

The mailbox was stuffed. Letters and catalogues were spilling out. Normally I would have left it alone, but I thought about how there was a last time for everything. This would be the last time I would ever check the mail at the house I spent the first ten years of my life in. After the destruction of the previous night, the enormity of what was happening hit me and I just wanted a few more seconds to feel like I had a home.

"I'm going to check the mail," I called to my dad. He just shrugged in reply.

As I pulled the plug of paper from the mailbox, I saw nothing but proof to support my father's theory. Final notices and incredibly early Christmas catalogues fell from my fingers to the ground. Utility bills that would never be paid and life insurance offers that would never be taken up were caught in a gust of hot wind that carried them down the street like autumn leaves. I let every document addressed to the house where we no longer lived fly free save for one: A postcard.

The picture on the front was of a golden city. The buildings were gleaming towers that shot miles into the sky and between the towers floated giant, pinkish whales. On the backs of these flying behemoths were green humanoid creatures with seven multi-colored eyes set in the center of star-shaped heads. Their arms and legs were covered in suckers that enabled them to cling to the whales even as one whale towards the back of the picture was ascending upwards at a 90-degree angle. The humanoids closest to the camera were waving and smiling, revealing toothless gums. There was writing on the front in an indecipherable language that looked like musical notes. I flipped the postcard over.

I recognized the handwriting immediately.

It was Darby's.

On the back was written the following:

From: Darby

To: Weirdo, Eddie, Jason, and The Anointed One

Hey guys what's up? I just wanted to let you know that I'm safe and that I'm sorry I didn't tell you I was leaving. I figured that if I did you would try to make me stay and I just couldn't. If I had to spend one more day in that town something bad would have happened. I am travelling now. What sucks is that this will be the last time you hear from me. Me and the house are getting further away from your dimension and it tells me that soon we'll be in realities so different from yours that I won't be able to send anything back. I've already seen so much cool stuff like an Earth where people ride giant spiders and use the vibrations of the webs to make sick music. There's another Earth where penguins wear these tiny hats and nobody can figure out where they get them from. Then there's the Earth I'm on now where I introduced skateboarding to these 7-eyed squid people who now think Tony Hawk is a god. There's so much more but not enough room to tell it all. It's really rad out here. You guys need to get out of Aickman as soon as you can. It's a deathtrap and the world is so much cooler than you can possibly know.

I love you all. I will miss you forever. You made my life suck less.

Darby

P.S. Sorry for getting so dorky at the end.

I stood there, rereading the message until my vision had been completely flooded by tears. I leaned against the mailbox and let the sobs come. Crying had never felt this good before.

Eventually, my father got out of the car. I could feel him behind me. I kept my face hidden against the mailbox. I didn't want him to see me smiling.

"I'm….I'm sorry," he said, putting a hand on my shoulder. "I'll try to do better," he lied.

I quickly slipped the postcard into my pocket and wiped the snot and tears from my face with my t-shirt. I turned to him.

"Time to go," I said.

"Do you want to say bye to your friends before we head out?" he asked.

I just laughed and got into the car.

As we drove through town for the last time, I looked out at all the people we passed who were busy with their Sunday morning rituals. These were the people I had known my entire life and as my eyes met with one or two of them, I realized that they couldn't care less that I was leaving, and it didn't really bother me that I would never see them again. Aickman was a town of strangers, but they were familiar strangers and the future seemed frightening as they disappeared in the rear-view mirror.

The last I ever saw of what I would recognize to be the town I grew up in was the sea of cars parked just off the farm road on the path that led to the Swap Meet. Hundreds of people were marching down that dirt and gravel track hoping to find what they were looking for beyond the mist. As we passed, I took Darby's postcard from my pocket and studied the golden towers and strange creatures. Darby had found what she was looking for. That gave me hope. Not only for myself but also for Eddie, Jason, and The Anointed One.

As I stared out at the endless expanse of road before us and contemplated my Aickmanless future, I was able to scream, "WATCH OUT!" about one second before my dad ran over the blood-soaked man with a machete. The events that followed happened well outside of Aickman and as such are of no concern to this book.

It would be nice if I could provide a postscript where I inform you of the accomplishments and triumphs of the friends I introduced you to, but anything of that nature would be complete invention on my part. I never saw or heard from any of them ever again. But that doesn't mean that I don't keep my ears open for news about strange messages from outer space, or keep my eyes peeled for articles about the latest breakthroughs in the field of trans-dimensional travel. I am also supremely interested in the recent reports of strange phenomena that seem to be emanating from the Antarctic and which the governments of the world are overly keen to convince us are not happening. And every ten years, I smile thinking about a fresh group of weirdos coming across a helpful little boy in the middle of a forest on the edge of a town that no one has ever heard of.

Acknowledgements

This book wouldn't have been possible without the love and support of my family and friends. Special thanks must, of course, go to Andrew Ferrell and Cloaked Press for believing in this incredibly odd endeavor. But my biggest thanks must go to one Mr. Gabriel Grant who read each story as they were written and told me again and again to keep on going. Thanks, Gabe.

ABOUT THE AUTHOR

Anthony D. Herrera studied playwriting at the University of
Texas at Austin but has only managed to write one full length
play which was never produced. In the intervening years his
creative focus has been split between YouTube sketch comedy,
TikTok videos, short stories, and a series of bizarre social media
posts about growing up in a strange town that would ultimately
lead to the book you are currently reading. If you would like to
learn more about this fascinating human being, you can follow
him at the links below:

Anthony D Herrera (@anthonydherrera) | TikTok

https://www.facebook.com/anthony.d.herrera.7/

Anthony D Herrera (@guacho_mufungo) on Threads

Anthony D Herrera (@guacho_mufungo) • Instagram photos
and videos

Made in the USA
Columbia, SC
24 January 2025

52468043R00181